I0672083

The Cursed Princess (Book 1 of the Eumetadotos Series)

Cover image: Virajitha Lanka (Fiverr name vira_lanka)

Cover design: Evan Schukis

Edited by: Sandra Rose (Fiverr name proofreadgirl)

ISBN: 978-0-9978449-0-0

ISBN-13: 978-0-9978449-0-0

DEDICATION

This book is dedicated to my late grandfather, William B. Carroll. A wonderful man taken away from us too soon. I love you forever, Boppy.

TABLE OF CONTENTS

Prologue

"Come, Ellavorn, there is no time to lose. The princess grows ever weaker with every breath."

"Father, why must we save this child…this *human* child?" Ellavorn sneered at the thought of squandering his healing gift on a mortal child. "She will die eventually anyway." The disdain that Ellavorn had for humans rolled off of his body in waves as he spoke to his father. "Why is this child so important? She is a mere human. Let her die. She will only come to that in the end anyway. Why prolong that agony?"

Armen turned his horse to face his son. He looked him up and down. Ellavorn's long, sandy brown hair was drawn back from his face; his blue eyes were narrowed in disgust. His lean body looked as if he were drawn tighter than a bowstring, ready to snap at a moment's notice. Armen knew that his son despised humans. He had a lot to learn still. Although he was 107 years old, Ellavorn was still considered young by elven standards. He was, however, the best healer in the elven kingdom.

"Humans are not as bad as you make them out to be."

"Then why do elves not mate with them?" Ellavorn mocked his father's compassion towards humans.

"That is a good question, my son."

"I will answer that for you. We do not mate with them so that we do not taint our blood with mortality. Death is a trait for them, not for us. They are all destined for it. Why not just let her die along with the rest of the human filth?"

"You know as well as I do that that is not true. Many Elves have met with death in battles. Besides, this is no mere human,

Ellavorn."

"What makes *this* child so special, father? Why are we rushing to aid her? Should we not be tending to our own people, instead of rushing to heal a human? If we were to rush to the aid of every hu-"

Armen cut him off. "She is the child born with violet eyes."

Ellavorn's eyes widened in surprise and he gasped. "Then, the prophecy is true?"

"It seems so. This child is to be the great savior of our land."

Ellavorn sneered. "Exactly what is she to save us from?"

"That, I do not know. But, I have seen what is foretold. She does not know it yet, but, she will save us all from an untold evil. We must save her or all of us will be doomed."

It seemed to Armen that his son finally understood how urgent it was to get to the little princess' aide. They turned and rode off at a full gallop as if their own lives depended on it.

As Armen and Ellavorn rode up to the castle, they dismounted their horses, leaving them in the care of the stable boy, who was alerted that they would be arriving at any moment. They raced to the princess' room and flung open the door. The sight before them was a heart wrenching one. Queen Alexandra sat on the bed by her daughter's side, holding her hand and weeping, while King Jasper sat quietly by the window, rocking back and forth in his chair, watching his daughter with a stoic face. Princess Arianna, only 9 years old, thrashed with a fever in the bed, eyes closed, alternating screaming and moaning in pain. Her chestnut hair was drenched with sweat, her face, ashen.

Ellavorn knelt next to the bed. Arianna thrashed some more in the bed as he took her free hand in his. He concentrated on her pale, sweaty face. He said the healing words in his mind, and slowly, Arianna's body relaxed. He held onto her hand for a few minutes longer, making sure that the sickness had entirely left her body. When he was sure that she was completely healed, he opened his eyes. His blue eyes were met with the midnight sky staring back at him.

Ellavorn's heart stilled at the sight. He had never seen anything so beautiful in his entire life. He had never felt anything like what he felt staring into this child's eyes, this *human's* eyes. In that instant, the wall of stone surrounding Ellavorn's heart shattered into a million pieces. He finally understood the compassion that his father was trying to teach him. He gasped inwardly when he realized that in that one instant, he had fallen in love with the Princess Arianna.

Chapter 1

9 Years Later

"I, King Sebastian of Goldlandia, present my son, Prince Ethan, to Princess Arianna for consideration of marriage."

King Jasper looked at his daughter, whose violet eyes had become glassy with boredom. Queen Alexandra nudged her with her foot, her emerald eyes blazing at the blatant disrespect her daughter was showing to her suitor.

"What? Oh, yes, thank you. I will take Prince, ummmm," she froze, looking sideways to her mother for help.

"ETHAN," her mother stage whispered to her, irritated with her only child.

"Ethan! I will be sure to consider Prince Ethan in my final decision for a husband. We will alert you immediately if I choose him," she said sarcastically. Arianna arose and sauntered out of the throne room, leaving her parents and her guests gaping in her wake.

King Sebastian was not amused by the actions of the girl. "Jasper! How could you allow your daughter to behave like this? Why, I have never been so insulted in my life! Ethan is a fine young man, and would be a great partner for her. He knows what it takes to run a kingdom."

Jasper looked over at Ethan, taking in the young man's slim frame and pasty white skin, which was accentuated by his jet black hair, giving him the look of death warmed over. The boy looked as though he would break under the weight of his stare. He was the complete antithesis of his father, who was quite a robust man with a rosy complexion and stark white hair. He tried not to laugh as he thought of his independent, willful daughter married to this waif of a boy.

"Sebastian, please accept my heartfelt apologies. Arianna has been rather difficult lately. I assure you that we do not mean any disrespect at all. We will deal with her accordingly. My friend, you have traveled far. Please, allow my servants to show you to your rooms. I trust that you will find them most comfortable. In the meantime, I will find my daughter and you can be assured that she will be reprimanded. Shall we see you at supper? The cooks are preparing lamb stew. That is your favorite, am I correct?"

King Sebastian seemed to be placated by his friend's offer of a comfortable room, good food, and the promise of a reprimand of his daughter. "Thank you, Jasper. We shall see you at supper. After tonight, we may be planning a wedding." He walked out of the room, following the servant, with a hearty chuckle and his son in tow.

King Jasper bowed and shook his head, his brown hair, falling in front of his soft brown eyes. He raised his head and looked around the throne room. The room was made entirely of stone with two thrones standing at the front of the large room at the end of a pink carpet. The crest of the kingdom of Eumetadotos, their kingdom, was embroidered in gold on a huge banner with a pink background that was hung between the two thrones. The sunlight streamed through the stained glass windows, painting beautiful murals on the floor. The torches that hung between the windows were unlit. He sighed, "I do not understand her, Alexandra. She has rejected every suitor we have brought here. She has even gone so far as to insult them, to their faces."

Queen Alexandra took her husband's face in her hands. "She is still young. She does not understand the way that things must be. She is holding onto her heart for one that she cannot have.

Give her time, Jasper. She will come to accept that things cannot always be the way you want them to be. She will see that a great ruler does what is best for the kingdom as a whole, not what is best for herself. She will give up on the dream that she holds onto so tightly and choose a suitor."

"How can you be so sure, my love?"

The queen smiled at her king and said, "Because she is your daughter. She may be proud, but deep down, she knows what is right. She has always chosen the right path. This time, will not be any different."

Jasper shook his head again, "Why is she being so difficult? We are asking her to marry, not pick her firing squad."

Alexandra giggled. "Well, marriage can be a scary thing, especially when you have held on to someone for so long, only to be told that it can never be. It is a life-long commitment, Jasper. It is not something to be taken lightly."

"You did not present such trouble when I was presented to you for marriage."

"No, but we had a bit of a history, now didn't we? Ari has never spent time with any of these young men. They are complete strangers to her. How do you expect her to choose the one that she will spend the rest of her life with? She will be sleeping next to him every night, bearing his children! We are expecting her to fall in love with a complete stranger at first sight, and choose to marry him and live out her days with him as her mate. That is a hard decision for anyone to make. However, I feel as if we are somewhat to blame. We have sheltered her ever since she fell ill as a child. This is partly our fault. We have spoiled her. But, we have also raised her to do the right thing. She will come around. I am sure of it."

Jasper wrapped his arms around Alexandra and whispered to her, “And how did you get to be so wise, my queen?”

Alexandra simply smiled and gave him a light kiss on the cheek. “That is my secret to know.”

Jasper sighed, “I guess we should go looking for Arianna, then, and scold her for being so brash with our guests.”

Alexandra shook her head, “No, she is long gone by now. Out riding her horse, I assume, going to clear her head of whatever thoughts are rattling around in there. We will see to it that we speak to her before supper. She does owe King Sebastian and Prince Ethan an apology.”

Jasper nodded and they walked out of the throne room together, arm in arm.

Chapter 2

After storming out of the throne room, Arianna raced to the stables and saddled up her horse, Lightning. His beautiful white coat gleamed in the sun as they streaked off to the meadow. Her long, chestnut hair flowing behind her, her violet eyes shining in anger. Her head swam with all kinds of thoughts that she just couldn't get rid of. She was furious with her parents that they continued this game of parading suitors in front of her, like she was just going to let go of her dream for some pretty boy, or, in Prince Ethan's case, a not-so-pretty boy, that she met five seconds earlier. No, thank you. Arianna had bigger dreams of married life and they did not include those boys.

They reached the far outskirts of the meadow and she dismounted, flopping down in a very unprincess-like manner onto a soft patch of clover.

"HA!" She laughed out a little too loudly, startling Lightning. "Sorry, boy, just had to get that off my chest. Can you believe them? They want to just hand me off to the first eligible male that comes along. I hate being a princess, Lightning. This doesn't happen to normal girls."

"You are no normal girl, Ari," a soft voice from behind her made her jump. She broke into a wide smile as the elven prince stood before her.

"Hello, Ellavorn. What brings you out here today?" She grinned.

"Something tells me I should be asking you that question," he smiled.

Arianna looked into the face that she had grown to know so well. The one that she had fallen in love with at the age of 9, when she lay in bed, sick with a fever so high that it threatened to kill her. A fever, that, today, they still had no explanation for. He had healed her and she had awoken to the sight of his face, so passionately concentrating on getting rid of the affliction that threatened to kill her. He had opened his eyes, and they bore straight into her soul and she knew that she would never love any other male as she did her savior. After that fateful encounter, she insisted that her father allow her to learn to ride a horse. When she had mastered that skill, she demanded the fastest horse that they could find, which is how she came to possess Lightning. She did some research and found the land where her elven prince lived, and learned that it was not a far ride by horseback. She made regular visits to the meadow, in secret, so she thought, hoping to catch a glimpse of Ellavorn. One day, about a month after she found the pasture, her patience paid off. He was sitting in the clover, almost as though he was waiting for her. She was overjoyed that she would have the chance to talk to him face to face and thank him for saving her life. Since that day, she would come to the meadow every day and he would meet her there. It was never a spoken agreement between them, but they seemed to both acknowledge it as though it were.

Arianna huffed, "Another stupid suitor."

Ellavorn laughed. "Was this one any better than the last? What did you call him, a blubbering buffoon?"

Ari snickered. "Well, he was. Any time he looked at me, he burst into tears. What am I supposed to think of that?"

Ellavorn chuckled. "What was wrong with this one?"

Arianna sighed. "He was too pale and skinny. He looks as though he's never done a day's work in his life."

"My dear Arianna, you have never done a day's work in your

life either."

Ari looked at him as though he'd slapped her. "Well, tell me how you really feel now, won't you?" She stood up as if to storm off. Ellavorn grabbed her hand and pulled her back to the ground.

"Don't go. I'm sorry. I was rude. Forgive me?"

"I forgive you. Just don't do it again, Prince of the Elves."

"Ok, Human Princess. I will try not to."

They smiled at each other and the silly nicknames that they had each given to the other.

"So, why do you keep rejecting these suitors, Ari?"

"I do not know them, nor could I ever love them as I do another."

Ellavorn looked at her profile longingly as she looked straight ahead. "Arianna, sometimes, as royalty, we need to make sacrifices in our lives to do what is best for the kingdom, as opposed to what will make us happy."

She turned towards him, glaring. "So, I am to just give my hand in marriage to the first boy that comes along? I am to just give him my body, my life? He will never own my heart, for I have reserved that for someone special. I cannot live like that and I will not. If I have to live my life as a lonely spinster and die alone with no heirs to the throne, so be it. I would rather be alone and see my line end than live a miserable existence with one that I do not love."

"You would give up everything? You would see your line end rather than get married?"

"If it meant that I didn't have to live my life with the one I did not love, yes, I would."

Ellavorn spoke softly, "Who is this man that holds your heart so tightly that you would end a noble line in his name?"

Arianna turned to look Ellavorn straight on. "If you do not know by now, then you need to be hit over the head with a brick. I must get back. They will expect me to be cleaned up and primped up for supper tonight."

She stood and mounted Lightning before Ellavorn could speak, or even process exactly what she had said. With a slight kick, Lightning sped off in the direction of the castle.

"No, my little human princess," he mumbled to himself, "I do not need to be hit with a brick. If only there was a way to make it happen. I would in a second, believe me." Ellavorn dropped his head and plodded his way back into the forest to his own castle, deep in thought.

That night at dinner, Arianna was even surlier than ever. It had become quite apparent to King Sebastian and Prince Ethan that she was not interested in marriage, at least not to Ethan. Instead of being insulted, however, Ethan seemed to be rather relieved, as he chattered happily to his father and King Jasper.

Queen Alexandra, however, noticed how miserable Arianna was, as she picked at her food and simply moved it around the plate.

"Ari, is there something wrong, dear?"

"No, mother, everything is just fine," she huffed.

"Well, I can see that is not the case."

Arianna rolled her eyes, "Well, then why even ask me?"

"Arianna, your attitude has gotten out of control. I demand that you knock it off this instant. The way you have been behaving is unfit for a princess."

"Well, Mother, I find it despicable that you are forcing me to marry against my will. I don't love any of the princes that you have paraded in front of me. Nor do they care for me, as you can see," she gestured to the men, deep in conversation on the opposite side of the table.

Alexandra sighed, "Arianna, what do you expect us to do? We have brought just about every prince in the realm here. They are all interested in marrying you and uniting our kingdoms."

Arianna glared at her mother, "Not all of them, mother. I notice one in particular has been absent from your parade."

Alexandra looked at her daughter with pity. "Ari, I do not know how to say it any more plainly. I know you are in love with him, but elves simply do not wish to pair themselves with humans. They do not wish to marry any mortal."

Arianna pushed her chair away from the table, noisily, and raced to her bedroom, sobbing.

Chapter 3

"Arianna?" Queen Alexandra poked her head into Arianna's room. It had been three days and the princess had not left her room, even taking meals there in private. She was met by a sniffle. "Arianna, get dressed. You are needed in the throne room."

"No, mother, I will not see any other suitors."

"Arianna, this is a direct order. You will get dressed and come to the throne room. IMMEDIATELY."

A half an hour later, Arianna pushed the door to the throne room open and was met by the sight of her parents sitting on their thrones, waiting for her.

"Arianna, come here," demanded King Jasper. Arianna trudged her way to the front of the room.

"We have one last suitor for you to meet. After today, you WILL make a decision on who to marry. If you do not, we will choose one for you."

Arianna's head snapped up, her eyes on fire. "Father! This is unfair! You cannot force me to marry someone I do not love!"

"SILENCE! I have had enough of your insolence, Arianna. You *will* choose today, or that choice will be made for you. You are a princess and it is time that you started acting like one! Now, sit down!"

Arianna stood between the thrones, sulking.

"Bring in the suitor!" King Jasper roared. The doors opened wide. Arianna turned her head to the left and refused to look at the guests as they entered the room.

A voice that Arianna found vaguely familiar rang out, “I, King Armen of Forest Glen, present my son, Prince Ellavorn, to Princess Arianna for consideration of marriage.”

At his words, Arianna’s head snapped around quickly, her eyes wide, and full of surprise. Her actions forced all in attendance to stifle their laughs. She looked back and forth at her parents’ faces, and they were watching her, smiling. She looked at Armen and his face held the same expression. She finally looked to Ellavorn and he looked as though he were going to jump out of his skin waiting for her answer.

Arianna slowly walked to Ellavorn’s side.

“I thought that elves don’t pair themselves with humans.”

“We normally don’t.”

“Why now? Why me?”

Smirking, Ellavorn said, “If you do not know by now, then, perhaps, it is you, Human Princess, that needs to be hit over the head with a brick.”

King Jasper, Queen Alexandra, and King Armen all gasped and widened their eyes in surprise. Arianna simply laughed, throwing her arms around Ellavorn’s neck. The rest of the royalty relaxed with a chuckle.

“Arianna, am I to assume that you have finally chosen your suitor?” Alexandra’s voice was uncertain.

Arianna looked at her mother with eyes swimming with tears of joy. “Yes, Mother! Yes! I choose Prince Ellavorn as my husband.”

Jasper jumped from his throne in excitement. “Armen, my

friend, should we give, say, a month's time for the preparation of a wedding?"

"Jasper, I think that would be perfect."

"Then it is set. In a month's time, Princess Arianna and Prince Ellavorn shall be joined in marriage. I am to assume that you both shall be staying in the palace during that time to help with the preparations?"

Armen smiled, "I cannot stay past tonight. Ellavorn, however, will be glad to stay on and help with any preparations that need to be done, if you will so have him."

"Indeed, my future son-in-law is always welcome here."

Alexandra ran to hug her daughter and future son-in-law. Jasper and Armen shook hands. Arianna and Ellavorn seemed to not be able to get enough of simply gazing into one another's eyes, finally able to publicly declare the love for each other that they had kept secret for so long.

"Armen, will you join me in my study? We must break out the good champagne to celebrate."

"But, of course, Jasper, we are to be a family in a month's time, not to mention that elves and humans are finally joining together. I find this a good reason to celebrate."

Alexandra also took her leave, claiming that there was so much to get started on for the wedding. She left the throne room, leaving Arianna and Ellavorn alone for the first time in three days.

"So, Prince of the Elves, you have decided to taint your bloodline with mortality, have you?"

"Ari, please, try to understand our people's way of thinking.

If you were given immortality, would you want to give that up? Would you want to mate with someone and give birth to children, who you would one day see perish? It is a curse, mortality. To have your life end, we do not understand it."

"Then what changed your mind?"

"These last three days, not seeing your face or hearing your voice. It drove me half insane. I could not bear the thought of not having you in my life ever. I knew then that I had to talk to my father. I needed to come and see if you would still have me. I want to make you my wife, for as long as you live."

"I will die one day, Ellavorn. That cannot be changed. Our children, if we have them, they will not be immortal. How will you face that? Death is irreversible."

"It is true, death is final. I could not, however, live my life knowing that I gave away my one chance at finding real love. Arianna, I love you. I didn't mean to fall in love with you, but I did. The day I saved your life and you opened your eyes. Something in me changed. I hated humans. I hated your weaknesses. I hated them because they could not live as long as we do."

"You hated us because we die? Because we cannot conquer death?"

Ellavorn hung his head in shame. "I did." He looked up and took her hand in his, bringing it to his lips and kissing it. "But, in my many encounters with you, I realized something. I realized that while death comes to all who are not immortal, it also comes to some who are. Just because we can live forever does not mean that we are invincible. We can be killed. In battle, many times, we are. I am so sorry, Arianna. My foolish pride got in my way of seeing that the best thing to ever happen to me is you. I want to spend the rest of our time together making that up to you."

Ellavorn then dropped to his knee and took Arianna's hand. He gently kissed each finger, looked up into her eyes and said, "Arianna, I am madly in love with you. I want to give you a proper proposal, not just the customary way of choosing. Will you please do me the greatest honor and take me as your husband? I will do everything in my power to love you, to protect you, and to help you in whatever you need to do, for all of our time together."

A single tear slipped from Arianna's eye, and she choked back a sob before pulling him up so that he was standing in front of her, she then threw her arms around his neck, saying, simply, "Yes!"

They embraced for a moment, before pulling away. Ellavorn leaned in close and kissed her lightly on the lips. Arianna closed her eyes, and pulled him back to her, their bodies fitting perfectly together. They began to kiss again, letting all of the unspoken feelings wash over them at that moment. They kissed until they were too tired to kiss anymore and simply fell into each other's embrace.

They held onto each other in that position until they heard Jasper clearing his throat in the doorway. Clearly embarrassed by his walking into the room on such a tender moment, his face blushed a crimson red and said, "We will be taking supper in the formal dining hall tonight to celebrate your engagement." He then hurried off to his chambers to change.

Arianna and Ellavorn looked at each other and burst out laughing.

"I should go to my room and change for supper as well. Will you escort me?"

"It would be my pleasure."

They walked arm in arm to Arianna's room, where she then asked her handmaiden, Abigail, to escort him to his. When she closed the door, her face broke out into a wide, triumphant grin, and she danced around her room with joy.

Supper that night was a glorious feast. It put all other feasts that they had ever held to shame. Three different kinds of stews and a multitude of every kind of meat and vegetable that one could imagine adorned the tables. The finest bone china was placed at each setting. The golden flatware was laid out as opposed to the silver. Arianna had never seen the dining room so gloriously laid out before.

She took her place next to her mother, who was seated to the left of her father, and across from Ellavorn, who sat next to his father. Jasper sat at the head of the table. Arianna could not help but beam at Ellavorn all throughout the meal. He had no choice but to return those smiles just as enthusiastically.

"So, Jasper," Armen's voice jolted Arianna and Ellavorn from their private world, "there is quite a bounty of food. What do you do with all that is left over?"

Jasper grinned. Arianna was interested to hear what her father had to say. She never really gave much thought as to where the leftover food went. "Well, whatever is left from our meals, I give to the servants. In times, such as this, when there is a feast as large as the one before you, I have my servants serve the remainder to the people in the village. So, my friend, though we five may be alone while we share our supper, we are not truly alone. The entire village will be celebrating with us and sharing our feast."

Arianna looked at her father, her eyes shining with pride. She had never known how the leftover food was disposed of. She only knew that she never saw it again. Ari felt a pang of regret of never having asked the same question. She thought of the way her father phrased his answer, "Though we five may be alone while we share our supper, we are not truly alone. The entire village will be celebrating with us and sharing our feast." She smiled at the thought. It was in that moment, that Arianna began to see what a true queen does, and how royalty should treat their people.

Arianna looked across the table at Ellavorn, and he seemed to be as humbled by the answer as she was. She decided that one day, when she took over as queen, and he as her king, they would keep that tradition. It seemed to her to be a generous one.

Chapter 4

The next two weeks passed in a flurry of excitement and planning for the upcoming royal wedding. The dress was being made, the menu was chosen, guests were invited, seating charts were arranged, and the list went on. Although it was all very exhausting, Arianna and Ellavorn never wavered in their enthusiasm. They were bursting with excitement over the upcoming wedding.

One morning, Alexandra and Jasper had made plans to travel to the next kingdom, Polýtimos, in order to purchase some jewels and to fashion some jewelry for Arianna's wedding present. Arianna begged her parents to go with them, but they refused, wanting everything to be a surprise. Ari was disappointed, but, at the same time, somewhat glad to be able to spend some time with Ellavorn alone without having to make wedding decisions. She decided to surprise him with a picnic in the royal gardens.

As night fell, Arianna started to worry about her parents. The journey to Polýtimos was not a long one, and they should have been home hours before.

Ellavorn came up behind her and wrapped his arms around her waist. "Don't worry. They probably decided to spend more time there and lost track of time," he whispered in her ear. "They'll come walking through those doors at any mom—"

He was cut off by someone crashing through the doors. It was a member of the royal guard, and in his arms was Queen Alexandra.

"Prince Ellavorn! Quickly! She's hurt. She needs help immediately!"

Arianna screamed as Ellavorn flew to the queen's side. He

located the source of the blood that was freely flowing. She was stabbed deeply in the stomach. He put his hands on her and they started to glow. The queen's body convulsed and then she lay still. Ellavorn looked at the guard in shock.

Arianna kept screaming as she looked at Ellavorn's hands, which were drenched with the queen's blood. She fled the room, yelling for her father. Ellavorn raced after her, dripping Alexandra's blood on the floor as he ran.

Down the hall, Arianna had found what was left of the entourage that had taken her parents into Polýtimos that morning.

"Father! Father, where are you?"

"Princess Arianna," one of the guards said her name sheepishly.

"Captain Oakford, where is my father?"

Captain Joshua Oakford stood just inside the doorway. He was just a few years older than she, and had only held his position for the last two years. His auburn hair was matted with blood. Whose, she couldn't tell. His blue eyes would not meet those of the young princess as he told her the tale of what had happened.

"We were riding back along the dirt road that connects our kingdom with Polýtimos, when a band of bandits jumped out and attacked us. They went straight for your parent's carriage before anyone knew what was happening. They pulled your parents out of the carriage and attacked your father first, hitting him on the head. He was barely alive. Your mother freed herself from their grasps and tried to defend your father. She fought heroically and killed two of their men before another one came from behind and stabbed her in the stomach. After they attacked your parents, they went after the rest of our caravan. Some saw how many of their men that we had killed and they ran off. Our men are still searching for them. Your father, princess, died on the way back to the palace. Your mother was gravely injured."

Arianna started to hear a wailing sound, thinking that it was an alarm to alert the villagers that they were in danger, she fell to her knees. Ellavorn came from behind and held her. It was then that she realized that the wailing she heard was coming from herself. Ellavorn held her and let her scream, cry, and grieve. He picked her up and carried her to her room. When he laid her on her bed, she looked at him and started to scream again. He had been so concerned about going after her that he had forgotten that he was saturated with the queen's blood.

"Ari, I'm so sorry. I should have at least wiped the blood off of my hands." He made sure that Abigail was with her and he left the room to go and clean himself up. When he came back, Arianna was lying in bed in a deep sleep, thanks to a special tea that Abigail had ordered from the kitchen. He pulled the same chair that King Jasper had been sitting in all those years ago over to the side of her bed and sat down, intent on keeping guard over her all night.

Chapter 5

Ellavorn kept his vigil over Arianna over the course of the next few days, while she planned the funeral for her mother and father. She seemed to want to be alone more than have his company, so he kept his watch from a slight distance. She barely spoke, even to him. She hardly ate anything at all, insisting that she wasn't hungry. Having never experienced grief over the passing of a loved one, he was confused and intended to ask her about it in the future.

The day of the double funeral arrived, and the weather outside was just as gloomy as the mood inside the palace. It was raining hard, with dark gray skies as far as the eye could see.

Arianna gazed out her window, seeming to be in a daze, as Abigail pulled her hair into a fancy braided up-do. Tears welled in her eyes, and spilled over her cheeks silently.

"Your Highness, is there anything I can do for you?"

Arianna looked at her, as though she had been so lost in her own thoughts that she forgot that she was there. She didn't think she would ever get used to being addressed as Your Highness, as opposed to Princess. She sniffed, "No, nothing can be done to bring them back. Death is irreversible," the last part echoing what Ellavorn had told her the day that they had become engaged. "Death is irreversible, and mortality is a curse," she muttered, under her breath, balling her hands into fists. Abigail gave her a funny look before she left the room.

When the door closed, Arianna buried her face in her hands and wept uncontrollably for a few minutes before regaining her composure. She stood up, smoothed down her black velvet dress and walked down to the small chapel to see to the final preparations of her parents' final good-byes.

The chapel looked beautiful, despite the solemn occasion of the day. There were bouquets of beautiful lavender roses, her mother's favorite, interspersed with gleaming white Shasta daisies, her father's favorite, throughout the room. Portraits of the king and queen rested on easels at the head of their closed caskets. Closed casket ceremonies were the tradition. The caskets, both made of deep mahogany wood and carved with the crest of Eumetadotos were situated side by side in the middle of the aisle. Their presence, marking the death of the two people that Arianna loved most in the world, were like a stab wound in her heart.

Ari tried to make herself go and stand between them. She knew that she should, but when she got within five feet of them, her entire body started shaking uncontrollably, and she collapsed into a heap on the floor and began to weep again.

Strong arms enveloped her from behind, and the voice that she so loved spoke to her, "I'm sorry, Arianna. I'm so, so sorry. Your parents were wonderful people and even better leaders. They deserved better than this."

His words seemed to steel her resolve again, and she pulled away, coldly saying, "Yes, they did. They should still be here with me. They shouldn't be lying in those caskets. We shouldn't be having this discussion at all!" She turned and stormed up the aisle.

Ellavorn watched her, thinking that it was good for her to be feeling that anger right now. It just might get her through the day. He followed her up the aisle to join her.

About fifteen minutes later, the doors to the chapel were opened and the entire kingdom of Eumetadotos filed in to pay their last respects to their slain king and queen. Some of them came by themselves, and others with their spouses or other loved ones, leaning on each other for support. There was not a dry eye in the entire place. The line of citizens seemed to stretch on forever. The procession took about three hours to filter through. The lucky ones were able to find a seat and the rest stood around the sides of the chapel, and spilled out the front doors.

When the last person had walked past and paid their respects to the fallen leaders, the clergyman walked to the front of the chapel and began his sermon.

"Today, we lay to rest two of the finest people I have ever had the pleasure of knowing. King Jasper and Queen Alexandra were two of the kindest, wisest, most patient and generous people I have ever known. They lived their lives in a peaceful and loving manner. They doted on their daughter, Arianna, and loved their kingdom of Eumetadotos just as fiercely. For them to have been taken from us in the manner that they were is just an unspeakable abomination. But, we must remember the good that they brought into our lives. They knew of all of your fortunes and misfortunes, and they celebrated and mourned along with you. To them, you are all a part of their family." He turned to Arianna.

"Arianna, it is our turn to share in your pain. Please know that we all feel your loss along with you. We grieve with you and we all hope that you know that we stand behind you in your time of great loss. I sincerely hope that the tragic death of your parents does not harden your heart to the love that they have taught you over the years and that you continue their legacy of love and devotion to Eumetadotos. As your parents so loved this kingdom, we love them just as much, and that love extends to you as well. You have grown up right before our eyes and we all feel a devotion to you, just as strong as we did to your parents. The entire kingdom grieves with you on this day, and every day after."

Arianna stood and embraced the clergyman. She then turned

to face the people of Eumetadotos. The same people that her parents had loved so fiercely. The same ones that she loved just as fiercely. She began to speak.

"Thank you all for being here with me on this day. I know that all of you loved my parents, and they loved you just as much. I can only hope to measure up to the people that they were to you, and to me as well. I am grateful for the time that I had with them, and my only wish is for more of it. They were taken from all of us too soon and too quickly. I promise you that everything in my power is being done to find the criminals who did this and to bring them to justice."

The kingdom burst into applause, and Arianna sat down again.

That night, Ellavorn went to Arianna's room and pulled the chair over to the side of her bed again. As he went to sit in the chair, Arianna's eyes flew open and she leaped out of bed and glared at him.

"What do you think you're doing?"

"I was going to sit here with you in case you woke up and needed someone to cry to."

"And you thought that you would be that person? Why won't you just leave me alone?"

"Well, yes, we are going to be married, are we not?"

Arianna scoffed. "No, we're not. You allowed my mother to *die*! You could have saved her, but you didn't! You barely even tried!"

Ellavorn gasped and looked at her as though he had been punched in the stomach by her words.

"You don't really believe that, do you?"

"I saw it with my own eyes. I knew that you hated humans for being mortal, but I didn't realize that that hatred extended to my family. I thought you had gotten past that, but obviously, I was wrong."

"Arianna, please, why would you think that I still have those feelings towards humans? I love you. You made me see that the hatred I used to feel was wrong, that humans are not a race to be hated simply because they are mortal. You are the one who changed my heart on that subject."

He reached out to hold her, and she pulled away.

"I saw everything with my own eyes, Ellavorn! You let her die. You could have tried harder to heal her, and you didn't. You didn't even try to deny that you let her die."

Ellavorn's eyes filled with tears. "Do you really believe that? Ari, you saw her wounds. I couldn't save her. I tried. Her wounds were too extensive. There was no way I could have saved her. It was too late. If they had gotten her back earlier, maybe I could have saved her, but I couldn't when she got home. She was on Death's door when she got here. I feel horrible that I couldn't save her. I tried, Ari, honestly, I did. I love you, why would I let your mother die, and right in front of you at that?"

Arianna glared at him with pure hatred in her eyes. "I want you gone by tonight. There will be no wedding. I will rule Eumetadotos alone. I don't need a king that will fall short of his duties. Now, leave my room and the palace altogether, and don't come back."

Ellavorn gasped, "You don't mean that."

She turned her back on him and growled, "I most certainly do.

Now, leave."

He looked at her, longingly, with a shattered heart, then turned and left the room. He went back to his chamber and, quietly, gathered his things and left the palace, pausing to look back one last time, willing Arianna to walk out of her door and beg him to forgive her and not to leave. She never came.

Arianna stood in the shadows in her room and watched Ellavorn leave the palace. When he passed through the gate, she buried her face in her arms and sobbed. In the course of a few days, she lost her family and the love of her life. Part of her knew that she was being unreasonable about breaking off her engagement. She saw herself that her mother would never have survived those wounds. Her grief was all-consuming, and she felt like the whole world had let her down. After crying to her heart's content, she raised her head and looked out at the kingdom that she loved so dearly. It steeled her resolve to be the best queen and ruler that she could hope to be. She left her room and began to make plans for her coronation. The coronation that she had hoped would not have been held for many years to come.

Chapter 6

Arianna set the date of her coronation as the date on which she was to be married. Although there was usually a grieving period before a coronation, she felt that, between the death of their king and queen and her broken engagement, the kingdom needed a reason to celebrate, and soon.

Since Arianna didn't have many friends, she had to rely heavily on the servants in the castle, and even they didn't really know how to help her. Her only friend was Ellavorn and now he was gone, and her parents were both dead. The custom in Eumetadotos was that when the king or queen died, the surviving ruler would then help prepare for the coronation of the heir and his or her chosen mate, who would rise to the throne. If there was no heir or the heir was too young to be married, the ruler must marry again within a year's time. Since both Jasper and Alexandra had perished in the attack, there was no one left to help Arianna with the preparations. Her grief was eminent in the daily tasks in preparing for the big event.

Arianna threw herself into the preparations like she'd never involved herself in anything before. The more she worked, the less she thought of her parents and Ellavorn. She worked until she was too exhausted to keep her eyes open, and would often collapse into her bed at the end of the day. Sleep is where the problems lay. When she slept, she dreamed. She dreamed of her parents, of them ultimately meeting their doom. She also dreamed of Ellavorn and the life that they should have had together.

Ari thought of sending for Ellavorn, or riding Lightning out to find him, but her pride got in the way. She was ashamed of how she had acted towards him, and she wasn't quite sure how to fix what she had broken. She refused to let herself linger in those thoughts for too long when she was awake, but the dreams played in her mind over and over while she slept.

On the morning of the coronation, she awoke to Abigail pulling the curtains open to let the sun shine in.

"I'm sorry, Your Highness, it is getting late and we need to prepare you for the ceremony."

Arianna smiled, but it didn't quite reach her eyes. "That's ok. I have a kingdom to tend to now, there is no time to be sleeping in." With those words, she felt a heavy burden bear down upon her shoulders. She had never realized how little she knew about running a kingdom, and it became apparent that this was why her parents were so adamant about her marrying sooner rather than later. This thought made her eyes well up with unshed tears. She closed them, took a deep breath and pushed those feelings away and got ready to prepare for her coronation.

She sat in her chair as Abigail worked her magic and put it up in a lovely, intricate braid, customary for the coronation ceremony. By the looks of it, she had trained for days to get it just right. When she was finished, she held the mirror up for Arianna to see her handiwork.

"It's just lovely. Thank you. And thank you for all of the years of work that you have done for me and my parents. I can see now that I truly am a spoiled, petulant child, who has never thanked anyone ever, but I am trying to change. I truly am."

"Oh, Your Highness, it has been my pleasure to serve you and your family. You are not so bad." She smiled. "I have heard stories of other princesses who are a lot worse than you are. You are going to make a fine queen."

Arianna hugged her tightly, taking Abigail off guard. "Thank you. I do appreciate those sentiments. They mean more to me than you will ever know."

They smiled at each other, and Abigail, overcome with emotions, straightened herself and said, "Now come, Your Highness, we must get you dressed and ready for the ceremony."

Arianna scowled at the heavy looking pink velvet robes. Summer had come early and they looked as though they would smolder her underneath their weight. She sighed.

"You know, Your Highness, the seamstress told me that these are the same robes that your mother wore for her coronation ceremony."

Arianna's eyes filled with tears again as she reached out and ran her hand down the soft, crushed pink velvet. The golden lace caught the light and the diamonds that were inlaid in the fur trim glinted in the sun. Ari smiled, really smiled, for the first time in weeks. The reflection danced around the room. She felt as though her mother was standing there with her, smiling with pride. Arianna sighed, closed her eyes, and thought, "If only you were here with me right now."

The thought pained her that neither of her parents was with her today to watch her take her vows, and she was also painfully reminded that the vows that she was supposed to be taking today were quite different ones.

"Shall we put your robes on now, Your Highness?"

"Abigail, you have been my handmaiden for the last five years. Please, call me Arianna. I don't have many friends. Well, I don't have any friends, really. I would like it if we could maybe consider each other friends?"

Abigail looked taken aback at this sudden change in her princess, now queen. She felt flustered at the request. "Your

High—I mean, Arianna, I would be honored to call you my friend." She smiled and helped her into her robes, which, indeed, were stifling in the heat.

Arianna turned to face her, and Abigail smiled. "You look like the queen that you were meant to be."

Arianna thanked her again, and held out her arm to join her on her way down to the chapel, where the coronation was to take place. Abigail's face brightened and she joined her until they got down to the chapel, where Captain Oakford was waiting, looking uncomfortable.

"Your Highness, usually it is the king and queen celebrating their coronation together, but, in this circumstance, there is no one to escort you up the aisle. Tradition states that the captain of the Royal Guard will escort the new queen if she is unwed or has no one to walk with her. Is this acceptable, Your Highness?"

A slight shadow of sadness fell over Arianna's face for a second, but she pushed it away. "Of course, Captain Oakford. I would be honored to have you escort me up the aisle.

He looked relieved that she did not rebuke him and held out his arm for her to take. "We are ready to begin when you are."

Arianna took a deep breath and said, "It looks like it's now or never."

"Your Highness, wait!" Arianna turned to see her mother's handmaiden, Arabella, was running as fast as her heavy gown would allow her to run towards her. She was out of breath by the time she reached Arianna's side.

"This just came. It was hand delivered from King Rubio and Queen Sapphira themselves. It was what your parents were going to order when they—on the day that—," her voice dropped, and she couldn't look Arianna in her eyes. Arianna looked at her with sympathy in her eyes.

"It's ok, Arabella. What do you have?"

Arabella held out a crushed pink velvet box with the crest of Eumetadotos emblazoned on the lid. Arianna gasped and held her hands out for the box, a little reluctantly.

"It was to be their wedding present to you, Princ—I mean, Your Highness."

Arianna looked up, tears welling in her eyes again. She was beginning to hate the feeling.

"Aside from having my parents back with me, this is the best gift that I could ever have received. Thank you, Arabella." She hugged her mother's handmaiden, who was taken aback by the gesture, and began to cry.

Arianna opened the box, and there, nestled inside was the most glorious necklace that she had ever seen. The focal point was a gorgeous, huge morganite gem, as pink as she'd ever seen. It was on a thick gold chain that held tiny diamonds, rubies, sapphires, and every other gemstone that could be imagined, including a few pure white ones that she had never seen before, ones that sparkled in every color that could be imagined, throughout the length. It was positively stunning. Arianna gasped, and looked up, showing Arabella and Captain Oakford what was inside the box.

She turned to Arabella, and asked, "Would you please put this on me? I want to wear it in honor of my parents. I should be wearing it today anyway." Her voice softened, and her eyes got a faraway look in them.

"I would be honored, Your Highness." Arabella took the

necklace from the box and placed it around Arianna's throat. She hooked the clasp, and when Arianna turned, she gasped at how glorious it looked on her.

Arianna looked to Captain Oakford and nodded that she was now ready to enter into the chapel.

Captain Oakford signaled to the guards to open the doors, and, as they did, every head in the chapel turned to see their new queen.

Arianna breathed, "Ohhh," as she looked into the chapel for the first time since her parents' funerals. She was stunned by the transformation. There were bouquets of the lavender roses intertwined with the Shasta daisies interspersed throughout the entire room again, as a tribute to her parents. In addition, there was wisteria, roses of every color and a plethora of other flowers intertwined into garland stretching down the length of every wall. The windows were open and sunlight was streaming into the room, making it brighter than Arianna had ever seen it before. The chapel was stunning and it looked as though the entire kingdom of Eumetadotos, as well as all of its allies, including Prince Ethan, King Sebastian and Queen Mary from Goldlandia and King Rubio and Queen Sapphira, from Polýtimos, were all in attendance, among other royalty from other neighboring kingdoms.

"Are you ready, Your Highness?" Captain Oakford asked.

"Yes. Let's go give this kingdom a reason to celebrate."

The music started, a tune that was centuries old, one which had been played at every coronation ceremony since anyone could remember. Arianna was escorted down the aisle by Captain Oakford. When they got to the front of the chapel, where the same clergyman who had performed the funeral for her parents stood, Captain Oakford bowed to her and stepped to the side, ready to walk her back down the aisle after the ceremony.

The clergyman cleared his throat and started.

We are here today to celebrate the coronation of Arianna. I have no doubt that she will make a fine queen." He droned on about the qualities it took to make a good leader for a kingdom and how he was certain that she would be able to live up to those values.

Finally, the time came for Arianna to take her vows.

"Arianna, will you solemnly promise and swear to govern the people of the kingdom of Eumetadotos, according to their respective laws and customs?"

"I solemnly promise."

"Will you be fair in your judgements, allow Justice to be served in a fair and merciful manner, and uphold the Laws of the Kingdom of Eumetadotos to the best of your ability?"

"I will."

The clergyman placed the crown that had belonged to her mother and all of the queens of Eumetadotos before her onto her head. He then presented her with the royal scepter and orb, and motioned for her to turn and face the congregation. She did so, holding up the orb and scepter. As she turned, the jewels on her necklace caught the sunlight and the reflections sparkled and danced around the room cheerfully. The morganite caught a direct sunbeam, and it seemed to glow as though it were lit from behind by a fire. Everyone in attendance gasped at the beauty of it.

"I now present to you, your new queen, Queen Arianna."

The applause was thunderous.

"Will everyone please move into the main dining hall for

supper after our queen has left the chapel?"

Captain Oakford stepped beside Arianna and, together, they walked back down the aisle, into the main dining hall. He escorted her to the front of the hall, where her seat, a golden high-backed chair with ornate carvings and a pillow cushion to sit on, and a single table setting were placed.

Arianna felt a lump form in her throat as she realized that she was meant to dine alone. She hesitated before stepping up onto the platform that was set up for her. She turned to Captain Oakford and asked him, "Would it be inappropriate if I asked you to dine with me tonight? I am a little uncomfortable being alone in front of everyone."

Captain Oakford startled. "Your Highness, it would be an honor to dine with you tonight. Are you sure that you wish to bestow such an honor upon me?"

Arianna giggled. "Of course. You are the Captain of the Royal Guard. You have earned that honor. You protect me, and you protected my parents before me, to the best of your ability."

Captain Oakford's head bowed, and when he looked back up, his eyes were swimming with tears. "Your Highness, I am so sorry that I could not protect them better that day. Everything had happened so quickly. I was too late to save them."

"Captain Oakford, I do not hold you accountable for anything that happened that day. I wish that we could find the people responsible and bring them to justice, but you are not one of those people. There is nothing to forgive on your part."

Captain Oakford looked at Arianna with a newfound respect. "Thank you, Your Highness. It was an honor serving your parents, as, I am sure, it will be an honor to serve you."

Arianna smiled, and they ascended the platform. She caught the attention of the maître d', and called him over. "Will you please set another place setting for Captain Oakford at my table? He will be dining with me tonight.

The maître d' looked surprised but did as he was asked.

The evening went splendidly. Since Arianna was not married, she asked Captain Oakford to dance with her for the first dance. She then took turns with every prince who was eligible for marriage all night. All of them hoped that she would take favor on him and choose him to be the next king and rule with her. Arianna, however, had no intentions of marrying any of them. She had given her heart once, and that had turned out to be a disaster. She was determined to never let that happen again. Besides, not one of these princes met her standards of what a good king for her people should be. She knew that she had to marry at some point or her line would die and leave Eumetadotos without a leader. As much as she had balked at the idea of marrying, she now saw what her parents were talking about. She needed to find the right king to rule alongside of her, but she just couldn't determine who would be the best person for the job.

The night ended, and when the last guest had left, Arianna flopped, in a most un-royal-like manner onto the throne, not unlike the way she had flopped into the clover not all that long ago. The memory made her frown. She heard a chuckle behind her, and she turned to see Captain Oakford standing next to her. She motioned for him to sit beside her, as he had for dinner. He graciously took up the chair, and she looked at him. Now that she noticed him, he was quite handsome. He had a strong, chiseled jaw, and if you looked close enough, you could see a small smattering of freckles across his nose. His blue eyes were soft, with just a hint of green in them. His auburn hair was done neatly, and fashionably according to the customs of the Royal Guard. Yes, he was handsome, but he did not come anywhere near the level of handsome of Ellavorn. Her heart ached when she thought of him, and how he should be the one sitting next to her. She furrowed her brow and addressed him, "What is so funny?"

"You are, Your Highness. You can carry yourself very regally, but the moment you are alone, and you don't think that anyone is around, you drop that regality and are so childlike. It is refreshing. You have grown a lot in these last few weeks. Everyone around the palace agrees. You are going to make a fine queen and I am honored to be the one in charge of protecting you."

Arianna smiled, "Thank you. I am honored that you feel that way about me. I just hope that I can live up to everyone's expectations."

Captain Oakford smiled and assured her that she would do a good job as their leader. He then offered his arm to her again.

"Would you allow me to escort you to your chambers?"

Arianna's ears turned pink and she took his arm. As she did, she felt as though she had made her second friend that day.

Chapter 7

After the coronation, Arianna took the title of queen very seriously. She was trained in the day to day activities that are required of the queen, and even did some research on her own family history. She fell into a fairly smooth routine. There was hardly a day when Captain Oakford was not by her side, standing guard, or just being a trusted friend and confidant.

One day, before anyone was awake in the palace, she slipped out of her room, unnoticed, and saddled up Lightning. "Hey, boy, I'm sorry I haven't been around much lately. Things have been kind of crazy. Have they been treating you well?"

Lightning raised his head high and shook it, neighing loudly.

"Shhhhhh, you'll wake someone up and they'll see us. I want to take a ride before anyone gets up. But, if they see me, the jig is up."

Lightning stomped his hoof in answer. She mounted him, and they took off at breakneck speed in the direction of the meadow. When they got there, she dismounted, and went to the edge of the forest, her eyes searching.

"He is not here, Arianna," a familiar voice said from behind her.

She whipped around to see Armen standing before her, with an unreadable expression on his face.

"Where did he go?" Her voice seemed small and lost, even to her.

"He left the day after you broke off the engagement. He said that he couldn't bear to be so close to you, yet not be able to go to you. You broke his heart, Arianna."

Tears now spilled freely over her cheeks.

"I'm sorry, Armen. I truly am. Where can I find him? I need to know. I made a terrible mistake. I need him to know that I don't blame him for anything. I love him. I was just overcome with grief. I lost both of my parents that day, and it was just so easy to lash out at him. I don't know why I did it. I have regretted it ever since."

Armen looked at Arianna with pity in his eyes. "Arianna, I do not know where he went. He left without saying a word to me or to anyone else. His mother has been beside herself with grief ever since. I know that you are sorry for the way that you acted, but you still hurt my son. You broke a pact that was made by your parents and by you, therefore, you are no longer welcome here."

Arianna felt as though someone has slapped her across the face. "What?" She whispered.

"I am sorry, but Forest Glen and Eumetadotos are no longer allies. You must leave now. If you are caught by my men, they will kill you on sight. I will never mention that you were here. But, you must leave now and never return. Am I clear?"

"Yes, Your Majesty. For what it's worth, should you ever need my assistance, you can depend on me and my people."

Armen simply smiled, and said, "Thank you, Your Highness."

Arianna ran to Lightning, mounted him as fast as she could and raced back to the safety of her own palace, where she ran to her chambers, collapsed in her bed and sobbed again for the lost love of her life.

A few hours later, Captain Oakford came to her chambers and knocked on the door. He was there to escort her on her daily errands. An idea came to Arianna. One night, after he had escorted her to her room, she pulled out the book of royal customs. She had to pick a husband and marry. She knew that none of the princes that she had met would ever measure up to her standards. None except one, and now she knew that, thanks to her own impulsiveness, he was permanently off limits. She had read the rules of marriage over and over again so that they were ingrained in her mind.

> *"Should the princess/queen not find a suitable prince/king within a year's time of his/her coronation, he/she may choose someone of royal appointment, such as The Captain of the Royal Guard...should he/she fail to marry within that time, a great curse will be placed upon the land."*

There were other titles listed, but that one stood out in her mind. As she took Captain Oakford's arm, she looked at him.

"Captain Oakford, in all of this time, I never asked you what your first name is."

He chuckled, a sound that was becoming familiar and quite pleasant. "It's Joshua, Your Highness."

"Joshua. I like that." She looked at him in the eyes and said, "Well, Captain Joshua Oakford, please call me Arianna. Your Highness is so formal, and I feel that we have moved past such formalities in our friendship."

He looked stunned. "Do you really consider me your friend?"

"Well, you and Abigail are the closest that I've got to friends."

Joshua smiled. "It is an honor to be considered a friend of the queen. More than you can imagine."

Arianna smiled. A lump formed in her throat, as she asked him, "Joshua, are you married, or intended to be married?"

The question seemed to take him off guard. "N-n-no, Arianna, I'm not. I am the Captain of the Royal Guard. I don't have much time for anything other than protecting my queen, and her future king." The last few words were said with just a slight hint of disgust.

"Oh," said Arianna.

"Why do you ask?"

"I was just making conversation. That is all."

"Oh. Have you thought any more of who you would intend to marry? We do need a king, after all."

"I've given it some thought. I don't know if I am ready to make a definite decision yet, though. It is a big step. This is the person who I will have to rule a kingdom with, and share a bed with, and probably raise children with. It is not to be made lightly."

Joshua looked a little disappointed, but he recovered quickly. "I agree. That is a decision that needs serious consideration. It is an important one and you want to make sure that the best possible person is chosen. Arianna, as your friend, I would like to impart just a little bit of advice."

Arianna's eyebrows shot up in interest. "OK, I am interested in what you have to say on the matter."

"Well, trust your instincts. Pick someone who is strong and dependable. But, also someone who thinks of you and has your best interest at heart. You are special, Arianna. Choose someone who sees that and will cherish you for that."

Arianna's jaw dropped in a most unladylike manner, and Joshua laughed at her expression. She shook her head to clear her mind, and spoke with her voice full of emotion, "Thank you, Joshua. I appreciate those words, and I will most definitely take them to heart."

Joshua nodded and they continued into the dining hall for breakfast. Arianna had started a new tradition, building on her father's. She now mandated that all servants in the castle were to eat their meals with her in the dining hall. She would address them every morning with her kind words. The new tradition was going quite well. The spirits of the servants seemed to be higher than ever before, and that, to her, was an accomplishment, for they were always very happy when Jasper and Alexandra were ruling. Joshua escorted Arianna to the front and pulled her chair out for her. He then took his usual place to her right, as was customary for the Captain of the Royal Guard. The place to her left was reserved for the King.

Breakfast was served to all of the tables, and when the servers and chefs themselves took their plates and sat in their seats, there was one table that was noticeably absent. Whispers abounded through the room. Arianna stood to address them all.

"Ladies and Gentlemen of the castle, Captain Oakford and I have some news on the status of my parents' murderers." Every eye was upon her and every ear was now open. The silence was deafening. "We have found two of them, and they have given us the whereabouts of the rest of their gang. They should be arrested by tonight and brought to justice swiftly."

The entire room erupted into applause, and Arianna smiled widely. When the clapping died down, she went on, "I would like to personally acknowledge Captain Oakford, and his guards for a job exceptionally well done. There will be a feast to celebrate after they are brought to justice. The entire kingdom is to be invited as well." Another cheer arose from the tables around the room. The atmosphere in the room was jubilant throughout the rest of the meal. Arianna sat, smiling quietly at the people who had worked so loyally for her parents and herself over the years.

"You are awfully quiet this morning." She jumped at the voice next to her.

"Well, yes, I have had a lot on my mind, Joshua."

He raised his eyebrows in interest, "Anything that you would care to discuss?"

Arianna hesitated, and then continued. "I know now why my parents were pushing so hard for me to marry. It seems as though I must marry within a year of my coronation or a great curse will befall the land. At least, that is what is written." She gazed off into the distance, a hint of longing in her eyes.

Joshua looked a little crestfallen. "You are regretting not marrying the elven prince?"

"Ellavorn. His name is Ellavorn, and yes, I am. I made a terrible mistake, and now it is too late."

Joshua took a deep breath and said, "I can send one of my men to the borders of Forest Glen to look for him if that is your desire."

Arianna's heart broke all over again. "No, it is not necessary. I rode out to Forest Glen this morning."

Joshua startled at the confession.

"I woke up early. Lightning has been penned up, and he needed a run anyway."

"Arianna! You should never have left here unguarded. Do you know what could have happened?"

"I had to try to see him, Joshua. I had to know that what I have done is permanent. It seems that it is. I've made such a mess of things with the elves."

"So, he would not take you back?"

"I wouldn't know. He left the day after I broke off the engagement. He didn't say a word to anyone as to where he was going. I was also made aware that I, nor anyone from Eumetadotos, is welcome in the forest or the meadow any more. I broke a pact with them. I am now considered the enemy. I didn't know what I was doing. How am I ever going to be able to rule the kingdom if I can make an enemy without even knowing it?" She looked away, and sniffed, blinking back the tears that threatened to fall, once again. "I can't even go one day without crying!"

Joshua put his hand on her shoulder, "Arianna, you have lost both of your parents and your chosen husband in the course of a few days. A few weeks later, you were sworn in as the queen. You were completely unprepared for the position. You are bound to be overwhelmed. You are dealing with a tremendous amount of stress and loss. To be honest, I would think less of you if you weren't so emotional. You are also dealing with this better than a lot of people would be. You haven't fallen apart publicly, and not once have I ever heard you say that you want to give up and quit. You are so determined to succeed. It is amazing to watch. You have grown so much in so little time. You need to give yourself more credit."

He smiled and turned back to the room. "They seem to be enjoying themselves. I have never seen morale so high in the palace."

Arianna looked at him, eyes shining with pride. "Really? Do

you mean all of that?" She managed to whisper.

Joshua looked at her and said emphatically, "Yes, I do. You are amazing. I hope that you will see that in time, and I hope that the prince that you choose will realize how lucky he is to have won, if not your heart, than your hand."

Arianna's jaw set at the mention of marriage again. She knew that she had to choose a king to help her to rule, but the list of prospects made her stomach drop. Each one felt wrong in her heart. If she was expected to marry, she wanted to at least be able to stand the thought of the person she was to be married to. She could not think of one of those princes that she could tolerate for more than a few moments at a time.

"That is if I marry a prince, or even at all, Joshua."

Joshua looked scared at that prospect. "Arianna, you cannot be serious. You read what was written. It was written for a reason. You *must* marry within a year of the coronation."

Arianna rolled her eyes. "Yes, I know what is written. I don't believe in curses."

"Arianna, these things were written for a reason. Do you not understand this?" Joshua rubbed his temples. "I thought that you had grown more in these last few weeks. I guess I was wrong. You need to think about what is best for your people. These people here," he waved his hand around the room to indicate the people who were still celebrating the news of the capture of the people who had murdered their king and queen.

Arianna's face filled with shame, "Joshua, I understand what you are saying. I truly do. I just am having a hard time with the idea of marrying someone that I don't love, and probably never will. I love Ellavorn–"

"Love or loved?"

"I love him, and I always will. You can't hold on to something so tightly and just let it go in an instant. I don't think that I have it in my heart to love another as I did him."

"Arianna, of course, you'll never love another as you love him. You can never love two people the same way. Love is as different as each person is. For example, I don't love you as I love my former girlfriend. You're a different person, so I love different things about you. It's the same with you. You will not love someone the way that you loved him. It will never be the same." When he looked at Arianna's face, there was an unreadable expression. It was only then that Joshua caught his mistake, and blushed a crimson shade of red. "I'm sorry, I was out of line. I should never have voiced that thought. I don't know why I said that. Please forget that I did."

Arianna simply looked at him. "Joshua, was that a declaration?"

Arianna had never seen someone go from that shade of red to the shade of green in a matter of mere seconds before, and she struggled mightily to hold in the giggle that was threatening to escape her lips.

Joshua looked down and began to pick at an imaginary spot on the tablecloth. He stammered, "Well, uh, I don't know. I mean, I feel something for you that I have never felt for anyone else before. I don't know if it's love, Arianna, but it is definitely along those lines, and the feelings are strong."

She had no idea how to take this information, nor what to do with it. When she had read that someone of royal appointment was eligible for consideration of marriage to the queen, she had felt a flutter in her heart, but nowhere near as strong as she felt for

Ellavorn. Suddenly, she was faced with a decision to make between giving Joshua hope for something that may never come to pass, or crush his dreams altogether."

"I need to go to my room." He made a move to escort her. "I need to be alone, Joshua. I have a lot to think about right now." He looked crushed, but nodded. Arianna stepped out of the dining hall as regally as she could manage. Once she had shut the door behind her, she broke into a run all the way to her room, where she threw herself onto her bed, too tired to cry anymore, but with too many thoughts to allow her to sleep.

Chapter 8

About an hour later, there was a small knock on her door.

"Who is it?"

"It's me, Abigail."

Arianna jumped out of bed and opened the door for her to enter.

"I figured you would need some help getting ready for the day. Oh, you look like hell. You do need help."

Arianna smiled at her friend. "No, but I do need advice."

Abigail's face lit up at the prospect of some actual girl talk.

"I guess you know that I am expected to marry within a year of taking my vows?"

Abigail simply nodded, and Arianna continued. "The problem is that I don't know of anyone that I would choose to marry rather than Ellavorn. I love him. I always will."

Abigail gave her a sympathetic look. "I saw the way you looked at him, and how he looked at you. It really seemed as though you were in love. What happened, Ari? You haven't really spoken of the broken engagement, aside to say that it was, indeed, broken off."

Arianna hung her head in shame. She hadn't wanted to admit to anyone what she had done. She didn't want to relive one of the worst moments of her life over and over. "He came to my room after the funeral and was ready to stand watch over me again. I became enraged and blamed him for my mother's death."

Abigail gasped.

Tears started flowing freely from Arianna's eyes, and she wondered just how many she had left in there, hidden. "I know it wasn't his fault. He tried to heal her, but she was too far gone. It was too late. I don't even know if he would have been able to heal her had he been at the scene. I was horrible to him, Abigail. Absolutely horrible. And now, it's too late."

"Can't you have Captain Oakford send a messenger to Forest Glen?" She asked excitedly.

"I went to Forest Glen myself this morning." Abigail looked just as shocked at the admission as Joshua had been. "He's gone. He left the day after I broke off the engagement. Armen has no clue as to where he is. Even if he did, I don't think he would tell me."

"Surely, he would, Ari. Armen was the biggest supporter of your marriage, aside from you and Ellavorn, of course."

"No, I spoke to Armen himself. I broke a pact. They are no longer our friends. I am no longer welcome in the forest or the meadow. I made a terrible mistake, Abigail, on many levels. I didn't know what I was doing at the time, but I certainly do now."

"There is no one that you can marry in his place?"

"Well, there are certainly prospects, but none that I could tolerate as my king."

Abigail raised her eyebrow. "Why is that, Arianna?"

Arianna smiled, a sad smile. "I always forget just how few friends I have until something like this comes up. I would tell Ellavorn all about the suitors that my parents would parade through here for me to choose from. He would often laugh at how I described them." She rolled her eyes, "Abigail, they were hopeless. Not one of them would make a good leader for our kingdom."

"Tell me," she said dryly, "What made them so hopeless?"

"Well, there's the Blubbering Buffoon. He would burst into tears every time he looked at me. I couldn't imagine being married to him. He'd drown us in our bed at night with his tears. Not to mention the hit that my ego would take."

Abigail burst out laughing. "Really? He burst into tears every time he looked at you?"

"*Every* time! Then, there was Prince Ethan. He looked as though he had never seen the light of day. He looked pale and sickly and like he had never seen a plate of food, let alone eaten it. Coupled with his jet black hair, he looked like a vampire."

Abigail clapped her hands and laughed even harder. "Tell me more, Ari!"

Arianna smiled, and said, "Another time. I need to figure this whole mess out."

Abigail pulled herself together, and sat straight up in the chair. "Ari, what if there are no princes that you would deem worthy? What then?"

Arianna sat down on her bed, and hung her head again. "I don't know. The Book of Customs says that if no prince meets my liking, then I can choose someone of royal appointment."

Abigail's eyes got as big as saucers, "You mean, like, the Captain of the Royal Guard?"

Arianna whispered, "Yes."

"I noticed that the two of you have grown close over the last few weeks."

"Yes, Joshua and I have become friends. I feel comfortable with him, but I don't know that I *love* him. Although, he made his feelings quite clear tonight at dinner."

Abigail clapped her hands together, loving the gossip, "What do you mean?"

"I mean," she bowed her head, "He pretty much told me that he loves me."

"Oh, Ari, what did you say?"

"I told him that I had a lot to think about and left to come here."

"No wonder he was in a right state. After you left, he looked so sad, it was almost like he was comatose. Does he know that he could be a possibility?"

"I haven't told him. I don't know if he's read the book or knows of that particular custom. I don't want to get his hopes up, Abigail. Please don't tell anyone about anything that I've told you here."

"I promise, I won't tell anyone. But, Ari, you need to talk to him. We have all seen such growth in you these past few weeks, but, this seems to be the one aspect where you're having trouble. You can't go storming off every time you hear something you don't like. You are the queen now. You have to hear these things and make decisions about them. Your responsibilities are far too important to be forgotten about because you are taking a temper tantrum."

"I have not forgotten my responsibilities," Arianna was getting annoyed with her.

"I simply mean that you can't throw a temper tantrum every

time something doesn't go the way you want it to. When you react that way, it looks as though you are shirking your responsibilities in order to act like a petulant child," Abigail purposefully used the same phrase that Arianna had used on the morning of her coronation in hope that what she was saying would get through to her.

Arianna looked at her with a fire in her eyes, but it quickly extinguished when she saw the look of concern on her friend's face. "You're right. I do need to control my temper." She sighed.

"What do I do, Abigail? I'm at a loss. I want to do what is right for my kingdom and my people, but I just don't know what to do.

"What is the worst that can happen if you don't marry?"

"The Book of Customs says that the land will be cursed."

"Cursed? Cursed how?"

"I don't know. I don't even know that I believe in curses. The book is so old, I don't know that it's true anyway."

"Arianna! Are you saying that you would risk the kingdom so that you don't have to make a decision?"

"No! I will not allow this kingdom to fall into disarray. I just don't know what I am going to do."

"Marry Captain Oakford. He is a good man. He would be a great king. You are comfortable with him, are you not?"

"I am, but I don't know that I am comfortable enough to *marry* him."

"Arianna, you need to think about this."

“I will. I have a year’s time.”

“Please don’t avoid this issue. It is important, Ari. All of our lives are dependent on it. Your parents wouldn’t have been so adamant that you marry if it weren’t important.”

“I said, I will think about it, Abigail,” Arianna snapped at her. “Now, if you’ll excuse me, I need to go and tend to the errands of the day.

Without looking back, Arianna left the room and closed the door behind her.

“Please do, Ari. Please do.”

Chapter 9

As Arianna stepped into her throne room, she felt the pressures of ruling alone fall onto her shoulders again. She took a deep breath and walked over and sat down on her throne.

"Your Highness, you have a message from Goldlandia."

Arianna looked at Joshua, confused. "Joshua, what is going on? I told you to call me Arianna."

"Yes, Your Highness, you did." He looked pained. "I think that it would be wise if I showed you the respect that the crown deserves."

"Should I revert to calling you Captain Oakford, then? Your title, as well, deserves some respect."

His jaw tightened. "If that is what you so desire, Your Highness."

"What I so desire is for you to tell me what is going on here."

"I do not think that this is a conversation that would be appropriate for this time."

Arianna pursed her lips and forced out, "Fine. Where is the message?"

Joshua handed the envelope over to her. It was beautiful. The entire envelope looked as though the paper were made of gold, which it very well could have been, considering that Goldlandia was known for their gold mining practices. They also love to keep the gold within the palace. The writing was a lovely calligraphy done with a quill pen in black ink.

Arianna read the letter and groaned.

Dearest, Queen Arianna,

It is with great regret that I hear of your broken engagement. Although, I am not surprised. Elves are a tricky bunch. I know that the pressures of ruling alone must be pressing to you, as you have not been properly trained in how to rule a kingdom. I would like to remind you that Prince Ethan has been properly trained in how to rule a kingdom flawlessly. I feel that he would be a perfect match for you. He is a fine young man and will produce healthy, strong heirs to the throne. There is no time to waste, Your Highness. You should choose your king soon. It would be wise to have a man by your side. Ethan would be your best choice. Our lands would be forever joined under the two of you, and you would enjoy all of the riches that you could possibly desire. I look forward to the acceptance of his betrothal.

Sincerely,
King Sebastian
King of Goldlandia

She screamed with rage, frightening everyone in the room, and forcing every head to turn to her in shock.

"That, that, that – ARGGGHHHHH! There are no words for him!" She threw the letter on the floor and stormed out of the room.

Joshua picked up the letter and read it to himself. He ran after her.

"Arianna, are you ok?"

"Oh, I'm Arianna now? What should I call you this minute?

Joshua? Captain Oakford? I'm confused. Are we friends, or are we not?"

Joshua grimaced, and blushed. "I'm sorry. My feelings were hurt. I didn't mean to hurt you as well. Yes, I still wish to be your friend. If I cannot have your heart, I would at least like to be a part of your life in some way. I understand that you have to marry someone of royal blood–."

"Or royal appointment."

Joshua looked confused. "What?"

Arianna eyed him carefully. "You didn't know?"

"Know what?" He looked genuinely confused.

"If I do not find a prince that I deem worthy of being my king, I may choose to marry someone of royal appointment, such as the Captain of the Royal Guard – you. I thought you knew and that is why you were professing your feelings to me."

"Arianna, I had no idea." Joshua looked hopeful and took a step towards her. She took a step back to match and his face fell.

"Joshua, I don't know what my feelings are towards you. I have been in love with Ellavorn for so long. I can't just kill that overnight. I don't know that I ever will. However, I do have feelings for you too. I just don't know what those feelings are. Please, I need time to figure this out." She gave him a pleading look. "I promise you, I will let you know my decision as soon as I make it. You will be one of the first, if not the first, to know.'"

His eyes lit up with the possibility, but he dared not let that shine through too much. He tried to keep a hold on his heart to keep it from soaring. However, the thought, "Maybe, just maybe she will love me back," kept running through his mind.

"Joshua," Arianna said, breaking his train of thought, "Please, do not get your hopes up. I don't know what is going to happen. I don't know how I'm going to feel. I have a little less than a year to make up my mind. I don't want to make a rushed decision on this. This is my life that we're talking about. I don't want to chance it to a maybe."

Joshua looked a little less hopeful, but he still had hope in his heart that she would possibly choose him. "I understand, Arianna."

"But, Joshua," she stepped forward a step.

He followed suit and took a step closer to her. "Yes?"

"If I run out of time, will you rule with me?"

"Arianna, I would be honored to rule with you. I would devote my life to you and Eumetadotos. You would never have to worry about having someone next to you to help you rule. I will stand with you to the very end."

Arianna sighed. "That is what I was afraid you would say."

Joshua looked stunned. "Isn't that what you want? Someone to help you, to stave off this curse? To help you rule this kingdom, and take some of the burdens off of you? I would treat you as an equal, not some lowly woman who is just a trophy on my arm, like it seems that King Sebastian wants Prince Ethan to do with you."

"Joshua, I do want all of that."

"Then what is the problem with my acceptance of your proposal?"

She looked at him and his face, and heart, plummeted.

"You want me to look for *him*."

"His name is Ellavorn. I would appreciate it if you would start using it. And yes, I want you to try to find him. I will make a pact with you. If you find him, and he will still have me, I want him to rule with me. If you cannot find him, or you do and he does not want me any longer, I will pledge myself to you. I know that I am asking you to choose to be second place in my heart. I am sorry for that, but I love him, Joshua. I need to find him. I need to know that he is safe, and I want to know that he does not hate me. I wouldn't be able to bear it if he reverted back to hating humans because of me."

"Wait, he hates humans?"

"No, he hated humans. He sort of had a change of heart at some point in time when he fell in love with me."

"So, he hates humans and you love him so deeply that you were going to *marry* him?"

"Joshua, please pay attention to *all* of the details, not just some. Yes, he hated humans. Yet, for some reason, he chose to save my life when I was nine. I still don't know the reason that he did, although, I am grateful to him for it. He has told me that it was the moment that I opened my eyes that his heart changed. We fell in love at that moment. Of course, being a child, I didn't fully understand what that meant. It was as I grew up and got to know him better that I grew to know what love truly is. I understand him, and he understands me. He knows me better than anyone in existence. Please, I know that I'm asking you to do something that could very well hurt you, but, please, try to find him."

"What if I find him and he refuses to come back?"

"Then I will know that he truly does not want me anymore, and I will marry you."

Joshua took another step closer to Arianna, and ran his fingers through her chestnut hair. "Why would you pledge yourself to me? I am sure that there is a prince somewhere who would love to be your king."

Arianna smirked and stared at the floor. "Yes, there are plenty of princes that would love to be my king. But, I do not trust one of them." Her eyes cut to him, and she trapped him in her gaze. "I trust you, Joshua Oakford. I trust you with everything."

"Except your heart."

"My heart isn't completely mine to give right now. Find Ellavorn. Once I know that he is truly done with me, I will have my answer for you."

Joshua nodded, biting his lip. "What if we are unable to find him in time?"

"I have already told you, I will marry you."

Joshua smiled, "I know, I wanted to hear you say it again."

Arianna smiled sadly and shook her head. "You are a terrible tease."

Joshua put his arm out and she took it. He escorted her back to the throne room, but didn't open the door.

"What's wrong?" She asked.

"Nothing. It's just that we forgot to seal our pact."

She looked confused. "What do you mean?"

"Well, usually when men make a pact, we seal it with a handshake. This is a little different, since what you are promising to give me is yourself."

Arianna looked at him, confused.

"Ari, I want you to seal this pact with a kiss."

Her eyes grew large. The request clearly had taken her off guard. She had never kissed anyone, aside from Ellavorn, and even that was not until after they were betrothed. She opened her mouth to speak, but could not think of anything to say, so she closed her mouth and simply nodded, looking scared.

Joshua burst out laughing. "You look terrified at the thought of kissing me."

She laughed, "It's nothing personal, it's just that I've only ever kissed one person before. Even then, I only kissed him after we had become engaged."

Joshua looked at her and stepped closer to her. Their mouths were inches of each other, and he said softly, "Well, I hope that I live up to his legacy."

He closed the gap and kissed her softly, then wrapped his arms around her, pulling her in and deepening the kiss. He poured all of the love that he felt into that kiss, hoping that she would see just how much he loved her.

Arianna melted, almost too willingly into his arms for a moment before she pulled away and took a deep breath, steadying herself mentally. She wasn't prepared for the onslaught of feelings and emotions that poured through her. She felt joy, peace, if not love, then fondness for Joshua. But, she also felt guilty. Guilt at having kissed someone who was not Ellavorn, but also guilt because she knew that, even if Ellavorn didn't want her anymore, or if they didn't find him, she would never be able to fully commit her heart to Joshua. And, judging by that kiss, that was exactly what he wanted from her.

Joshua looked at her and smiled, then put out his arm to escort her back into the throne room. “Are you ok, Ari?”

Arianna looked straight ahead and nodded, too distracted by her own thoughts about the kiss that had just rocked her entire world. She knew that if Ellavorn wasn’t found, or that if he didn’t want her, Joshua would be the perfect companion to help her rule.

Chapter 10

The doors to the throne room crashed open, in marched five filthy, smelly strangers wearing shackles on their wrists, flanked on all sides by twenty guards. The oldest looked to be about 50, the youngest seemed to be younger than Arianna, by at least 3 years. She had to wrestle with herself to keep her hand from covering her nose from the stench. These men clearly had not bathed in weeks.

"Queen Arianna, we present to you the final five members of the band of bandits that murdered King Jasper and Queen Alexandra."

The guards lined the prisoners up in a straight line, on their knees, facing Arianna. They then fanned out into two lines behind them, on guard to make sure that they did not go anywhere or try anything to harm her.

Arianna looked into the faces of the men who were accused of killing her parents in cold blood and she tried to not let her heart turn to stone. She motioned for Joshua to come closer.

"Please bring me the two bandits that were captured earlier."

Joshua bowed, summoned some more of his guards and they set off to retrieve the prisoners from the jail cell.

While he was gone, Arianna rose from her throne and stepped down on the floor. She paced up and down the line, looking down at each of the bandits in utter disgust. In turn, each of the bandits sneered at her. One even going so far as to pull his lips back as if to spit at her. The look on her face alerted the guards to something happening, and one stepped up and hit him in the back with the hilt of his sword.

Arianna looked horrified as to what had just transpired.

"Why would you hit him? I did not ask you to."

"Your Highness, he was making a move to do something. What, I do not know, but the look of horror on your face said it all."

Arianna stood as straight as she could and fired back, "I do not condone that type of violence. Please do not ever act that way in front of me again. You did not see what had happened, or was going to happen. You had no right to lash out like that."

The guard looked embarrassed, and apologized to his queen, who seemed to accept the apology readily before turning her attention back to the five prisoners kneeling before her. She went to the young boy and stood, looking into his eyes. She was met by a glare full of hate, which she did not understand.

"What is your name?" She demanded.

He simply sneered at her.

"Do you always ignore direct questions from your queen? I asked you what your name is. If you will not answer that question, how will you answer the more difficult ones?"

She heard the guards stifling their laughs. She gave them a look that silenced them all.

She turned her attention back to the man, who was no more than a child, kneeling before her. He simply continued to stare at her, his gaze blazing with hatred.

"Are you going to answer me?"

He shot her a look of disgust before replying, "I don't answer to pigs like you."

Arianna's eyebrows shot up. She then turned her own heated gaze onto him and said, "It would be wise not to anger the person who holds the fate of your life and the life of your friends in her hands."

He gave a short laugh and said to her, "You think you have my fate in your hands, but who holds your fate in their's?"

Arianna looked confused. The four other bandits began to laugh at what the youngest of their band had said.

"So be it. I can see that you want to do this the hard way."

She turned and walked back to her throne. The five bandits continued to laugh for a moment, before Arianna gave the guards the signal to quiet them, which they did, but by less violent methods than hitting them with the hilts of their swords.

No sooner had they been quieted down, the doors swung open yet again. In walked Joshua with the two bandits that they had captured previously. They were even dirtier than the five recently caught ones from being locked in the dungeons. They were forced to kneel and face Arianna as well.

Joshua gave Arianna a signal that they were secure, and she rose from her throne again and began pacing, thinking of the right questions to ask. She had tried compassion with the youngest one. He didn't seem to comprehend that emotion. All seven of the prisoners glared at her with unbridled hatred.

She suddenly turned to them and demanded, "Are you the ones who killed my parents?"

All seven stretched their faces into broad smiles, and each one, in turn, admitted to doing the unthinkable and killing two people on the road.

Arianna then asked, "Why would you kill them?"

The oldest one spoke, "We act on its orders."

Arianna and Joshua exchanged confused looks. Arianna asked him, "Whose orders?"

The seven of them all burst out laughing as though they had just heard the funniest joke ever told.

"The one who dwells afar," one started chanting.

"The one who lives to mar," the next one chimed in.

"The one who teaches what is right," the next in line said.

"The one who will diminish your light." The fourth one finished, menacingly.

All seven started laughing again, as Arianna and Joshua exchanged another look of confusion.

"What is its name?" Arianna demanded. She was beginning to lose her temper.

The youngest of the seven chortled. "Names do not matter. Names hold no bearing."

Arianna stood before him again. She dropped to one knee, and looking in his eyes said to him, "Names matter more than you know. Your name is what makes you who you are. They are what defines you. I pity you that you do not see it." It was her turn to show her disgust at the group.

She strode back to her throne, and addressed them as a whole.

"Do the seven of you admit to murdering my parents? King Jasper and Queen Alexandra of Eumetadotos?"

Each one gleefully took their turn acknowledging that they played a part in the death of Arianna's parents. The youngest one looked her in the eyes and added, "It was a pleasure to do it. I would do it again if I could."

Arianna felt as though he had stabbed her with a knife in her heart, as opposed to just with his words. She then looked at Joshua, who nodded his ascent.

"It is my duty, as Queen of the Kingdom of Eumetadotos, to accept your guilty pleas and sentence you all to death. Your execution will be held in the courtyard, and you will all be beheaded by the guillotine, one by one."

As she stood, she made eye contact with Joshua, who nodded in agreement. Inside, she felt terrible. She was sentencing seven people to die. She wanted justice for her parents, but, at the same time, how could she live with herself for sentencing seven people to death?

"Guards, please take them away. Their sentence will be carried out in three days' time." She then motioned for Joshua to come closer. "Please sound the signal that I wish to address the village."

"Arianna, are you ok?"

"No, I am not, Joshua," she yelled. "I just sentenced seven people to death! How can I be ok?"

"Ari, it's the law. You need to follow the law when sentencing."

"I know that. It doesn't mean that I feel any better about it. What makes me any better than them? They killed two people. I've just killed seven."

With that, Arianna turned and stormed out of the throne room to address her kingdom.

Chapter 11

Arianna stepped onto the balcony and looked out at the people of Eumetadotos. Joshua walked out behind her, and stood to her left as she walked to the edge and addressed them.

"People of Eumetadotos, I have summoned you all here with terrific news. Captain Oakford and the rest of the royal guard have been working tirelessly to find the bandits that murdered my parents, your king and queen, and bring them to justice. Today, that justice has been served. There were seven surviving bandits. All seven have been caught and sentenced to death by beheading. The sentencing will be carried out in three days' time. We will raise red flags, one by one, as their sentences are carried out in the courtyard. That night, we will have a feast in the castle in order to celebrate the victory of having found these criminals and bringing them to justice."

A cheer went up from the crowd, and the rejoicing had begun. Arianna's heart swelled as she watched the villagers and servants below hug one another, and be happy that her parents' murderers were finally caught.

Arianna turned to see Joshua staring at her with mixed emotions on his face.

"I thought that you would be happier that we have caught these criminals and that they are now going to die."

"Arianna, you know that I am glad that they are caught, and I am glad that they are going to die. But, I am also worried about you."

"Joshua, I will not speak of this anymore. I need to be alone."

"Arianna, I don't think that it is wise for you to be alone right now. You feel too much guilt. Please talk to me."

"Joshua, I think I made a mistake. I want to rescind my sentence of death and just have them imprisoned for life."

"Arianna, it is the law."

"Aren't I the one who is in charge of making the laws? I can change this."

"I don't think that you should. It will speak of weakness in you."

Arianna glared at Joshua. "Are you calling me weak? I find greater strength in what I am doing than killing them."

"Killing them would rid the world of their filth."

"And killing them would also make me a murderer."

"No, Ari, you are not a murderer. You are simply doing your duty."

"My duty? No, Joshua, my duty is to be merciful. This is not mercy. I have three days to make a decision. I need to be alone to think."

Arianna turned on her heel and stormed off to her chambers, where Abigail was anxiously waiting for her, excited to rejoice with her.

"Ari, is it really true? Did they really find all of the bandits?"

"Yes," she answered flatly.

"This is wonderful news! You don't seem so happy about it. What is wrong?"

"I got into a disagreement with Joshua."

"Over what this time? It must have been bad, judging from the look on your face."

"Abigail, I'm sorry, I really don't care to discuss it." Arianna knew that the sentence that she handed down to the men was what the law dictated, but it still did not seem right to her. She also knew that if she told Abigail how she felt, she would disagree with her as well, and she wasn't up to dealing with another argument on this matter.

"I should get ready for dinner. Would you help me fix up my hair, please?"

"It will be my pleasure."

Abigail began styling Arianna's hair for dinner, and she noticed how quiet she had grown.

"Ari, I thought you would be happier that they found the bandits and that they were brought in."

"I am. I'm just worried that I handed down the wrong sentences. I'm supposed to be merciful, but yet, all I could think about is vengeance for my parents. It scares me."

"What scares you? The fact that you are human and have emotions, or the fact that you sentenced seven men to death? Ari, it is a death that they deserve. They murdered your parents in cold blood. They deserve death."

"It's not as simple as that, Abigail. Yes, it is upsetting that I just condemned these men to die. I know it won't be me pulling the lever on the guillotine, but am I any better? I'm the one giving the command. Does that make me a murderer as well?"

Abigail pulled a chair over and sat across from her friend, looking her in the face, "Ari, do you really think that these men are obsessing over these thoughts? Do you think that they feel guilty about what they've done? Did they show any remorse?"

"No. Not one of them. In fact, they were ecstatic that my parents are dead, and that they were the ones to do it. They would not even tell us their names, the cowards. The youngest is only about 15. He was the worst. He tried to spit on me. He also told me that he killed my parents with pleasure and that he would do it again."

Abigail gasped, and reached for her hands. "Oh, Ari, I'm so sorry. I can't imagine how that must have felt."

Arianna couldn't meet her friend's eyes. "It was hard. It made me so mad," she said softly. "But, I still think that I made a mistake."

"No, the law of Eumetadotos states that murderers must be punished by the penalty of death."

Arianna sighed. "That's the thing. When I passed the sentence down, I wanted that boy to hurt. I wanted him to hurt as badly as I do, every day. I am reminded of what happened to me every day, and yet, he deemed it funny. He mocked me. They took away my parents, and laughed at me for it. I know that the law demands death. I hate them for what they did. But, I also don't want blood on my hands. Hasn't enough blood been spilled as it is?"

Abigail tilted Arianna's face to meet her's. "Ari, you did what was necessary. Those men killed your parents with no remorse. They seem to be taking pleasure in what they did. It's disgusting. It is your duty to uphold the laws of our kingdom. You did the right thing."

"You sound like Joshua. He said pretty much the same thing."

Abigail smiled. “I knew I liked him. He’s a smart man. You should listen to him, Ari.”

Arianna turned and gazed out the window. “This would be so much easier if Ellavorn were here. I miss him so much.”

Abigail’s face softened. “I know that you love him. But, Ari, he’s gone. He left. It doesn’t sound like he is coming back.”

“I asked Joshua to find him.”

“What? Arianna! Why won’t you just marry Joshua? Ellavorn is an elf. He gave his heart to you once. No offense, but you pretty much stomped on it. Do you think he’ll come back?”

“I have to try.”

“And if he doesn’t? What then? What will you do then?”

“I promised Joshua I would marry him.”

“What? Ari! When were you going to tell me? When did this happen? How did this happen?”

Arianna took a deep breath and blew it out in a most un-queenly manner. “Before they brought the bandits in. We were talking about finding Ellavorn and what I would do if he can’t find him, or if he does find him and doesn’t want me anymore. I promised him that if that were the case, then I would marry him.”

“Gee, how romantic, Ari,” Abigail grumbled, rolling her eyes.

“What was I supposed to do, Abigail?”

“I don’t know, Ari. Maybe not treat him like he’s second best? Listen, I know how you feel about Ellavorn. I’ve been your handmaiden for years. I’ve seen the look in your eyes when you got back from seeing him every day.”

Arianna looked up in surprise.

"Do you really think no one knew where you were going? Your parents knew all along. Why do you think that they called on Armen to discuss your betrothal? You were so adamant that you didn't want to marry any of those other princes, and from what you've told me, rightfully so. They wanted you to be happy, Ari. In the last few weeks, you have been anything but. I know that you just lost your parents and the love of your life, but you can't treat people like they're second best. Joshua is a good man. He deserves better than that."

Tears welled in Arianna's eyes. "The problem, Abigail, is that *everyone* is going to take second place in my heart. No matter who they are. I need to marry someone by the one year anniversary of my coronation. I trust Joshua. I know that he will take the best interest of the kingdom to heart. But, I still love Ellavorn with all that I have. He knows me, heart and soul. I can't just give that up in an instant."

"I understand, Ari. I do, honestly. But, you did this to yourself. You threw him out of the palace and broke off the engagement. No one is to blame but yourself."

Arianna's eye blazed. "Don't you think I know that, Abigail? Don't you think that I'm reminded of that every single day? I was foolish and I made a stupid mistake. I know that. I just can't accept that it is really over between Ellavorn and me until I hear him say it. What would you do in my shoes?"

Abigail's jaw had dropped at her friend's outburst. Her eyes started to fill with tears. "Ari, I'm sorry. I didn't mean to push you. I know how much you love him. It's just that he is gone. How are you going to find him?"

Arianna lets a few tears slip down her cheeks. She looked her friend in the eye and whispered, “I don’t know.”

Chapter 12

The next three days were a blur as the palace got ready for the execution of seven murderers. Arianna walked around in a daze. She still could not come to terms with the fact that she had sentenced seven people to die. When she was alone in her room, she would pull her chair over and sit and gaze, longingly, at the Forest Glen, silently willing Ellavorn to appear, charging his horse towards the palace in order to tell her that it was all a nightmare from which she could now wake up. That never happened.

On the morning of the executions, Arianna woke up early and had Joshua escort her to the dungeons in order to have one last look at the men that would no longer be alive at sundown. They walked to the dungeons in silence.

"Ari, what do you expect to gain from this visit?"

"I don't know. Maybe hope that they will repent for what they did?"

"You know that isn't going to happen, right?"

"I expect not." She hung her head sadly for a moment, before picking it up and looking at Joshua head on and with a half-smile, said, "I can hope, can't I?"

"You can always hope." He returned her half smile with a broad one. "Just please don't let your hopes get too high. They are quite despicable."

She nodded as he held the door open for her as she walked in. As soon as the men heard the door creak open, they all lifted their filthy heads. Arianna didn't even try to hide the look of disgust on her face as she caught the first whiff of prisoner funk. She held her hand to her nose as she walked in.

“Do you not believe in bathing?”

One of the men sneered. “We do not bathe. Bathing is for pigs.”

Arianna looked at him with an amused look on her face. “Is that so? The pigs I’ve seen bathe in mud or dirt, much like you. So, I ask you, who is the pig now?”

The man looked as though he had been slapped, and just stood speechless.

Arianna turned to Joshua with an unreadable expression. “Please ask the guards to send in seven buckets of well water. I will also need some old clothes for myself, a long handled scrub brush and some soap. Abigail will get the clothes for you.”

Joshua nodded, biting his bottom lip to keep himself from bursting out in laughter, figuring out what she was about to do. When he returned a few moments later, he was bursting at the seams from keeping his laughter at bay.

Arianna moved into the solitary confinement stall because it was heavily boarded for privacy. When she emerged, she was dressed in her old riding clothes. She smiled at Joshua and asked, “How do I look?” With this, the dam that Joshua had been holding back burst, and he broke down into uncontrollable laughter.

“You look like you’re about to clean some livestock.”

“Good, that is the look I was going for.”

The bandits had all been watching everything with fearful eyes and they all tried to retreat to the backs of their cells. Joshua ordered the guards to bring the men back to the front of the cells, remove their shirts, and chain them so that they could not get free, and so that they were not able to reach Arianna as she gave each one of them their baths.

The guards then stood at the front of each cell while Arianna moved to and fro, cleaning each one the best that she could to remove the stench that permeated their skin. When she was done scrubbing them down with the soap, she took great pleasure in dumping the freezing cold well water all over their bodies to rinse them off. When all seven were cleaned to the fullest extent possible, she moved back into the solitary confinement cell and changed back into her clothes. She then stepped out and stood in the middle of the aisle, greeted by seven pairs of glaring eyes.

"Today, you all will die. You will all meet the same fate that you doled out to my parents. Do you have any remorse for what you've done?"

All seven men burst out laughing at her question, causing the guards to bang the bars of their cells in order to try to silence them.

"Very well. That is your choice to die with this on your soul. At least you won't foul up my executioner's nostrils with your stench." Arianna turned to leave. When she reached the door, she turned back and addressed them once more, stepping forward slowly as she spoke, as if those steps were spurring on her speech.

"The word Eumetadotos means generosity. It is the name of my kingdom, and it is how we try to live our lives, in a generous manner. I have tried to be generous with you. I have given you the chance to repent for the horrendous things that you have done. That generosity has been thrown back in my face time and again. You all mock me. I don't know why, but I am assuming that it has something to do with my showing you generosity. Mark my words. Generosity is not a show of weakness. No, quite the opposite, really. Generosity is a sign of strength. Strength to care for another person, no matter what they have done. Strength to forgive, even if that person isn't willing to ask for forgiveness. It is the strength to do good in this world, no matter the consequences. But, I must also have the strength to do what is right for my people and my kingdom. You killed my parents, and my people's king and queen. The penalty for that is death. In a way, maybe that, too, is generous. Not for just you, but for me as well. You see, knowing that you are all down here is too tempting for me to sentence you all to torture. There is no justice in that. So, you all must die, and die you will."

With that, she turned and walked out of the dungeon, and walked swiftly to the throne room, where she collapsed onto her throne. Joshua came up beside her, kneeling so that they were face to face.

"That was a brave thing to do, to address them like that. Are you still unsure of the death sentence?"

Arianna sat straight up. "No, I know that they must pay that ultimate price. I still don't like it and I will carry that guilt with me forever, but I know that they have to die." She buried her face in her hands. "I, however, cannot bear witness to it."

Joshua put his arms around her, pulling her into a hug. "It is not written that you need be present for the execution. Stay in the palace, where you cannot see what is happening."

Ari looked up and gave him a sad smile, "Thank you."

Joshua looked at her face, so sad, yet so unbelievably beautiful. He had to restrain himself from kissing her, so he stood up. "I will oversee the executions. There are things that need to be done still." He turned and walked out of the room, closing the door behind him. With the door closed, he leaned against the closed door and took a deep breath before heading down to the guillotine.

The area was ready, including the basket under the opening of the guillotine to catch the head of each of the bandits after the lever was released. That thought made Joshua's stomach turn a little as he thought of the fate of each of those men. He knew how Arianna felt, to a point. He hated the idea of the death of seven men coming at the hands of his own people. But, he also knew that the law needed to be upheld. This was what the law called for.

He thought about the young queen in the throne room, and his heart clenched. After today, he knew that he would have to start the process of finding Ellavorn. He hated that idea. Before King Jasper and Queen Alexandra had been murdered, he thought of Arianna as a spoiled little brat who had no concept of how to run a kingdom properly. He felt that she behaved selfishly and didn't care about anything except how things affected her.

Over the last few weeks, he realized that he had, mostly, misjudged her. Yes, she preferred to do things her way. Yes, she was being obstinate about marrying someone. But, hearing her reasons behind her actions, he couldn't help but to sympathize with her. He knew that Ari had lived a sheltered life. Her parents did not do her any favors in that aspect. As he watched her over the last few weeks, however, she blossomed into the queen that she was born to be. She truly loves her kingdom.

Joshua just wished that she would come around and realize that he wanted all of those things too. He wanted them with her. He knew that he had to keep his word and look for Ellavorn. He would not be able to bring himself to lie to her. He knew what he had to do, no matter how badly it hurt. Joshua knew when he signed on to be the Captain of the Royal Guard, what the consequences were. He would probably never marry. His duties were far too important, and he would have to be away much of the time. No wife that he knew of would be happy with that arrangement. He sighed and shook his head to clear his thoughts just as the gate opened and the seven bandits marched in, their heads covered with black cloth bags. Joshua made a gesture and the guards lined the seven men up in a row and removed their bags.

"Have you anything to say before we carry out your sentence?"

The youngest bandit smirked, "Where is your queen?" He spat out.

Joshua walked over to him calmly, looked into his eyes and said, "She is of no concern of yours."

"Couldn't handle the show, could she?"

"Is there anything else that any of you would like to say?"

"This land will not survive its wrath!" One of the other men yelled out. "It will have all that it wants. It wants her dead."

Joshua whipped around and grabbed the man by the throat. "Who are you talking about? Who wants her dead?"

"The one who is all powerful. It will not be seen until it wishes to be. We are simply a few of its army. All who oppose it will die. Your little queen is in its way. It wants the throne. It will have its way." The man began to laugh maniacally.

Joshua squeezed his throat and the man began to choke. "I will never allow that."

"In love with the queen, are you? I can see it every time you look at her. She will never have you. The bitch needs a royal sire to breed. It will kill any little bastards she has too."

Joshua reigned in his anger and tossed the man backwards. He gave the signal and the guards put the bags back over their heads. He pointed at the vile man who had just threatened

Arianna's life to be put to death first.

Two guards flanked him and marched him up the steps to the guillotine. They placed his head in the hole, locked him in and removed the bag. Joshua closed his eyes and gave the signal. The guillotine crashed down and the man's head fell into the basket with a "thunk." He signaled for the first red flag to be raised.

Joshua felt sick to his stomach, knowing that he would have to endure this six more times. He refused to look up at the guillotine, instead, he pointed to the youngest of the bandits, indicating that he was next. The process was repeated over and over until all seven men were dead. Their bodies and heads were piled on a cart to be burned. The decision had been made that the bodies of these vile men would not sully the ground of Eumetadotos with a burial.

Joshua turned and went into the castle, sick to his stomach. Arianna would be awaiting his arrival to inform her that the bandits were dead. He stopped just inside the castle doors and leaned against the wall to compose himself. His head was spinning and he felt as though he was going to be sick. After a moment, he stood and walked to Arianna's chambers.

Arianna waited by her door for Joshua to come back with news that the bandits had been executed. When she heard his footsteps, she opened the door. She looked up at him and his face was very pale. He looked sick. She invited him in and gestured for him to sit in her chair and asked Abigail to get him a glass of water. When he looked as though the spell had passed, she asked him, "Is it done?"

"Yes, it is." His voice seemed far off.

"Are you alright?"

"I don't know. I didn't think that it would affect me like this.

But, I just handled the execution of seven men. It's a little much to take in all at once."

"I knew that I should have changed their sentences. I knew that this was a bad idea."

Joshua stood up and took her in his arms, and looked into her eyes. "No, Arianna, this is what had to be done. This was the right choice. I will be ok. It was just a little much to take in all at once."

Arianna realized that he had pulled her a little too close, and pulled away from him a little, causing him to release his grip and sit back down. "I'm sorry. My first instinct is to want to hold you and to console you. I didn't mean to overstep my boundaries."

She had felt the loss of warmth on her arms the instant that he released her, and surprisingly, she missed it. "It's ok. I understand. Will you be well enough for the banquet tonight?"

"Of course. I will go and change. Would you care for me to escort you to dinner?"

"That would be lovely. Thank you, Joshua."

He smiled and left the room. As soon as the door had shut, Abigail turned to Arianna, with wide eyes.

"Well, that was intense!"

"I guess you could say that a discussion about the execution of seven men would be intense, yes."

"Honestly, Arianna! That man is head over heels for you! Can't you see it?"

"Abigail, I am not really in the mood to discuss this."

"So, you're still going to go forward with your search for Ellavorn?"

Arianna's heart skipped a beat at the mention of his name. "Yes. I need to find him. I need to know if what I did is final, or if he will give me a second chance. I have explained this to you before. I need to know."

Abigail simply nodded her head and began to help Arianna get ready for the banquet.

Chapter 13

Arianna took her time getting ready for the feast. She knew that she should feel glad that the men who had killed her parents were brought to justice, but she just could not shake the guilt that she felt by sentencing them to death. She also felt guilty about leaving Joshua to handle the executions on his own. As the queen, she should have been there to order each execution herself.

She had had a gown made of the brightest red silk. The bodice was form fitted with the skirt flaring out beautifully, the whole dress accentuating her hourglass figure. Throughout the dress were crystals that were embedded into the fabric. Around the collar dangled prisms of different sizes. When they caught the light, they threw rainbows around the room. Her chestnut hair was styled into an elaborate up-do with baby's breath pinned at intervals.

As she stepped out of her room, lost in her thoughts, she didn't notice Joshua standing outside waiting to escort her.

"You look beautiful, Arianna."

She jumped, and noticed that Joshua held his arm out to her. She took it. "Thank you. I owe you an apology, Joshua. I should have been there for those executions. I should not have made you handle all of that on your own. I am sorry."

Joshua stopped and turned her so that he could look into her eyes.

"Arianna, there is nothing in our laws that say that you have to be at the execution. As the Captain of the Royal Guard, it is my duty to handle the executions. Unfortunately, this was my first experience with it as well. It was a little harder than I thought it would be, being that there were seven at once, but it was necessary. I do not hold any ill feelings against you." He brushed a stray lock of hair that had fallen onto her face away. "If I were in your position, I don't know how I would have handled it. I may have done the same thing."

Arianna smiled a slow, sad smile and shook her head gently. "Somehow, Joshua, I don't believe that. I appreciate what you are trying to do, though. You are a good man."

They continued their walk to the banquet hall in silence. Once they got to the doors, they looked at each other and plastered on the most genuine looking smiles that they could muster. The guards opened the doors and they were announced. The entire room fell silent and turned to watch their queen and the Captain of the Royal Guard make their way to the front of the room. As they walked through, Arianna caught wind of a few whispers among the townspeople.

"The Queen and the Captain have become quite close as of late, have they not?" She heard one woman say to her spouse.

"I have noticed that as well, my dear. I wonder if there will be an announcement of another royal engagement soon," her husband responded.

"Well, after the fiasco that was the last engagement, I would hope that he would seriously think it over. She seems to enjoy her freedom. It makes you wonder if she will actually go through with a marriage or if she will get cold feet again."

The words that the woman spoke stung. Arianna's shoulders stiffened, and her step faltered for a moment. Joshua looked down at her, concerned and asked if she was ok.

She refreshed her smile, which had fallen just a little and told him that she was fine and they continued their walk through the banquet to the front of the room, where their place settings sat waiting for them. The crowd looked to them, anxiously, waiting for them to speak.

Arianna picked up her golden goblet and looked out to her kingdom. She took a deep breath and began.

"Ladies and Gentlemen, it is my pleasure to announce that the men who killed my parents are dead. Their filth will haunt our lands no more. They have paid for their crimes and my parents deaths have been avenged. Let us now offer a moment of silence for my parents."

The room fell silent until Arianna began speaking again.

"Let us all raise our glasses in a toast to my mother and father and their memory. They were wonderful leaders and the best parents anyone could ever ask for. I miss them every day, as I am sure all of you do as well."

A chorus of cheers to the fallen king and queen could be heard throughout the room, and the room began to break out in merriment as Arianna and Joshua took their seats.

"Ari, is everything ok? You seem as though something is bothering you."

Arianna looked into his eyes, with tears glistening in hers.

"Do you think I am flaky in regards to marriage?"

He laughed and said, "Where would you get an idea like that?"

"I overheard a woman speaking to her husband about me, and that is the gist of what she said. She noticed that we have gotten closer and said that you should seriously take my broken engagement into consideration if you are thinking of marrying me."

Joshua's face grew red with anger. "How dare she? She doesn't even know you, and yet she passes judgement on you? Who said it? I would like to speak with her."

Arianna reached out and covered his hand with her own, a gesture that shocked Joshua into silence. "Don't worry about it. She is right. I acted impulsively, and I am aware of how that looks. I just never thought that my kingdom would think of me as being ambivalent towards getting married. That wasn't the reason that I broke off my engagement with Ellavorn."

"I know, Arianna. I know your reasons. I know where your heart lies. I promise you that I will do everything in my power to find him for you." Joshua's face fell at that last part, and he began picking at an imaginary piece of lint on the tablecloth.

Arianna again covered his hand with hers and said, "I'm sorry to hurt you like this, Joshua. If I could change my heart, I would right now."

"I know that you would. But, I wouldn't let you. If you love me, I want you to love me on your own terms, not because you feel guilty. If you give me your heart, I want you to do so because you want to. I would do anything for you, including finding Ellavorn."

Arianna's eyes opened wide in shock that Joshua had finally said Ellavorn's name.

"Don't make a big deal out of it. I figure I had better get into the practice of using his name if my men are to go out looking for him. We begin our search the day after tomorrow."

Arianna's face broke out into a radiant smile, the first genuine one that she had smiled all night. She leaned in and hugged him.

"Thank you, Joshua, for understanding how much he means to me."

With that, the food began to be brought out. Arianna and Joshua were served first, and the rest of the kingdom was fed immediately after. After everyone had eaten, the music started playing, and Joshua offered his arm to Arianna.

"It is a tradition that the queen should dance the first dance. May I have the honor?"

Arianna accepted, and Joshua led her down to the dance floor, where they began dancing a waltz. About half way through the dance, the doors slammed open, and the wind blew out half of the candles in the room. A few people screamed in fear, and Joshua shoved Arianna behind his back, while drawing his sword in front of him to defend her from any intruders.

In walked a figure, heavily shrouded in a black cloak. It was impossible to tell whether the person was male or female, or even a person at all. The figure seemed to look around at the merriment taking place. Joshua signaled two of his guards to grab the intruder. With a flick of its wrist, the figure flung the guards backwards, sending them crashing against the wall. The entire room gasped.

"Magic!" Arianna gasped, her eyes were as large as saucers, and Joshua turned to look at her.

"That's impossible. There is no magic in Eumetadotos, save for the elves, and they can't do that. They can only use their magic for good. The wizards left years ago, there is no magic here."

"Joshua, there is no other explanation. No one could have done that without magic."

The figure seemed to have overheard their whispered

conversation, and turned their way. When it spoke, the voice was shrill and indescript.

"Yes, magic. Magic is coming again. You will know the effects all too well, little queen."

Arianna, in a burst of courage, stepped out from behind Joshua, and boldly asked, "What do you want from this kingdom?"

"To rule it, and rule it, I shall."

"You have no claim to the throne. This land will never see you as the true ruler."

The figure threw a fireball at her feet, barely missing her. She jumped backwards as the flames extinguished themselves, while the figure cackled its horrible laughter.

"It will if you are dead, little queen. You will join your parents in death."

Joshua leapt in front of her again, which made the figure cackle again.

"Oh, captain, I will not kill her today. I like to play a little. I want to see her suffer some more."

"Be gone with you, demon!"

The figure cackled again, "Demon? No, I am no demon. I am, however, a force to be reckoned with. I want this land. I will have it as my own. I will rule, and you all will die." It swept its arm, indicating Arianna and her guards. "Be warned. The curse is coming."

With another cackle, and a burst of smoke, the figure disappeared, leaving the room in silence.

The woman who Arianna had overheard talking about her earlier started to scream. Joshua grabbed Arianna's hand and dragged her back to the head table, throwing her underneath to shield her from the crowd that was now stampeding towards the door, despite barked orders from the guards to remain calm.

After the people had all fled, Joshua bent down to tell Arianna to come out. When he lifted the table cloth, however, he was met with the sight of her sitting curled up under the table, sobbing into her knees.

"Arianna, I will not let that figure harm you."

She looked at him with tears streaming down her face. "Joshua, you can't. You cannot protect me against magic. The only thing that can fight magic is magic. We are doomed."

"No, we're not. We can call on the elves."

"The elves are no longer our allies, remember? This is all my doing."

"Then we must find Ellavorn right away."

Arianna nodded, and Joshua helped her out from under the table, and escorted her quickly to her chambers, where Abigail was waiting, anxiously.

"I will post a guard by her door tonight. Please see to it that she goes directly to bed. I will also stand guard by her window, after she is in bed."

Arianna made a move to protest Joshua sleeping in her room, and was met with fire in his normally bright blue eyes. She swallowed back her argument for the time being and went to get dressed for bed.

After the door was closed, Abigail started firing questions at her.

"Ari, who was that figure? What did it want? Are we in danger? Should we leave the kingdom?"

"Abigail, slow down. I know as much as you do. I don't know who that figure is, or what it is. You saw what happened at the banquet. I think that we are in grave danger if we do not find a way to counter its magic. We need to find a way to make peace with the elves, or to find someone who is magical."

"But, there hasn't been magic in Eumetadotos in decades. Not since *he* left."

Arianna shook her head, "I know. I don't even know where he went. He left long before my grandmother was even born. I don't know where we could start looking. I don't even know his name. I just know that he was a great wizard who served on my great-grandfather's court. There is nothing else said about him. It looks as though all information about this great wizard was destroyed for some reason. If only I could make things right with Armen. He would surely know what happened, or where to find him."

"What would happen if you went to see him?"

Arianna huffed, "His people would kill me on sight."

"Well, that seems a bit harsh."

Arianna smiled sadly at her friend, "Well, I did break a pact with them. That broken pact also sent his son running away. I need to find Ellavorn. I need to set things right with Armen and the elves, and possibly get rid of this threat to Eumetadotos."

"Do you think it will work?"

“It has to, Abigail, it’s the only way.”

Chapter 14

The next day was spent making plans on how to find Ellavorn and try to persuade him to return to Eumetadotos, or at least to the Forest Glen. Arianna did not miss the agitation that Joshua was feeling. She tried to limit the hurt that she was inflicting on him, but that proved to be impossible, given the task at hand. Arianna didn't try to deny her feelings for Joshua to herself. That would just be a lie. She did care for him, she just didn't care for him with the same intensity as she loved Ellavorn.

"Don't look at me like that, Arianna." Joshua's voice broke into her thoughts.

"How am I looking at you?" She asked, a little defiantly.

"Like I am broken. I am not a broken man. It is true that I love you fiercely. I have been completely honest with you about that. I know why you need to find him. Your heart needs closure. If this will help you to move on, I will do it, Arianna."

"Joshua, I do not wish to move on. I love him. I know that this hurts you to hear it, but it is true. I love Ellavorn. He owns my heart almost completely. I need a chance to make right the wrongs that I have done to him. I need a chance to see if I can work things out with him. Not just for me, but the entire kingdom of Eumetadotos is at stake now. I need to be able to save my people."

Joshua grabbed her arms, a little rougher than he meant to. Her eyes widened in fear. When he realized what he was doing, he loosened his grip a little and spoke. "What of me, Ari? How do you feel about me? I've kissed you. I felt the feelings that you have. Please don't deny that."

"I can't deny that I do feel something for you, Joshua. It is why I made the pact with you to marry you if you cannot find Ellavorn, or if he does not wish to return. I have to see things through with him first. I could never just walk away from him without making an effort to find him. Besides, if I did that, wouldn't you always wonder about me? Wouldn't you become wary of the thoughts of him returning and what I would do? What would you do in my situation? To me, it seems like an impossible choice."

Joshua released her from his grip and turned his back so that she wouldn't see the tears that were forming in his eyes. He drew a shaky breath.

"I understand why you are doing this, Ari. I would do the same thing if I were in your shoes. Just don't expect me to like it."

He started to walk off, but Arianna's voice stopped him, but he didn't turn to look at her.

"I never asked you to like it, Joshua. I would never ask you to like it. I don't like it myself. I do not wish to hurt you. I do care for you."

"Just not enough. My men will leave in the morning." With that, he stormed out of the room and slammed the door, rattling the windows and leaving Arianna speechless.

Arianna stared at the door for a few moments, trying to compose herself and to squash the guilt that she felt for making Joshua plan to find Ellavorn. She sat down on the cold floor, bringing her knees to her chest and she cried softly. She felt terrible to be tearing Joshua's heart out like this. But, she knew that she had to know where she stood with Ellavorn. If there was any chance at all of his return, she had to take it. After a few more moments, she composed herself, pushed herself up off of the floor, brushed off her gown and made her way back to her room to prepare for dinner, where Abigail was waiting.

"*What* happened between you and Joshua *now*?" She asked, exasperated.

Arianna looked at her friend sadly, drew in a shaky breath and said, "The guards are going to look for Ellavorn tomorrow. Joshua is angry with me because I still want to find him."

"Ari, I don't understand why you still want to look for him. Don't you think that he would have come back to you if he still wanted you?"

Abigail's words hit her hard. "No! Abigail, I turned him away, not the other way around. I was horrible to him. I said some downright ugly things. I accused him of allowing my mother to die! I don't understand why you are not comprehending this. I need to at least try to rectify this! Besides, I love him. I have loved him deeply for almost my entire life. You don't just let that go!"

"But, he's gone now. You have Joshua who loves you just as much. Just give up on Ellavorn and move on."

Arianna rounded on her friend, her eyes burning with anger. "You do not give up on the one you love so easily. Don't you realize how much trouble I have caused over this?" Her voice started to rise. "I not only lost the love of my life, but I have made enemies of the elves! How are we supposed to fight this magical being without their help? Are you really so stupid to think that I could just walk away from all of that? I need to fix this as fast as I can! It's called being a good leader."

It was Abigail's turn to look as though she'd been slapped. "Well, Your Highness, I guess that settles that. Let's just drop this subject and get you ready for dinner."

Arianna rolled her eyes at Abigail's use of her official title, but she was growing tired of arguing with everyone over this issue. The fact remained that Ellavorn held the majority of her heart still. She needed to find him. Not only that, but she needed to make reparations with the elves and mend that allegiance. If Abigail and Joshua didn't want to see reason and listen to what she was saying, that was something that she would have to accept. She didn't like it, but there was nothing to be done about it.

After helping Arianna into her dress and fixing her hair for dinner, Abigail turned and left the room without another word. Arianna felt her absence as soon as she had left and buried her face in her hands and wept. This day had turned out terribly. She now had her only two friends angry with her and she had no idea how to change that. No matter what she did, she was bound to lose.

Arianna thought of Joshua with his bright, blue eyes, and the way he looked at her and spoke softly to her. He did seem to love her. She knew that he was a good man and that he would make a great leader of the kingdom. However, she also knew that she could never completely love him. Would it be right to expect him to always be second place in her heart? And what about the elves? If she didn't fix relations between Eumetadotos and the elves, how would they handle this magical being?

Thinking of the elves brought the image of Ellavorn's face to her mind. She couldn't help but smile at the way even just the thought of him could still make her breath hitch. He was so much more to her than just a handsome face. He was the embodiment of true love to her. When she was with him, he gave her everything. His ears, his heart, everything. He knew her true heart and he loved her completely. If they couldn't find him, she didn't know how she would be able to let him go completely. In addition, if they did find him, and he didn't want her anymore, how would she be able to live with herself? She knew that it was a risk that she had to take. She just hoped that it would pay off in the end.

A soft knock on her door startled her out of her thoughts. She opened the door to one of the kitchen boys, who could have been no more than eight years old, standing there. His flaxen hair was sweaty, and his white clothes were covered in food stains. He looked at her with intense blue eyes. He looked like he was scared and excited all at the same time. She smiled at him. "Can I help you?"

"Um, yes, Your Highness, um, I just, um, I was sent to, um, see if, um, you were ready to come to dinner. Your Majesty."

Her face broke into a wide smile as she watched the boy shift from foot to foot as he spoke. "I am ready to come to dinner. But, I have no escort. Would you be so kind as to escort me down?"

The young boy's face grew as red as a cherry, but his face broke out in the biggest smile she had ever seen. "Wow! Really? I get to escort the queen to dinner? Are you sure?"

Arianna let loose a little giggle. "Of course! A queen needs an escort to dinner, does she not?"

"Well, goodness gracious! I would love to escort you to dinner, Your Highness!" He straightened his back, puffing out his chest, and offered Arianna his arm. She had to bend down slightly, but she took his arm, and they made their way to the dining room.

"What is your name, boy?"

"I am called Charlie."

"Well, Charlie, I am pleased to officially meet you. What is it that you do in the kitchens?"

"I cut the vegetables!" He said this as though it were the most important job in the world. "I make sure that they are all cut up just the way the chef likes them for dinner! Sometimes, he needs them cut up real small, like, bite sized, even, but sometimes, he needs them to be big chunks! I never know what I'm going to have to do when I wake up in the morning." His enthusiasm was catching and Arianna felt her spirits lift, at least a little. This little Charlie was certainly a ray of much needed sunshine in her day.

"Well, cutting the vegetables is certainly a very important job, Charlie. I have noticed how they are always cut just right."

"Really? You mean, you've noticed my work? Well, goodness gracious! I can't wait to tell everyone how the queen thinks that I do a good job! They are going to be just so jealous!"

Arianna had to bite her lip to keep from laughing. This young boy certainly seemed to enjoy his job. His enthusiasm was quite catching, and by the time they made it to the dining room, Arianna's spirits had been lifted even more than when they first began speaking. She immediately was quite fond of the little boy. His whole demeanor seemed to sparkle.

As they reached the doors, Charlie started to pull away, but Arianna stopped him. "Aren't you going to escort me to my table?"

The little boy's face lit up with excitement. "Really?"

Arianna smiled and said, "Of course!" She nodded to the guards at the door, and they opened them, smiling at Charlie as they walked past.

Everyone in the room rose to greet the queen and froze when they saw this young boy in stained clothing escorting her to her table. Whispers rippled through the room about what could have happened between the Queen and the Captain of the Royal Guard, who was nowhere to be seen.

They got to the front of the room and Charlie turned to leave, but, again, Arianna stopped him. "Aren't you going to eat with me?"

He looked down at his clothing and said, "But, Your Highness, I am not dressed suitably to eat with you. My clothes are stained and my hair is a mess. I should go and eat with the kitchen staff. We always eat together."

Arianna looked him over and said, "I see nothing wrong with the clothes you are wearing or your hair. But, if you wish to eat with your friends, that is ok. Thank you, Charlie, for escorting me to dinner."

Charlie looked between Arianna and the kitchen staff, unsure of which table to sit and eat. Arianna smiled at him, and he ran over to the table with the kitchen staff with an ear to ear smile on his face. She couldn't help but giggle at his enthusiasm as she sat in her own chair.

"Well, you certainly made his night," a cold voice said behind her. She turned to see Joshua standing there, scowling.

"I needed an escort to dinner, and you didn't seem up for the job tonight," Arianna said with a chill to her voice that could freeze a running river.

"I would have still walked you down here."

"Well, I found someone who was willing to relieve you of that duty tonight. Besides, look how happy it has made him." They both looked over to see Charlie excitedly chattering away, bouncing up and down in his chair, his smile never wavering, obviously recounting his walk with the queen.

Joshua relaxed a little and gave a small, tired smile of his own. "He does seem excited. Of course, who wouldn't be? He got to walk a beautiful woman to dinner, a beautiful woman who happens to be the queen."

Arianna sighed. "Joshua, please. I don't want to fight with you, and I definitely do not wish to hurt you. I know that this must be awful for you, but I love him. I would do anything to find him. I don't know how I can make it any easier on you. I hate that this is hurting you. You are my friend and I hate seeing you like this."

"You may not have to for much longer."

Arianna's eyes grew wide with fear. "What do you mean?"

"I have been thinking of joining the search for him."

"You mean leaving me here? Unguarded?"

Joshua gave her a look of disbelief. "You will be guarded. I wouldn't leave you without someone to defend you. It would just make it easier for me to not see you every day. If he does come back, that is."

Arianna swallowed a bit, choking back tears and nodded. It was then that they were served their dinner, and they ate their meal in silence.

Chapter 15

Early the following morning, Arianna heard noises outside of her window. She rose to see what was going on and saw Joshua suiting up in his armor and mounting his horse. One of the other guards handed him his sword, which he sheathed in his belt, and a pack of food and water for his journey. When he was settled on his horse, he turned the steed towards the gate to leave. At the last second, he turned and looked at Arianna's window. She lifted her hand to wave to him, but he did not wave back. He simply turned and set the horse at a gallop out of the castle gates.

Arianna turned and collapsed back on her bed, sobbing. She knew that she had hurt Joshua. She didn't mean to, and it was the last thing that she wanted to do. But, in her heart, she knew that she had to find Ellavorn. She still had time to make a decision on who she would marry, but she could feel the time slipping away. Action needed to be taken, and she knew what she wanted, but now, she found herself wondering if it was the right thing to do.

She cried herself back to sleep, and before long, Abigail came knocking at her door to get her up and ready for her day. As her friend came into the room, Arianna could tell from the chill that she brought with her that she had not forgotten their argument from the night before. As Abigail started arranging things around the room, Arianna just sat on her bed, feeling miserable.

Finally, Abigail turned and looked at her. When she saw her friend's face, her own softened a little. "What happened, Ari?"

"Joshua left this morning. He's gone to join the search for Ellavorn."

"Oh." Abigail's demeanor stiffened a little again. "Well, shouldn't you be happy that he is putting such an effort into finding him?"

Arianna felt something snap inside of her and started yelling at Abigail. "Do you really think that all of this is easy for me? Do you really think that I enjoy hurting him? Can you really be so narrow-minded? You have no idea what I have been dealing with, Abigail. Your parents weren't murdered simply because of who they were. You didn't have an entire kingdom thrust on you with no idea of how to run it. You didn't make the biggest mistake of your life, only to find that it could cost the lives of thousands of people! People who depend on you to do the right thing no matter what! I threw away the person I loved most in the world. I chose him to be my husband. In a moment of grief and fear, I threw it away. He's gone! Yes, it is my fault, and I own up to that, but that doesn't mean that I can't try to make it right. I love him, Abigail. I love him more than I can put into words. I will always love him. Why can't you understand this? Why can't you see that there is no one who will ever come close to him in my eyes? Yes, I have feelings for Joshua as well. He is wonderful. But, he is not Ellavorn."

Her voice softened. "You saw what happened the other day in the dining room. I need someone to help me. I don't know how to handle this on my own. Ellavorn and the elves know about magic. I don't. I need help. Even if he won't return to me, at least I have tried. Maybe then Armen will forgive me for what I've done and help."

When Arianna had finished her tirade, she looked Abigail straight in the eye, and continued, "You may think that I am being selfish. Maybe on some level, I am. I don't deny that. I *won't* deny that. But, you have no idea what it is like to live my life. Why is it so wrong to want to find the man that has held my heart in his hands for so long?"

Abigail simply looked at her friend and said, "We need to get you ready for your day."

"That's it? That is all that you have to say? Abigail, I just poured my heart out to you, and you have nothing to say about it?"

"Ari, no matter what I say, you are going to do whatever you want. You always have and you always will. To you, it doesn't matter who you hurt, so long as you get what you want. I have seen it happen so many times over the past few years. Why should I think that this is any different?"

Arianna looked at her friend, who was glaring at her with such contempt, bewildered. "I can't believe that you actually believe that about me. Do you really think that I am that selfish? Do you really think that I don't care about my kingdom? How can you think that I would risk any of your lives for my own happiness? I am not the spoiled little princess that I was a few weeks ago. I may not be the perfect queen, but I have made progress. Do you really think that I am so selfish that I don't see what this is doing to Joshua? Do you really think that I don't care? If that's the case, then you don't know me at all."

"Maybe I don't know you like I thought I did."

"I don't understand where all of this hostility is coming from, Abigail. I thought you were my friend."

"I did too, but I don't like the decisions that you've been making lately, Ari."

"So what? Do you think that friends always agree? They don't. I may not know a lot about friendship personally, but I have seen it. People argue. People disagree. Not everyone thinks the same way all of the time. That doesn't mean that they stop caring about each other, or let petty differences get in the way of their friendships. It means that they work together to overcome those differences. I still don't understand why you are so angry with me. I hope that you will see that I don't have selfish intentions in doing this." She turned and looked out her window. "I don't want to hurt anyone. I have been honest from the beginning about my feelings. I wish that things were different, but they're not. Life isn't all rainbows and unicorns, you know. I need to face up to my reality and deal with the choices that I have made, and the consequences of those choices. I also need to try and make things right where I can." Arianna turned and looked at Abigail again. "If you don't understand that, then maybe it isn't me who is the immature one. Maybe, it is you."

It was Abigail's turn to look as though she had been punched in the stomach, and she didn't like it. "So, you're going to lecture me on friendship and hard choices? You don't know much about my life, Arianna. I lost my parents too. Granted, not in the same manner as you lost yours, but I did lose them both on the same night. So, yes, I do know what it feels like. You threw away Ellavorn. He reached out to you, and you just cast him out! Now, you have someone else who loves you and you are throwing him away too! Do you know what I would give to have someone love me like that?"

"I'm sorry about your parents, Abigail. I truly am. I'm also sorry that you feel that way about my situation with Ellavorn and Joshua. I am lucky that I have two men in my life to choose from, but one holds my heart completely, the other doesn't. You say that you envy my position, but do you really? I am being forced to marry someone in order to save the entire kingdom. Why wouldn't I want to have the chance with someone that I love more than anything? Why would I choose to spend the rest of my life with someone for whom I hold lukewarm feelings if I have the chance to be happy? I do have feelings for Joshua; that is true. But, the feelings that I have for Ellavorn are a million times stronger. He is the other half of my soul. I was stupid and foolish to send him away. I have regretted it ever since, and I do not need anyone, especially not you, to rub that in my face every chance that presents itself. Yet, that is exactly what you do."

"I want the best leader for our kingdom, Ari. Joshua has proven himself to be a great leader."

"And so has Ellavorn. He is the prince of the elves. He has had training in how to run a kingdom. And now, I fear that he alone can bridge the rift that I created between elves and humans. Do you know that he is the first elf to ever even think of pledging himself to a human? He did that for me. I made a mess of things when I sent him away and I fear that if he doesn't return, we may never become allies with the elves again."

"You talk as though we need the elves, Ari. We don't need them. We're just fine on our own."

Arianna turned to the window again. "You're wrong. You saw the dark figure. It knows *magic*, Abigail. I know nothing of magic. The elves do. They are the only ones who can help us right now. I don't think that you understand how vital it is that we bring Ellavorn back and make things right. Even if he does not wish to marry me, I need to make amends."

Abigail scoffed. "We can wage a war on this hooded figure without magic. Even magical beings can be killed. Even elves, who claim to be immortal, can be killed in a battle or an assault."

Arianna whirled around to face Abigail again. "Yes, elves can be killed, as can any creature if you take the correct approach. But, this is magic we're talking about. It's not even white magic, like the elves possess. Abigail, this is dark magic." Arianna's eyes grew fearful. "Dark magic knows no rules. Those who possess it are hungry for power and greed. They don't care who they hurt to get it. We need help with this matter."

"How do you know this much of magic, Arianna? You claim you don't know much of it, yet you seem to be pretty well-versed on the workings."

"Ellavorn has told me some things over the years during our chats in the meadow." She sat back on the bed and put her head in her hands, thinking of the times that she would ride out to the meadow to meet her love, and missing the talks that they would have, and wishing that she could turn back the clock and go back to those days.

Abigail looked at her friend, as the realization slowly started to dawn on her. "You really do miss him?"

"More than anything, even more so than my parents."

"Do you really intend to marry Joshua if he does not wish to return?"

"I will if I have to. I care for Joshua. I do. But, I have a love for Ellavorn that burns deeply."

"You really don't see any other way out of this whole magical mess?"

Arianna looked up at her friend, and Abigail saw that she had started to cry. A single tear was making its way down her cheek, and it thoroughly melted Abigail's resolve to stay mad at her. "I see no other way. I need him to return. We all do, Abigail. If not, Eumetadotos is doomed."

"OK. Ari, please, promise me that you won't break Joshua's heart if Ellavorn returns."

"I will try my best not to. I don't want to hurt him. I honestly don't."

The women embraced, and Abigail said, "Now that this nonsense is over, let's get you ready to start your day." Arianna smiled and let her friend style her hair, but she couldn't help but cast a few furtive glances at the window, hoping against all hope that someone would approach with news of either of the two men that she held so dear.

Chapter 16

Three weeks passed with no news from Joshua. Arianna was getting worried. Every morning, when she woke, she would go to her window and look for any sign of the return of either of the two men, only to be disappointed to find that there had been no word of the return of either of them.

Abigail noticed her anxiety and tried her best to comfort her friend. Charlie, however, took great delight in being asked to escort his queen to meals every day. The request had been by Arianna after Joshua had left. He was so excited with the new clothes that Arianna had sent down to the kitchens for him to wear while he served as the queen's official escort. He was a ray of sunshine in her days that had become so dreary with the absence of both Joshua and Ellavorn. Arianna loved to hear him babble away on his vegetable cutting adventures. She found it refreshing to have such a youthful presence around in such a time of despair. Charlie even started to sit with her at her table so that she wouldn't be dining alone, much to the envy of the rest of the kitchen staff.

One night, the castle staff was dining when the door slammed open again, and in rushed the dark hooded figure with a vengeance. It stormed into the middle of the room, and pointed a gloved finger at Arianna.

"Little queen, where is your guard? Is that little boy going to be enough to protect you?" It moved its hand so that it was pointing directly at Charlie.

"Leave him alone! What do you want?"

"I told you what I want. I want your kingdom. Abdicate your throne to me or you will suffer!"

"I will never abdicate to you. You, who can't even show your face. You are a coward."

The figure stepped closer to Arianna. "Do not provoke me, queenie. I will make you wish you had never been born."

Arianna stood taller, and took on a regal manner. "No one will dictate what I do or do not do, not even one who wields magic."

The figure laughed its shrill laugh. "So, you think you can intimidate me with your regality? Little queen, take notice."

The figure made a gesture with his hands, and Charlie was swept out of his chair and pinned against the wall. Something invisible seemed to be choking him.

"No! Stop!"

The figure laughed that horrible laugh again and let the little boy breathe.

"Abdicate your throne to me, queen, or I will end this little boy's life right now."

Charlie looked at Arianna worriedly. Arianna looked at him with tears in her eyes. He shook his head and said, "Don't do it, Your Majesty. Don't let him ruin our kingdom."

The dark figure laughed that shrill laugh again. "Don't try to be noble, boy. Make your choice, queen."

Arianna looked from the dark figure to Charlie again, unable to decide what to do. The occupants of the dining room were deathly quiet, eager to see what their queen would decide.

"There has to be another way," she said.

"You try my patience," the voice screeched. Charlie began to choke again. Arianna ran to his side, screaming and weeping. The figure again loosened its invisible grip.

Arianna turned to face it, throwing her hands out in front of her to try to shield herself from any attacks it may throw at her. As she did, she screamed, "Leave him be!" Her hands began to glow a bright white glow, and from them, beams of brilliant white light erupted forth and slammed into the dark figure, knocking it across the room into the other wall.

Arianna stared at her hands in disbelief. The entire room gasped at the same time and started to chatter amongst themselves. The dark figure stood and proceeded to walk towards the queen again. She flung herself in front of Charlie, who was coughing and forcing air back into his lungs and forced him under the table. His face was an ashen white and he looked as scared of Arianna as he was the dark figure.

"Well, little queen, it seems that you have been keeping secrets from all of us. You do possess magic. Although, it doesn't seem that you know quite how to use it! That could be an advantage to me."

The figure, laughing maniacally, advanced towards her. Arianna didn't know what to do, so she tried to mimic what she had done moments earlier, and threw her hands out in front of her again screaming, "Stop! Leave my people in peace!"

Again, two bolts of pure white light erupted from her hands and slammed into the dark figure, sending it crashing into the wall again.

"You will curse the day you discovered your magic and used it against me! Your title will be cursed! I promise you that. You may still be the queen, but you will not rule this land for long. Your white magic will be no match for me! I will find a way to rule this land. If I cannot have it, no one can!" The dark figure then disappeared in a blast of smoke, leaving the room in utter chaos.

Arianna was oblivious to the pandemonium around her and collapsed into her chair, staring at her hands. She was completely lost in her own thoughts when she felt someone pulling at the skirt of her dress. She looked down to see the pale face of Charlie, still under the table.

"Oh, Charlie! Are you ok?"

"Y-y-y-yes, Your Majesty."

"I am so sorry that you were attacked. Are you hurting still?"

"N-n-n-o, Your Majesty."

"Charlie, are you afraid of *me*?"

"A little."

"But, why?"

"You did magic!"

She looked at her hands again, in complete disbelief. "Yes, I know I did. I don't know how I did it, though. I didn't even know that I *could* do it! It scared me too."

"You saved me. I told you not to. To save the kingdom, but you saved me. Why?"

"Charlie, I saved both you and the kingdom. I couldn't just let him kill you. You are part of my kingdom, but more importantly, you my friend."

"But, I am only a kitchen boy. I'm not anybody."

Arianna slid to the floor and sat in front of Charlie, taking his face in her hands. He flinched at first, but quickly realized that she wouldn't hurt him. "Charlie, everybody is somebody. Everybody has something to contribute to the world. You are still so young. You have a lot to learn and one day, you will be a great man."

"Do you really think so, Your Majesty?"

"I really do." She grabbed him and hugged him tight. "Don't ever let anyone tell you that you are simply a kitchen boy. You are destined for greater things in life."

"How do you know?"

"I don't know how I know. I just do. Now, will you please escort me to my chambers? I am sure that Abigail will have plenty to ask me about this debacle."

Charlie smiled, stood, and turned to offer his hand to help Arianna up. He then offered her his arm and they walked up to her chambers, where, as Arianna had predicted, Abigail was waiting, not so patiently. As soon as the door opened, she flung herself at her friend, asking a million questions at once.

"Arianna! How could you not tell me that you can do magic? Where did you learn it? Who is this figure that keeps appearing and threatening you? Why would it go after Charlie?"

It was then that she saw Charlie standing with Arianna, and she ran over to him, hugging him almost as tightly as Arianna had.

"Oh, Charlie, are you ok? Are you hurting still? Can I get you something? You poor, poor boy."

Charlie smiled, savoring the attention, and said, "No, I'm fine. I was scared, but Her Majesty talked to me and made it ok. I'm just going to get some hot water and honey."

Charlie left the room to wander down to the kitchens.

"I'm sure that he will have quite a captive audience when he gets down there," Arianna said with a small smile.

"Arianna, the entire castle is a captive audience. What is going on?"

Arianna looked at Abigail and told her the truth, "I have no idea."

"I didn't know that you know how to do magic!"

"I don't! I don't know where that came from! It was just as big of a surprise to me as it was to all of you. I didn't even know that it would work the second time around. I took a chance, and luckily, it worked."

"Poor Charlie. He must have been so frightened."

"He was. Abigail, he was scared of *me*. Is everyone scared of me now?"

"I don't know. They are all in shock from what happened tonight. You really need to call everyone together to talk about this, Ari. We need to figure out what is going on. You said that the elves know white magic. That's what you have got. We all saw it. It was the most brilliant white glow!"

"Yes, but the elves won't help us, Abigail. Don't you remember? They are no longer our allies. I broke that alliance by breaking off my engagement."

"There has to be a way, Ari. There just has to be. Surely, they will want to know of this…development. No human here can do magic! They must know something of this." Abigail stopped talking for a moment, and looked at Ariana in wonder. "Ari, do you think that you may be part elf?"

"Abigail, don't be silly. We all know that elves don't mate with humans. The first one to choose to do so never got the chance. No other elf has ever wanted to mate with a human, so there is no possible way that I could have elvish blood in me."

"What other explanation do you have for you to be able to do magic?"

"The only other humans who could do it were the wizards. There haven't been wizards here in almost a century. I wouldn't even know where to begin looking for one. Besides, most of the guard is out looking for Ellavorn. I can only hope that they find some trace of him soon. It's the only hope of a chance of reuniting elves and humans as allies."

"Isn't there some kind of research that you can do? Maybe you have wizard blood in you! Maybe trace these wizards to wherever they went? We need to find them! They could be your family! They couldn't have just disappeared from existence, right? I mean, an entire race of people just disappeared?"

"I guess we could try to find something in the castle library, but I don't know. It has been so long. Plus, there may not be any documentation as to where they went. Remember, we haven't heard much about them in almost a hundred years. Wherever they went, they didn't want to be followed."

"This is a dire emergency, Ari. Don't you think that they would want to help? I mean, this is their home!"

"It *was* their home, Abigail. I don't know that they would even consider this their home anymore. We don't know why they left, but they did, and they obviously have no intention of returning."

“You need to try, Ari. What other choice do we have?”

“I don’t know.” Arianna stood and walked to the window. “I wish that there was a way to get to the elves. They know magic. They would know what to do.”

“Send someone to summon Armen!”

“I can’t, Abigail. They would kill any messenger that I were to send. I couldn’t risk the life of one of my guards.”

“They would kill a guard?”

“Yes.”

“But, what about a commoner?”

“I’m not willing to take that risk.”

Abigail flopped onto Arianna’s bed, pouting.

“I will figure this out, Abigail, I promise.”

“I know you will. You have to.”

Chapter 17

News of the dark figure's return reached the far corners of the kingdom by the next morning. Arianna decided to address her kingdom before breakfast. As she stepped onto the balcony, she felt the fear blossom in her stomach again. She had her speech written down, but she was afraid of the backlash that she would receive. She took a shaky step to the front of the balcony and began talking.

"Ladies and gentlemen, you may have heard rumors of a dark figure that has visited the castle twice now, threatening our kingdom." She was confirming the people's worst fear. She swallowed and continued. "These rumors, unfortunately, are true. This figure is determined to claim the throne as its own. I do not know who or what this figure is. I do know that it is very dangerous." She paused. "It has brought magic back to Eumetadotos. Not just any magic, but black magic. It attacked someone last night with it. That person is fine and recovered, but I warn everyone to be on guard and to report anything that they see to the guards immediately."

As she finished, she turned to walk back into the castle, but someone yelled from the crowd, "Your Highness, is it true that you, too, possess magic? Didn't you save the child that was attacked?"

Arianna gasped. She had forgotten that the townspeople would find out about her magical outburst last night. She turned back to face her kingdom, shaken, and looking for the right words to say to assuage their fears. The only thing that she could think of was the truth.

"I don't know. It is true that last night, it seemed as though I am in possession of some kind of magic, but I don't know where it came from, nor do I know what I am capable of. I was able to defend my friend, yes, but the magic came to me without my knowledge of its existence. You can all be rest assured that I will be researching all that I can to figure out how to handle this situation and to come to the best conclusion as to where to go from here."

The crowd erupted in confusion. Another person asked, "Does this mean that the wizards will return? Are you a wizard?"

The question took Arianna off guard. Abigail had brought that very possibility to her attention earlier, but she didn't see how it could be true. Her heart began to beat wildly.

"I know as much as you do on the matter. As for the wizards returning, I do not know where they have gone. I don't know if they would come back and help. I know nothing of their plight. As for me, I am still the same queen that you saw grow up as a princess. Nothing has changed." In a whisper she added, "Except that I can now do magic."

"Well, if this figure has brought black magic back to Eumetadotos, how can you be trusted with your magic? How do we know that your magic isn't black magic?"

"I assure you that I mean no harm to anyone. I don't know what my magical abilities are. I am just as ignorant about magic as you are. But, I do know that I have not changed in any other way."

"Your Highness, what is being done about finding out who this dark figure is? How do we know that it will not harm us?"

"As of right now, nothing is known of this creature. Its sole purpose as of now is to gain my crown. I know nothing more of its plan. I vow to you all that I will do everything in my power to protect you all from harm. If any of you know anything of the wizards, I beg of you to come forward and tell me in person. Are there any more questions?"

"What about the elves? Wouldn't they know something? Can't they help?"

"No. The elves no longer consider themselves allies to Eumetadotos due to the broken engagement between their prince and myself. They will not help."

The crowd grew silent and simply stared at their queen, some in wonder that a woman so young could be so strong against an unknown adversary, but most, in fear.

"I need to retire to the library to do my research. Please, if anyone has any information about where we may be able to find the wizards, come to the castle to discuss what you know. Any information, even an old fairy tale could be of help."

Arianna turned and walked back into the castle, leaving the crowd behind to absorb what she had just announced. As she walked in the doors, Abigail fell into step beside her.

"Ari, I am going to help you with this."

Arianna smiled. "Abigail, you don't need to help me. I know that you have other duties to tend to."

Abigail took Arianna's arm and turned her to face her as they both stopped walking. "Do you really think that any of those other duties compare to helping you save the kingdom, and quite possibly yourself? Arianna, I am your friend. You are in danger. We need to work together to figure this out. Both Captain Oakford and Ellavorn are gone. You need someone to help you. You cannot do this on your own." She hesitated. "Well, I'm sure that you could, but you don't have to. I am here to help you."

Arianna hugged her friend, and tears of relief started to well in her eyes. Blinking them back, she said, “Thank you, Abigail! You’re right, I can use the help. I can’t do this on my own. I don’t even know where to begin. I would be honored to have you help me.”

Before they could start their walk to the library, they heard a commotion from outside. Arianna turned and started to run back to the balcony, but was stopped by a guard before she went outside again.

“Your Highness, it may not be a wise idea to go out there.”

“I am still the queen here. I need to see what is wrong with my people.”

“With all due respect to you, I have sworn to Captain Oakford that I would ensure your safety while he is gone. I swore with my life to protect you. I am not willing to be careless with my oath and to pay the price.”

Arianna straightened her back and, in a regal tone, announced, “I command you to allow me out on that balcony to tend to my people! Whatever oath you have sworn to Captain Oakford is not my problem. I need to be present for my people and I will not allow anyone to keep me from that responsibility. You will not pay a price. I will see to it.”

The guard looked unsure, so Arianna raised her eyebrows at him and asked, “Do you dare defy an order from your queen? The way I see it, I could consider that an act of treason and have you sent to the dungeons.” It broke Arianna’s heart to threaten the guard who was just doing his job, but she needed to hear what her people had to say.

The guard relented and she stepped back out onto the balcony.

She heard a lot of shouting, which got louder as she walked farther and farther out. Finally, some of the townspeople realized that she was watching. The shouting intensified, and she could make out accusations of her being a witch and of being evil. These words screamed by those who supposedly loved her were enough to break her heart.

She dropped down to her knees, crying. A hand on her shoulder made her look up. It was the guard who had tried to stop her from coming out in the first place. He looked at her gently and offered a hand to help her up. She wiped her tears on her sleeve and took his hand. As she made her way back into the palace, her resolve steeled again, and she turned and stormed back to the edge of the balcony, screaming over the noise.

"Ladies and Gentlemen, I do not know why you are accusing me of these horrible things! I have done nothing wrong. I did not ask for this magic. It was thrust upon me! I did not use it for evil purposes. I saved the life of a young boy. I drove the dark figure out. Does this not count for something? Do not let your prejudice against magic blind you. I only have the best of intentions for this kingdom at heart. I need your support more now than ever."

She turned to walk back in, but heard a loud scream. She turned to see a spear flying towards her. She held her hands up, and two bursts of pure white magic flew from her hands, the same way as they had the night before. The spear burst into flame. The ashes blowing away in the breeze. The silence from the crowd was deafening for a moment before utter chaos erupted again.

Arianna rushed to the side to see the guards pushing their way through the crowd to find the person who had thrown the spear at her. She witnessed them knocking people over and throwing them out of the way.

"Stop!" Arianna screamed down. "Everyone stop!"

The crowd quieted and the guards continued to fight their way through.

"Guards! Stop!" They turned and faced her in surprise.

"I understand your fear. I feel it too. I don't know what is happening to me. I don't like feeling this way. I need your understanding in this. As long as I have been alive, no one has been able to do magic in Eumetadotos, white or black. I am at a loss of what to do. If you cannot be understanding, you are free to leave the kingdom. I cannot keep you here against your will, nor will I try to. However, I wish that you would give me time to figure out this matter before making that decision. This incident with the spear will be forgotten."

She signaled to the guards to retreat. "In the future, however, the attacker will be found and justice will be served."

She turned and walked back into the palace and was met by astounded stares. "I know. It is unconventional to free someone who just tried to assassinate the queen, but they are afraid. I am afraid as well. I will allow one slip, only one. Now, I must go and research."

She signaled for Abigail to follow her and they fled to the library, locking the door behind them.

Chapter 18

"Ari, where do we start? This library is huge!" Abigail exclaimed as she marveled at the vast expanse of the room filled with books.

Arianna was just as overwhelmed, but determinedly walked over to the book catalogs. "I guess we look up magic here?" She started thumbing through the cards, but came up with nothing. She tried several of the catalogs with no luck. Frustrated, she kicked the wall next to the catalogs. The vibrations from the kick knocked a brick loose a little way down the wall. She knelt down and called Abigail over to help remove it.

Inside, was a wooden box with intricate carvings in the lid and sides. She had never seen the markings before. She opened the box, and inside, found a card simply marked, "Magic," with a key attached to it. The key was beautiful. It was long and looked as though it was carved purely from a single ruby. The handle was fashioned into a beautiful, intricate lotus pattern. The bottom was shaped like a dragon's wing. She had never seen anything like it before. It was truly a one of a kind key. The question was, to what?

Abigail gasped behind her. "Ari, that is beautiful!"

"Sure, it's beautiful, but it's not much good without a door to open with it." She picked up the box again, turning it upside down, hoping for something else to fall out, but was met with no luck. She sighed and righted the box again, placing the key back into it. "We need to find the door that this key opens."

The two women started walking around the room, trying to catch a glimpse behind bookshelves, and making special note of the markings on the walls, all with no luck. After spending several hours searching, both Arianna and Abigail were starving. They were both scared to go down to the dining room because of the events of earlier in the day. Arianna opened the door to find a guard standing outside. She asked him to have someone bring up some food and drink for them to replenish their strength. He nodded and walked off.

Arianna and Abigail sat down on a couple of the comfortable chairs that were set up in a semi-circle in a sunny nook. The key lay on a table in the middle of the area. Both women sat with their elbows on their knees and their chins resting on their hands, staring at the key. Neither one knew where to look next. Both were growing weary and desperate when a knock on the door came in and Charlie came bouncing through the door with a pitcher of water for them. He was followed by a surly looking man pushing a dinner cart.

Charlie bounded across the room and half placed, half threw the pitcher on the table, spilling a little water on the table, which elicited a sneer and a growl from the surly looking man. He ran over to Arianna, throwing his arms around her in a huge hug. She couldn't help but hug him back. "Thank you, Charlie. I needed that."

The surly man grumbled and removed the plates for Arianna and Abigail from the cart and placed them on the table. Charlie poured them two glasses of water, handing one to each of the women with a huge smile. The grumpy man placed another platter half full of cheeses and crackers and the other half full of fresh fruit and desserts for them to pick at as they continued their exploration. They thanked him. He simply grunted and turned and left the room.

"Gee, he's a real ray of sunshine," Abigail quipped.

Charlie giggled. “He’s the head chef. He’s a bit cross that he was asked to actually serve some of his food, even though it is for Her Majesty.”

Arianna shook her head slightly and muttered sadly, “Or, maybe because it *is* for me.”

Charlie looked at her with such confusion that she had to give a short laugh.

“Your Majesty, I don’t understand, why are so many people so mad at you? You saved my life. They should be happy.”

“Charlie, people often fear what they don’t understand. They don’t understand the magic that I conjured yesterday. I don’t even understand it, and it scares me too. It’s the unknown that is feared. Magic has been gone for so long that no one here knows what to do with it now that it’s back. I don’t even know where to begin to find anything about it either.”

“Did you look under magic in the catalogs?”

Arianna gave him a curious look. “How do you know about the catalogs?”

“I ummm, I uhhhh,” He looked down at his shoes, guiltily. “I like to come in here and read the books.”

Arianna smiled widely. “Do you now? Well, Charlie, you may come in here any time you like. Someone needs to read these dusty old books.”

He smiled widely again. “I’ll go look for magic.”

Arianna stopped him. “It’s ok, Charlie. We looked. There is nothing under magic.”

He flopped down on the chair next to Arianna and sighed.

"Well, that's just unlucky!"

She smiled at him and said, "Well, we did find this." She picked up the key and held it out to him.

"Woah! Where did you find that? It's beautiful!"

She explained what had happened, and then told him about the lack of success in finding the door in which it fit.

"Well, of course, you didn't find it here. That door isn't here."

Arianna looked at him incredulously. "Charlie, have you seen the door that this key belongs to?"

"Well, I don't know if it's a door, but there's a carving in a stone in the kitchen that looks just like that."

Arianna knelt in front of him, "Can you take us there? After we're finished eating, of course?" She threw a glance at Abigail, who gave her a grateful look in return.

"Sure! It's in the kitchen pantry! I know where it is because we keep a lot of vegetables in there. No one knew what it was for. We just thought it was a decoration in the stone."

Arianna couldn't believe her luck. She jumped up and hugged Charlie tightly. "Oh, Charlie! I could kiss you right now! Oh, what the heck?" She bent down and kissed him on the cheek. His face turned beet red and his smiled stretched across his face in a broad grin.

Arianna and Abigail rushed through the rest of their meal quickly as Charlie chattered on about his duties in the kitchen. When they were finished, they left the library and started down to the kitchens. They didn't make it very far when they heard a commotion coming from the Great Hall.

"Stay here," Arianna said to her friends. She thrust the box into Abigail's hands and she started to race towards the noise. "I will see what is happening and come back."

As Arianna turned the corner into the Great Hall, she heard a voice that she had grown to know so well. It lifted her heart, as she turned the corner.

"Joshua! You've returned!" Arianna smiled broadly at him. She had truly missed his companionship in the weeks that he had been gone.

Joshua walked briskly to her, and enveloped her in a huge hug and Arianna took the opportunity to chance a glimpse over his shoulder.

Joshua held her back at arm's length and looked into her eyes.

"I'm sorry, Arianna, we searched far and wide."

Her chin began to quiver slightly. "So, you did not find him?"

Joshua's jaw tightened. "No, we found him."

Her eyes lit up with a hope that was quickly squashed.

"He refused to come back with us. He said to tell you not to look for him again and he gave us a peace offering for his father to make amends with the elves. Although, I do not know what it is."

He held out a locked box with symbols carved into it. The carvings matched the box that Abigail held in her hands. Arianna gasped.

Joshua looked confused. "Do you know what it is?"

"No, but we found a box that matches it perfectly."

Joshua narrowed his eyes at her, skeptically, and asked, "What do you mean you found a box that matches it perfectly? Arianna, what has been going on?"

"Oh, Joshua, there is so much to tell you. So much has happened the past few weeks, in the past few days at that. But, you look exhausted. Maybe you should go get a bath and get some sleep."

"No, Arianna, sleep can wait. I want to know what is going on."

She shook her head, knowing that he wouldn't listen to her. "Come on. There's no time to explain right now. I have to meet Abigail and Charlie. You should come along. I think you'll have to see it to believe it anyway."

Arianna and Joshua made their way back to Abigail and Charlie in silence. As they turned the corner, Abigail gasped in surprise to see the Captain of the Royal Guard back in the castle. She smiled broadly at Arianna, who returned her smile half-heartedly. Abigail read what that meant in her friend's face and, wisely, said nothing as they all turned and followed Charlie to the kitchen pantry.

Once they arrived, Arianna was amazed at how busy the kitchen was, preparing for their dinner. The chef caught sight of Charlie and made to yell at him for not doing his duties. Arianna held her hand up and he closed his mouth and continued on his way, glaring at the group.

"It's this way, Your Highness!" Charlie grabbed Arianna's hand and dragged her into the pantry with Abigail and a very confused looking Joshua right behind her.

"Right there! That's the stone!" He was hopping from foot to foot, pointing at a bleached white stone that had a carving that matched the ruby key perfectly.

Arianna's breath caught and she smiled. She bent down and kissed the top of Charlie's head.

"Thank you, Charlie! You are wonderful!"

"Arianna, will you please tell me what is going on here?" Joshua looked even more confused than ever. "I don't understand why we are looking at carved stones in the pantry wall. Is there some kind of meaning to this?"

Arianna looked at Joshua, straight in the eyes and said, "I sincerely hope so. Things have taken a very…interesting…turn since you left."

Abigail and Charlie laughed, which just made Joshua even more confused.

"Let's hope that this works." She held out her hand for the box, and Abigail handed it over to her. Joshua's jaw dropped when he saw an exact replica of the box that Ellavorn had given him. Arianna opened the box and withdrew the key, and Joshua looked as though he were going to pass out from the surprise.

Arianna caught sight of his face and burst out laughing. Joshua realized how foolish he must look and composed himself.

Arianna walked over to the stone and placed the key into the carving sideways, so that it fit. She heard a click and was able to push the stone with her hand. As she did, the floor began to move. Abigail, Charlie and Joshua all ran to stand next to Arianna, all four of their faces were frozen into masks of shock as the floor began to unravel itself into a spiral staircase.

Joshua was the first to speak, leaning over to Arianna, but never taking his eyes off of the stairs that had just formed in front of his very eyes. "Arianna, what is going on here? How is this possible?"

Arianna looked him straight in the eyes and uttered one word, "Magic."

Chapter 19

Joshua looked from Arianna's face to the staircase and back again in utter disbelief. "What do you mean by magic? That is impossible. There hasn't been magic in Eumetadotos in at least a century!"

Arianna held his face so that his blue eyes bore into her violet ones. "That was true, up until the figure appeared. You know as well as I do that it set these events in motion."

Joshua made a move to remove her hands and paused, staring at Arianna's wrist. "Arianna, what is this mark? It was never there before."

"What mark? I don't know of any mark."

She turned her wrist to take a look and there was a black mark. It was beautiful. The pattern was that of interlocking bows that danced across her wrist. Horizontally, through the middle, was an arrow. The arrowhead was the most interesting part. Lined on the edges were beautiful patterns, however, on the inside, it was marked with a decorative "A." The mark had not been there in the moments before. It had suddenly appeared, and it scared Arianna.

She looked up at her friends with fear in her eyes. "I have no idea where this came from. It was not there until just now. What could this possibly mean?"

Joshua pulled the box that Ellavorn had given him out from his cloak pocket. "That symbol looks familiar. I think it's Elven."

"That's impossible, Joshua."

"Obviously not, Arianna," he retorted, indicating her wrist. He held his hand out for her to give him a better look and he began scanning the box. "A-ha! Here it is!" He turned the box and pointed to almost the exact marking, carved into the wood.

Arianna could hardly believe her own eyes. "What does this mean? I don't understand."

"Well, there's someone we can ask now, so long as he accepts the peace offering."

Arianna gulped. "Armen."

Joshua nodded. He wouldn't meet her eyes at the mention of the man who was supposed to be her father-in-law. He knew that much of her heart still lay with Ellavorn, even though he had rejected her. He couldn't imagine how she was feeling in that moment, knowing that she would have to face Armen again.

"Ari?" Abigail spoke softly.

Arianna had forgotten that she was there and turned to look at her friend.

"What are we going to do about that long spiral staircase that seems to go into the dark abyss? Should we explore it?"

Arianna's mind snapped back to the present. "I think that we should. We can fill Joshua in on the rest of the news of the past few weeks as well."

"Oh, boy," Abigail groaned. She was met by a glare from Arianna.

Joshua sighed as he replaced the box in his cloak pocket. "What other news, Arianna? What else could have happened?"

"Let's see what's down here. Hopefully, it's more private. We can tell you everything down there."

Arianna walked onto the first step down, turned and motioned for her friends to follow. She walked a few more feet, and a torch flared to life next to her, startling her sideways, and almost causing her to fall. Joshua caught her by the waist and helped her to steady herself. She gave him a small smile and said, "Thank you."

He nodded and they continued on their way. Every few feet, another torch would ignite itself, lighting the way. With every flame flaring up, Joshua looked more and more uncomfortable. Finally, they reached the bottom of the steps.

The room was pitch black. Arianna took a few steps into the room. After about five steps, the torches all around the room lit, one by one. She looked around. They were in a round room. One half of the circumference of the room was lined with books, covered thickly with dust. The other half was lined with all kinds of flasks and beakers, and other glassware full of different colored liquids. The glassware looked as clean as though it had just been washed. The liquid looked as though it had just been poured, even though, it couldn't possibly have been. This room had been abandoned for at least a hundred years. In the center stood a tabletop, where it looked as though experiments with the liquids were performed. On top of the table were a few candles that had collected dust over the years.

The liquids caught Arianna's interest, and she started walking towards them. She got about 2 feet away from the shelves, and was met by some sort of invisible barrier that glowed a pale yellow when she touched it.

"Arianna!" Joshua yelped and ran towards her.

"I am fine, Joshua. It's just a barrier of some kind. This must have been the wizard's laboratory. Those liquids could not have lasted this long without magical help."

"I'm not comfortable with this, Arianna. Why are you so

obsessed with magic all of the sudden? Nothing good can come of magic."

Arianna wrenched her arm from his grasp. "Is that so, Joshua?" She growled at him.

"What do you mean? You know nothing of magic."

"Oh, don't I?" She walked up to him so close that they were standing nose to nose. She glared at him and said, "I know that I can do magic."

Joshua took a step back, eyes narrowed. "What do you mean that you can do magic? That is not possible. Only the wizards and the elves can do magic. You are neither." As he finished, his eyes flicked to her wrist, which she quickly hid behind her back.

"I don't know how it is possible, Joshua. I just know that I can. I have. The Dark Figure came back last night. It attacked Charlie. I put my hands up to try to help, and white beams of light shot out from my hands and hit it. That happened twice. I didn't even know if it would happen the second time, but it did. Then, this morning, after I addressed the people, someone threw a spear. I held my hands up and the spear just…disintegrated in front of me. I don't know how I did it. I don't know why it happened. I just know that it did happen, and that I have saved Charlie's life, as well as mine. If that is evil, Joshua, I don't know why."

Joshua's face had grown paler and paler as Arianna spoke. He looked at her as though he didn't know her, and like he was terrified of her.

"Don't look at me like that! You know that I'm not evil! I didn't even know that I could do magic until I saved Charlie's life! I wouldn't call that evil either. The Dark Figure is the evil one."

Abigail stepped forward, looked at Joshua and said, "Captain, what she says is true. I saw the magic that she possesses. It is the purest white. Isn't that a good thing? If it was dark magic, wouldn't it show differently?"

Joshua still looked unsure, but he acknowledged that if Arianna's magic were dark, that it would not be as pure white as they claimed it to be. Once it seemed as though they had persuaded him that not all magic was evil, they began to explore the laboratory. Arianna stepped up to the barrier again, only to be met with resistance in the form of the yellow light once again.

Joshua said softly, "I really wish that you wouldn't do that. It makes me nervous."

Arianna simply smiled and began to try to feel for another way through the barrier to no avail.

Meanwhile, Charlie and Abigail began to look at the books on the shelves. They were covered with inches of dust on the shelves, but none of the books looked as though there was any damage done to them through the years.

"That is strange, isn't it, Charlie? There is not one book damaged by mice or rats or bugs. Every last one is intact. A bit dusty, perhaps, but intact." She picked one of the books off the shelf and blew the dust away. The dust billowed out into a thick cloud that left both of then coughing. Once it had settled again, Abigail read the title aloud, "The Thaumaturgy of Magus." She opened the book, but found nothing but symbols instead of words. She snapped it shut and put it back on the shelf. "How are we going to figure out how to stop this creature if we can't even read these dusty old books?"

Charlie looked at her, confused, "What do you mean?"

Abigail gave him a look that spoke of equal confusion. "I

mean, this book here," she plucked the same book off of the shelf again, "is written in symbols, not words."

Charlie gave her a funny look again. "Are you daft?"

"What do you mean? I can't read this."

"I mean, I don't understand what you're talking about. There's nothing wrong with the way the book is written. It looks pretty clear to me."

Abigail looked at Charlie in astonishment. "Are you saying that you can read this?"

Charlie smiled, "Sure! This here," he pointed at a group of symbols, "it says, 'diafotízios.'"

Abigail glanced at him sideways, doubtful, until Charlie pointed at an unlit candle on the tabletop and exclaimed, "Diafotízios!" All of the candles on the tabletop jumped to life. Charlie clapped his hands together in sheer delight.

The commotion caught Arianna and Joshua's attention and they hurried over to the other side of the room. Arianna saw the now lit candles, and, astonished, asked, "How did that happen?" She then caught a glimpse of Charlie's gleeful face and raised her eyebrows in amusement. "Charlie, did you do that?"

Charlie looked as though he were about to jump out of his skin in excitement. "Yes, your highness, I just pointed at one of those candles, and said, 'diafotízios,' and they all lit up! It's that amazing?"

She chuckled softly and agreed that it was. Behind her, Joshua was shaking his head in disbelief. She turned to ask him what was wrong, and he sat on the bare, dusty floor and put his head in his hands. Arianna knelt in front of him, taking his hands in her own and tilting his head so that their eyes met.

"Joshua, what is bothering you?"

"This, all of this." He pulled his hands from hers and spread them as to indicate the entirety of the room. "It's all too much to take in at once. Magic has not been a part of this kingdom in over a hundred years. Now, all of the sudden, there are two – well, apparently three," he indicated Charlie, whose smile got even bigger than they ever thought possible, "people who can now do magic. Two of whom were just revealed within a day of each other. Why now? Why—you?"

Arianna looked at him intently and answered him honestly. "I don't know, Joshua. I honestly don't know. I wish that I did. I wish that I had more answers. But, I don't. I am as confused about this as everyone else is. I want the answers, but all I seem to uncover is more questions. Joshua, I need your help with this. I don't know what to do here. I'm completely lost."

Joshua, feeling weary from his journey, and the revelations that he experienced in the last few hours, held his hands out for hers again. When Arianna had placed her hands in his again, he squeezed them gently. "Arianna, I will do whatever you need me to do to help you with this, and to protect you as much as I can. I just need to process everything. It's just a lot to take in all at once. There are so many questions that I have, and you don't seem to have any answers. It doesn't seem as though anyone here does."

"No one in Eumetadotos has those answers, Joshua. You know where we need to go."

Joshua nodded, "The Forest Glen. Do you think that Armen will recognize this gift from his son? We are taking the word of someone who, truthfully, you hurt pretty deeply. You don't think that he would trick us into doing something foolish, do you?"

Arianna shook her head slightly. "No, I may have hurt him, but Ellavorn is not the spiteful type. If he told you that the box will help to mend an alliance with the elves, then it must be so. It is something that we desperately need right now."

Abigail and Charlie had been very quiet during this whole encounter, so quiet that Arianna and Joshua had forgotten that they had company. "Ari, I think that we should get out of here and plan out what we should do next," Abigail said quietly.

"Svino!" Charlie exclaimed excitedly, and the candles sputtered out immediately. He whooped with excitement and raced up the stairs, with the book tucked tight under his arm. Arianna, Joshua and Abigail all laughed at his enthusiasm, and Abigail yelled, "Show off!" up the staircase to him as she began to ascend back to the pantry.

Arianna began to make her way over to the stairs as well, but Joshua had gotten up off the floor and took hold of Arianna's arm. "Arianna, there is something that I think that we should discuss privately."

Arianna took a deep breath and turned slowly to look at him.

"When I left, you made a promise to me that if Ellavorn did not return to you, that you would accept my marriage proposal. Are you going to hold up that bargain?"

"Gee, Joshua, that is a proposal that every girl dreams about," Arianna said jokingly. "Of course I will hold up my end of that promise."

Joshua's face broke out in the first genuine smile of the day. He then dropped down to his knee, took Arianna's hand in both of his, looked up at her and asked, "Arianna, will you do me the greatest honor of becoming my wife?"

Arianna's heart constricted some when he asked the question, but she smiled brightly, looked him in the eyes and said, "Yes, Joshua, I would be honored to be your wife."

Chapter 20

The next morning, Arianna dug the engagement ring that she had worn on her finger not long ago out of her jewelry box. It had been in her family for generations and was only worn during the engagement period. She placed it on her vanity and looked at it for a few moments, feeling the weight of her decision on her shoulders. She had agreed to marry Joshua. She had to come to terms with the fact that Ellavorn no longer wished to take her as his wife. So many emotions rushed through her heart. She wasn't sure exactly how she felt. As she picked up the ring and twirled it around with her fingers, a knock came at her door.

"It is open," she called. The door opened and Abigail came in to help her get ready for the day. Abigail started chattering, but Arianna didn't hear a word that she had been saying, as she was lost in her own thoughts.

"Ari, are you listening to me?"

Arianna snapped to attention, "I'm sorry, what were you saying?"

Abigail looked at her and her eyes fell upon the ring in Arianna's hands. A look of amusement crossed her face.

"Is there something that you would like to share with me?"

Arianna sighed and gave her a small smile. "I have agreed to marry Joshua."

"Oh, Arianna! That is wonderful!"

Arianna gave another small, sad smile, and looked out her window, wistfully, with tears in her eyes. "Yes, I guess it is."

Abigail huffed, "Well, for someone who just got engaged to be married, you sure look like a rain cloud."

"I don't mean to. It's just that --, well, you know."

Abigail rolled her eyes at her. "Yes, I know, Ellavorn. Arianna, you need to let him go. He isn't coming back. You have to move on."

Arianna shook her head. "I know. But, for so long, he was what my heart wanted. You can't just change years of longing overnight. There is always going to be a part of me wondering about him. I will marry Joshua, but I will never fully love him."

Abigail shook her head slightly and hugged her friend. "Well, the fact that you are getting married is exciting! Why don't you focus on that? Surely you will want to start planning your wedding soon? You're running out of time."

"I am very well aware of my time constraints, Abigail. There are very important matters to tend to first, though. The wedding can wait for a while longer."

Arianna realized that she had grasped the ring in her hand and was now squeezing it so tightly that she had a perfect indentation on her palm from it. She looked at her hand in wonder for a moment, took a deep breath and placed the ring back in the box and closed the lid.

"Aren't you going to put it on?"

"I will. Just not right now. I guess I just need to let it sink in for a little while. I have time."

Abigail made a disgruntled noise.

"I will, Abigail. Just give me time. This isn't your decision to make anyway. It is mine. I will choose when I put that ring on my finger."

Abigail threw her hands up in frustration. "Ok, ok, fine. But, you also should make an announcement as well."

"Can we figure out the bigger problems first? For example, how are we going to get close enough to the Forest Glen in order to give Armen this box that Ellavorn gave to Joshua? We need to make amends with them. I need to get answers from them."

"You have magic now. If they fire on you, just melt their arrows."

Arianna looked at her in bewilderment. "I don't think that's how this works. I'm not fully in control of my powers. I don't know how this works. That's another reason that I need to talk to them. I have to find out if I am a part wizard."

"Or part elf. Didn't Joshua point out that the mark on your wrist matches the marking on the box?"

"It's impossible, Abigail. Elves don't mate with humans."

"Well, maybe someone broke the rules."

Arianna sighed. "Can we just get ready to start the day? I have a lot of things to do."

"Of course." Abigail helped Arianna get dressed and style her hair.

As they were finishing, there was a knock on the door again. Arianna opened the door to Joshua standing on the other side. His smile was radiant as he looked at her.

"Good morning!"

Arianna couldn't help but return his smile. While she still didn't have the same feelings for him as she did for Ellavorn, she could not deny that she had strong feelings for him. She took his arm and they made their way to the hall for breakfast.

"You are awfully quiet today."

Arianna smiled. "I just have a lot on my mind."

Joshua nodded. "Ari, we don't have to make an announcement about our engagement if you don't want to at this time. We can give it time."

Arianna relaxed a little at his words. "Thank you, Joshua. That means a lot to me. I won't make you wait too long, I promise."

Joshua stopped and stepped in front of her, facing her and put his hands around her waist. "Arianna, take as much time as you need. We have other battles to fight as well, ones that are more important. After breakfast, we need to meet to discuss how we will handle these issues."

Arianna smiled at him and nodded her head in agreement. Joshua fell back into step with her, she took his arm and they continued on to the dining room.

The entire room seemed to be abuzz with gossip on the return of the Captain of the Royal Guard, and none of them seemed too concerned about keeping it quiet. Arianna looked at Joshua, who returned her gaze with a reassuring smile. It did little to soothe her nerves.

The meal seemed to drag on forever, but it finally came to an end. Joshua stood and offered his arm to escort her to the throne room. They made their way in silence. When they had reached their destination, Joshua took her aside before entering. "Arianna, talk to me. You are not acting like yourself today and it is starting to worry me."

"You're right, I am not myself. Joshua, you have been away for quite some time. So much has happened in that time. I don't know myself anymore. I look into the mirror and I don't recognize myself. It's the same face I've always seen, but different somehow. I have never known magic, but yet, now, it flows through my body. I don't know how to control it. For as long as I can remember, I have been in love with Ellavorn. I finally got my heart's desire and I threw it away in a moment of grief and foolishness. I am finding more and more that I do not know much about myself at all, even though I thought I did."

Joshua could not meet her gaze. "So, do you regret agreeing to marry me?"

Arianna took a deep breath, and gently raised his face to meet her own. "No. You are a good man, Joshua. You will make a wonderful king. I do not regret accepting your proposal. I just need a few days to process everything. I am honored that you wish for me to be your wife. I am sorry if I have led you to believe otherwise. It was never my intention."

"I understand. I know that your life isn't what you had planned. I am sorry that things have not gone the way that you wanted them to. I want you to be happy. I will admit to you, though. I am not sorry that I will be able to call you my wife. I love you, Arianna. I love you more than I can ever express. I hope that, one day, you will be able to return that love completely."

"What if I can't, Joshua? What if we go to our graves and I still cannot give you my whole heart? What then?"

"I will take whatever you have to give to me. I intend to spend the rest of my life trying to make you forget about him. I hope that one day, I will be successful in my endeavor."

Arianna simply smiled at him. "I hope that you will be successful too, Joshua." She knew in her heart, however, that he never would be. She turned and entered the throne room.

Inside, she was met by several members of the Royal Guard, Abigail, and an overly excited Charlie.

"Your Majesty! I figured out a bunch of spells last night! I'm getting good at this magic thing!"

Arianna chuckled softly and said, "Very good, Charlie. Those skills will come in handy. Keep practicing."

Charlie's face fell a little. "I was told to stop practicing and to focus on my work. Your majesty, I love chopping vegetables, but I think I like learning magic better."

Arianna knelt down on the floor so that she was eye to eye with Charlie. "Well, Charlie, then I am issuing a royal decree. I no longer want you to work in the kitchen. You are to be my wizard-in-training. How does that sound?"

Charlie's entire face lit up with joy. "Goodness gracious! That sounds amazing! Thank you, Your Majesty! Thank you very much!"

Arianna hugged him tightly. When she released him, she said, "After our meeting, we will collect your things from your room and I will show you to your new chambers."

Charlie's eyes grew wide in excitement, "I get my own room? Goodness gracious! I've never had my own room before!"

Arianna laughed. "Yes, you will get your own room. We will also have to spend time in the chamber we found yesterday in order for you to have a proper place to practice. I also want to see if we can get the barrier down from around the liquids. I want to know what is in there."

Charlie looked as if he were going to burst with joy at her words. Arianna smiled at him and then turned to address everyone else as well.

"There are some matters that need to be discussed. First, Captain Oakford has returned with an item that may help us to repair the broken alliance with the elves." She nodded to Joshua and he produced the carved box and laid it on a table. Several members of the Royal Guard looked at it, unimpressed.

"How will this make amends?" One of the guards asked.

"I am not sure, but it was given to me by the prince himself. He did not explain what it was, but merely told me that it would bring peace between Eumetadotos and the elves again."

"The prince? Does that mean that he will return?"

Arianna's eyes fell to the floor. She answered, "No. He will not return." The expression on her face warned everyone in the room not to broach the subject any longer.

She continued, "What this means is that we now have a way to repair the rift that I caused. We can hopefully form an alliance with the elves again and learn about the magic that has manifested in me. We may be able to find answers to the questions that we have about the wizards and maybe come up with a plan to defeat the dark figure that has been tormenting us. It also means that we need to figure out how to get into the Forest Glen without being attacked."

"Your Majesty, wouldn't you be able to just melt their weapons like you did that spear?"

Joshua shifted uncomfortably. "I would prefer her to not use her magic unless there is no other choice."

Arianna gave him a heated glare. "What Captain Oakford means is that we do not wish to go into the Forest Glen and do anything that would give the impression that we are there to harm the elves. This is a peace mission. I do not wish to drive our peoples farther apart."

Joshua and Arianna exchanged a look of disagreement for a moment.

Arianna continued. "Now, we must come up with a plan on how to approach them. Are there any suggestions?"

One of the guards spoke up, "We could go in with our white flags waving. Your Majesty, with all due respect, you should be well protected in this group. We should have you flanked on either side, and to the front and back. Would your magic harm anyone who was in the way, should it be necessary to use it?"

"I'm not sure. I've never had anyone in the way of it before, aside from when it was directed at the dark figure when he was harming Charlie. I would rather not find out."

The guard looked at Joshua before continuing. "Well, I think that your magic is the best defense when approaching the Glen. We could ride in this formation until we make our final approach and then reorganize so that you are in the front."

"No!" Joshua yelled out. "She will not be the first to go into a slaughter. We need to protect our queen! Not send her into the butcher shop first."

Arianna gave a frustrated cry. "Joshua! Please! You know nothing of what I am capable of doing. You were not here to see it."

"I was not here to protect you, is that what you are saying? If I remember, Your Majesty, you sent me away!"

"I most certainly did not. You volunteered for that mission. I would have preferred you to stay here. You went on your own volition. Do not blame me for that. By doing so, you missed out on some vital information that surfaced here."

She stepped across the room, and motioned to one of the guards. "You, there, please, stand across the room and throw your spear at me."

The guard looked shocked at her request. Joshua wore an expression of murderous rage. "Don't you dare!"

"Joshua, please stop talking. I am trying to show you what you won't listen to me say." She turned back to the guard. "Do not disobey a direct order from your queen. Throw your spear at me."

The guard stole another glance at Joshua, whose jaw was set so tight that you could see the muscle twitching. He then looked at Arianna, who gave him a look that said, "Hurry up." He took a deep breath, and hurled his spear as hard as he could at her. She threw her hands up, and the white light erupted from them again, spewing out and disintegrating the spear to mere ashes. She turned to look at Joshua, whose jaw hung open, and his eyes opened wide in equal parts surprise and fear.

He looked at her again and said, "Fine, Arianna, you will lead the final approach into the Glen. We leave in the morning." He then turned and quickly walked out of the throne room, slamming the door behind him.

Chapter 21

The next morning, the sun was shining brightly. Arianna got out of her bed and sat by the window for a few moments, thinking about Joshua. He barely spoke to her for the rest of the day before and refused to go to dinner last night. She wasn't sure what he was thinking. Her thoughts were interrupted by Abigail coming into the room to help her get ready.

"Have you seen Joshua yet?" Arianna asked, desperate for any information on her fiancé, since he was obviously not in the mood to be forthcoming.

Abigail shook her head, sadly. "No, I haven't. But, I did hear him shuffling around in his room."

Arianna nodded and the girls got her ready in silence.

After Abigail had left, Arianna decided to confront Joshua on her own. She opened the door, and found him standing outside, looking apologetic.

"Joshua, please come in and talk to me." She opened the door farther, and he stepped inside, closing the door behind him. He made his way to a chair in the corner of the room while she sat on the bed.

"Why are you avoiding me? What did I do that is so wrong?"

"I'm sorry, Arianna. I don't know how to act around you now. When I left, you were simply the queen. You needed protection. You were vulnerable. Now, you can melt spears in mid-air. I don't know what to think of that. I don't know how to make sense of your new powers."

Arianna smiled at him and said, "Well, that makes two of us. Joshua, I didn't ask for this. I don't know why this happened to me. I don't know how this happened to me. As far as I know, there is no magical blood in my family. I'm starting to doubt that right now, but I have no proof. I have just as many questions as you do on this matter. But, I don't have any answers at all. I don't know anything about this at all. But, I will tell you what I do know."

Arianna stood from the bed and crossed the room. She slipped her arms around his neck and eased herself onto his lap. Joshua was startled for a moment, but he circled her waist with his arms. She looked deeply into his eyes. "I know that I need your support. I need to know that you are on my side. Joshua, I need to know that you will stand by me, and even love me, through all of this, maybe even in spite of all of this. You are to be my king. I need to know that my king will stand by his queen through everything."

Joshua didn't answer with words. He pulled her into him and crushed her mouth with his. It was a frantic kiss, one filled with longing and desire. He knew that he loved her unconditionally. He would stand by her until the very end, no matter the outcome. He kissed her for what seemed like an eternity, and a millisecond at the same time. When he broke the kiss, both of them sat, pressing their foreheads together, breathless.

"Arianna, I will follow you to the end of the world."

"That's what I was hoping you'd say."

They got up and started to walk out of the room, but Arianna stopped.

"What is it, Ari?"

"There's something I forgot."

She made her way over to the jewelry box and retrieved the engagement ring. She twirled it in her fingers for a moment and then slipped it onto the appropriate finger. She turned, faced Joshua, smiled, and took his arm again and they started walking to breakfast.

Joshua looked at her and asked, "Are you sure that you're ready to take that step?"

She nodded. "Yes, I think that it's time that I stop pushing you away and start to move ahead with you by my side. We should make an announcement after we've had a chance to go and speak with the elves. I would like to address everyone in the same day."

Joshua beamed at her. He couldn't remember a time where he felt happier.

As they made their way to the front of the hall, they heard some whispers among the crowd in regards to her ring. They simply ignored them and ate their breakfast together. Afterwards, they made their way to the front of the castle, where their horses were being prepared for the journey to the Forest Glen.

Lightning stomped the ground in greeting of his mistress. Arianna was equally elated at seeing her beloved horse, and feeling a little guilty that she hadn't been able to make time to get down to the stable to ride him as often as she used to. She mounted him, and bent down to whisper, "Good boy. I'm sorry I haven't been to see you. There's a lot going on now that I'm queen."

Lightning tossed his head as if to tell her that it was ok and that he understood. She patted his neck and hugged him. She would have to remind herself to give him a sugar cube and an apple when they got back. They were his favorite combination.

Once all of the guards had mounted their horses, they fell into formation. Arianna was in the middle, Joshua at her right, and three other guards to her left, in front and to the rear. They were about to leave when Charlie came riding up on a pony.

"Your Majesty, I want to go too. I might have some questions for those elves about magic too. I can do magic very well now."

Arianna looked at Joshua, neither of them knew what to do. The thought hadn't occurred to them to take Charlie to ask about how he could conjure magic and understand the language. Joshua simply shrugged.

"Charlie, fall in next to me," Arianna said. "You will be protected inside this circle. When we change positions, stay in the middle. Do not leave yourself vulnerable to any attacks. If we are attacked, you get out of there as quickly as you can. Do you hear me?"

"Yes, Your Majesty. I'll get out of there really fast. You don't think that we'll get attacked, do you?"

She smiled, "I've traveled to the Forest Glen hundreds of times. I think we're pretty safe."

Once they had all fallen into their new formation, they set off out of the castle gates.

They had only ridden a short way when a dark figure stepped into the road. The front guard's horse reared up on his hind legs, throwing the guard to the ground. The horse took off. The guard was unhurt aside from a few bruises.

The figure began to speak in the shrill voice that Arianna would recognize anywhere. The other horses, aside from Lightning, all began to grow uneasy.

"So, queenie, you're leaving your throne behind? Do you think that is wise? Anyone could go in and steal it from you."

"The throne of Eumetadotos is not easily stolen. If it were, I suspect that you would have tried a long time ago. You cannot rule my kingdom unless I abdicate to you or I am dead."

"The latter can be arranged quite easily."

Joshua growled quietly, but grew silent at Arianna's fierce look.

"You keep threatening to kill me, yet you have never made a move, dark one. Why is that?"

"It is not yet your time. You have much still to complete for me. I will tell you, though. The curse is coming, and coming soon. You will be powerless to stop it."

With that, it disappeared in a cloud of smoke.

Arianna and Joshua looked at each other. "Well, I'll give it one thing. It sure knows how to make an exit," Arianna tried to make a joke, but Joshua was not ready to just brush it off.

"Arianna, that thing has yet again threatened you. It has hurt one of my men." He motioned to the guard who was now going to retrieve his horse. "This is serious."

"I know that. Isn't it part of the reason that we are going to visit the elves? To try to figure out what this figure is, where it comes from and what it wants?"

Joshua nodded. "Yes, it is. I'm sorry. I can't break the habit of worrying about you. It is still my job."

Arianna smiled at him. "I know. I am grateful that you take your job so seriously."

The guard came riding up from behind. Joshua motioned for him to fall into position at the front of the line again, and they continued onto the Forest Glen uneventfully.

Chapter 22

The group traveled on until they were almost at their destination. Arianna and the front guard switched positions and the guards all raised their white flags as they made their final approach into the Forest Glen.

They had traveled just over the border when the first arrow started to fly out of the woods. Arianna held her hands up and white light erupted from them and disintegrated the arrow into a pile of ash. Several more arrows flew into the air, all meeting the same fate. After another wave of arrows all disintegrated without touching one of the entourage that had crossed into their lands, Arianna heard an unfamiliar voice yell, “Hold your fire!”

From out of the tree line stepped a rather tall elf. His hair was a chestnut brown. His body was muscled heavily, indicative of a trained warrior. His face held an expression of a fierce man who would not play games. He stepped farther into the clearing and motioned for Arianna to dismount. She got down from her horse and took a few steps closer to him before he held up his hands for her to halt. She stopped walking and stood very still.

“Why have you come here? You are not welcome here.”

“I have come to try to make amends with Armen and the elves.”

“We have no use for your treaty.”

“Please? We come bearing a gift.”

The elf scoffed at her. “We have no use for human gifts.”

“I never said it was human-made.”

The elf looked at her curiously. "And what wonderful gift could you possibly have that we would be interested in?"

"I sent my men out looking for Prince Ellavorn. They found him."

The elf looked at her in disbelief. "And just where is he?"

Arianna's shoulders sagged a little when she said, "He refused to return. However, he gave something to my captain. He said that it would repair the rift that I have foolishly caused."

The elf said nothing, but gave her an expectant look.

Arianna motioned for Joshua to step forward. He came to her side and handed her the box. She held it up in both hands for the elf to see.

The elf's expression molded into one of disbelief. "That cannot be. It's a myth."

Arianna and Joshua exchanged a look of curiosity.

"I don't know what myth you mean, but this was given to me by Prince Ellavorn himself. He told me to return it to his father and that he would be able to help us."

The warrior elf's face blanched and he motioned for them to follow. He called over his shoulder to them, "Leave the horses behind. My men will see to it that they are fed and watered."

The group followed him into the tree line. Arianna had never been past that point in all of her visits. When they stepped beyond the trees, the sight she beheld was breathtaking. An entire kingdom was standing before her. Buildings made of pure white stone and thatched rooves stood all around. Gleaming streets wound themselves all around the kingdom. Several elven children were playing a game in the street. They stopped to watch with curiosity as the group of humans passed through. They walked to the center of the city where a humongous castle with gleaming white walls stood before them. It dwarfed the castle of Eumetadotos by twice the size. It took Arianna's breath away. The elf held up his hand for them to stop as he made his way up the stairs.

"I will be but a moment. Wait here."

He made his way through the enormous front doors of the castle and they closed behind him. The group stood in silence, taking in their surroundings, for a few moments longer. When the castle doors opened, the elf appeared again with Armen by his side. Arianna looked at the elf that was supposed to be her father-in-law, trying to figure out his expression. It remained neutral as he approached them.

"Adasser said that you have something of interest for me from my son."

"Yes, your majesty. I sent my Royal Guard out to look for him. My captain found him, but he would not return. Instead, he sent this, saying that it would help to mend the rift that I have caused by my foolish actions." Arianna held out the box to him.

Armen gasped and reached out to take it gently from her grasp. He looked at her in amazement.

"Do you know what this is?"

"No."

"This is the Koutí Profiteíavoun. It was said to be a myth. No one thought that it actually existed."

"Is this a good thing that it exists?" Arianna looked worried.

"Yes, Arianna, it is a good thing. All of you, come inside. We have much to discuss."

Arianna and Joshua both blew out deep breaths. They ascended the stairs to go into the castle and followed Armen into a huge throne room.

Arianna couldn't help but look around. At the front of the room stood two gigantic thrones, made of pure gold. Between the thrones hung the banners of the Forest Glen. The background was hunter green and the symbol of the leafless oak in a circle was gold. The carpet was a rich, plush hunter green with shoots of gold thrown in throughout. It ran the aisle up to the thrones. The rest of the floor looked as though it were made of granite with beautiful white gems scattered among the stone. These gems held Arianna's interest most of all. They were the same gems that were inlaid in the necklace that her mother had made for her wedding day. Armen noticed her curiosity.

"I see you recognize the white gems?"

"Yes. They are beautiful. My mother had them put into a necklace that she had made for me. What are they?"

"They are fotovólos stones. You can only find them in the Forest Glen, and even then, they are very rare."

"They are beautiful."

"That they are. But, I sense that you did not come here to discuss stones."

"No, Your Majesty, I didn't. I've come to discuss some rather serious incidents that have been happening in Eumetadotos."

"Adasser tells me that you disintegrated our arrows with your bare hands. He said that you somehow had white light coming from your hands and it just burned them up. Can you explain that?"

"I was hoping that you could help me with that. I think that it would probably be good to start at the beginning."

Armen nodded. He motioned for some of his guards to fetch some chairs. Once they were all seated, he motioned for Arianna to begin.

"A few months ago, a dark figure appeared in our dining hall. It made some threats."

"A dark figure? Why do you call it an 'it?'"

"Well, we don't know whether it is male or female. It speaks with a shrill voice and wears a hooded cloak. It never reveals its identity. It makes threats and leaves."

Armen nodded, looking quite serious.

"It appeared, and as I said, made some threats and disappeared. It is pretty certain that it is going to take over my throne. We did not see it again until a few days ago. Joshua had gone away to try to find Ellavorn. The figure, once again, came into the dining hall and made threats. This time, however, it tried to hurt little Charlie." She pointed at Charlie, who sat up straight and smiled his most dazzling smile. "When I saw that it was going to kill him, I didn't know what to do. I threw my hands out at it and these white beams of light just shot out of them and hit it, sending it flying backwards. It made some more threats and disappeared again. The next day, I was addressing my people, and someone threw a spear. Again, I threw my hands up to protect myself and the spear just disintegrated."

Armen was giving her a curious look. "Is that the end?"

"No."

"Of course not," Joshua muttered. Arianna shot him a look that screamed for him to just stop talking.

"My handmaiden and I went to the library to try to find something to read on the subject of magic."

"Let me guess. You found nothing?"

"Well, not exactly. At first, we couldn't even find it in the card catalog. But, then, I found a box, similar to the one that we just gave you hidden behind a brick."

Armen looked startled by this revelation. "Where is this box now?"

"I have it hidden."

"Did you open it?"

"Yes."

"What was inside?"

"A key."

"A key?"

"A beautiful key. It looks as though it is cut from a single ruby. The handle is a complicated lotus pattern. The bottom is a dragon wing."

"It cannot be."

"It cannot be what?"

"Continue."

Arianna eyed him suspiciously. "What do you think it is?"

"Continue your story. I will tell you my thoughts after."

Arianna took a deep, frustrated breath and continued. "We had no idea where the key went. Charlie told us that it would fit into a stone in the pantry of the kitchen."

"You built a pantry at the entrance?"

"I didn't build anything. How did you know it was an entrance?"

"I'm sorry. Go on."

Arianna was beginning to get frustrated with Armen's interruptions, but she continued on to finish the rest of her story.

"As we were making our way down to the pantry, Joshua arrived back. He told me of his meeting with Ellavorn and showed me that box." She indicated the box that Armen still held tightly in his hands. "He also noticed this." She rolled her sleeve up to expose the mark on her wrist. Armen looked at it in disbelief.

"How can this be? This is an elven mark. How would you come to bear an elven mark?"

"Again, I was hoping that you might be able to shed some light on that subject."

He shook his head and she continued.

"We all continued to the pantry, where we found the stone. We placed the key in the slot and it disappeared into the wall. A set of spiral stairs began to form from the floor, and we followed them down. Torches began lighting themselves. We came to the bottom and noticed that we were in some kind of chamber."

"You have found it?"

"Found what?"

"Continue."

"There were all kinds of books that none of us, save Charlie, could read. There are liquids down there, but we can't get to them. There is some kind of barrier around them, preventing anyone from stepping in too close. I couldn't make out any names. But, Charlie could read the books. He began performing simple spells and he's gotten quite good at those."

Charlie grinned and sat even straighter in his chair.

"We looked around a little more and then we left. We figured we should come up with a plan to make amends with you to try to figure out what is going on. Our kingdom has been void of magic for so long that no one knows anything of it. You are the only magical beings that we could think of that may be able to help us. Can you? Help us, that is?"

Armen looked at Arianna with a mixture of amazement and fear in his eyes.

"And so it begins."

Chapter 23

The room fell completely silent. Arianna stood, started pacing and broke the silence. "What is beginning?"

Armen stood in front of her and grabbed her by the arms. "Arianna, there are many things that you don't know yet. You were destined for greatness before you were born."

Armen sat down again and slid the box that Ellavorn had given to Joshua in front of them. He motioned for Arianna to sit.

"Arianna, this box contains your destiny."

Arianna's face contorted in confusion. "What do you mean my destiny? If that's so, why did Ellavorn have it?"

Armen continued to look at the box, unable to look at the woman who had broken his son's heart.

"I suspect that Ellavorn retrieved this box from the Hall of Prophesies in order to have something left of you. He must know what is coming. That is why he handed this over to Captain Oakford so freely, so that you knew of the danger that you were facing and that you could mend some fences, so to speak. By giving me this box, it was his way of reminding me that you would need help."

Arianna simply looked at him, willing him to go on.

"Long before you were born, there was a prophecy made about you, Arianna. Not by name, but by the one physical feature that sets you apart from everyone else."

"You mean –"

"Listen." Armen unlocked the box and turned it to face her. He lifted the lid and a figure of a female elf stood up. She looked as though she were made of smoke. The figure didn't seem to take notice of anyone in the room, as she spoke.

"Take heed, a great evil will threaten to befall the entire land. The child born with eyes of violet skies will hold the power of victory."

The figure then dissipated in front of their eyes.

Arianna looked up at Armen, confused.

"What does this mean?"

Armen finally looked up at her, with tears swimming in his own eyes.'

"It means that you are meant to save us all from this evil. You are the one who holds the key to defeating what is threatening us."

Joshua finally spoke up. "Why her? Why can't the elves use their magic?"

Armen shook his head, sadly, "I do not know why it must be her. I know as much as you do about the prophecy. It was spoken long ago, long before even I was born."

Joshua gave a frustrated sound and pushed himself up from his chair and took Arianna's place pacing the floor.

"How can she possibly save us all? She's just a human! She doesn't –." He stopped mid-sentence and looked at Arianna, who knew what he was going to say, but couldn't because he knew that the words were no longer true.

She looked at Armen. "Is this why I can now do magic?"

Armen shook his head. “I don’t know. Let me see that symbol on your wrist again.”

Arianna held out her arm for him to see.

“Adasser, come forward.” Armen’s voice was neutral, betraying nothing in his tone.

“My Lord?”

“Adasser, hold out your crest.”

Adasser hesitated for a moment before holding out his arm, wrist up. Armen put his next to Arianna’s. The symbols matched perfectly.

Angrily, Armen growled, “How can this be, Adasser? How does the child bear the crest of your family?”

Arianna snatched her arm away. “What do you mean, the crest of his family? What is going on?”

Adasser sighed. “I am sorry.”

Armen stood, looking at the commander of his army. “What have you done, Adasser?”

“She is my granddaughter.”

“No! My grandfather was the king of Eumetadotos.”

Adasser shook his head. “That is what everyone has been lead to believe, at least up until this point.”

“No! You’re lying!” Arianna was screaming at this point.

Armen looked at her. “Please, Arianna, please, calm down. Let’s hear what Adasser has to say.” He motioned for Adasser to sit.

Once they had all settled back into their seats, Armen gave him the signal to begin his story.

"I met your grandmother before she married your grandfather. She was so beautiful." He smiled wistfully, remembering her.

"She would go down to the river quite often to sit and watch the water rush past. She always looked so serene as she was lost in her own thoughts. I watched her for weeks before I mustered up the courage to speak to her. I knew that she was the princess to take over the throne. She was off limits to me. Elves don't marry humans and princesses don't marry common folk.

"One day, I decided to make myself known to her. I stepped out of the shadows, and she looked at me as though she knew I was there all along. She looked at me and said, 'It's about time you revealed yourself. I was starting to worry that you were plotting a way to kidnap me.' She then threw her head back and laughed. It was the most beautiful thing I had ever heard."

"So, you fell in love with my grandmother?"

"Yes, I did. We talked that day, and for months after. I tried to fight those feelings, as did she. Neither of us knew how to stop those feelings. Her parents began parading suitors in front of her, one by one. She rejected them all. She said that she just couldn't feel the way that they wanted her to feel about these men. She said that she only felt that way about me. No one else."

"So, you're saying that my grandmother never even loved my grandfather?"

"I don't know, Your Majesty. Her parents told her that she needed to make a decision. They told her that she had to get married. She told me that she could never marry any of those men. She told me that she wanted to run away. I talked her out of it. I told her that it would never work the way that she wanted to. I tried to make her see that she couldn't leave her kingdom. They needed her. She finally relented and agreed not to run away. She told me that she refused to marry any of them. Her parents, however, were insistent that she marry."

Arianna stayed quiet. Her story held so many parallels to her own, that her heart broke for both her grandmother and Adasser. She was dealing with conflicting emotions. On one hand, she wanted to cheer Adasser on because she knew how he felt. On the other hand, she wanted to believe that her grandparents were truly in love. She couldn't think of anything else to say, so she motioned for Adasser to continue.

"One day, she came to me, in tears. Her parents were dead set that she marry. They were not taking no for an answer. She begged me to come and ask their permission to marry her. I couldn't. Elves don't marry humans. Princesses only marry royalty. It broke my heart to tell her no. I wanted nothing more than to go and request permission to marry her."

"Then why didn't you?" Arianna could only manage to whisper.

"I told you why. It was stupid. I should have asked. I should have fought for her. It is something that I regret to this day. But, I couldn't. I was afraid."

"Then what happened?"

"Your grandmother stormed off. She told me that she was going to have to marry one of those men and that she was making her decision that night. She took off and I couldn't find her. A few days later, it was announced that she was marrying your grandfather. My heart broke. I didn't see her again until about a week before the wedding. She came to the river bank, sat there and wept. I approached her and we held each other for hours, weeping together for the life we should have had."

"And then what?"

Adasser grew uncomfortable. "We started to kiss. Things started getting heated and one thing led to another. We made love for the first time on the river bank. Afterward, we promised to meet up every day until the wedding. If we couldn't spend our lives together, we would have that precious week to act as though we were man and wife."

"I think I'm going to be sick. This is my grandmother that you're talking about. She wouldn't do that."

"I'm sorry, Your Majesty, but she did. We did. Every day for the rest of that week, we would meet up and let our passions go unbridled. We poured all of our love for each other into those moments that we had together, praying that we wouldn't get caught. Thankfully, we didn't. It would have meant the end of our time together, and we weren't sure of any other consequences."

Armen was the one to speak this time. "What do you mean, other consequences?"

"We weren't sure of what would happen in accordance with our laws."

"None of our laws forbid elves mating with humans. That is a choice that we, as individuals, make for ourselves. As for Eumetadotos law, I do not know what consequences would have befallen her. Please, continue."

"When our week was up, we knew that we could never completely say good bye, but we had to. She was getting married the next day. She would be pledging her life to another man. She would no longer be mine. After we made love, we lay there for hours, just lying there together. We made love one last time, and said our good-byes forever. She went off and married your grandfather. I watched from afar. About 2 months after they were married, she announced her pregnancy. I always suspected that the child that she carried was mine, but I could never ask her. I never spoke to her again."

He turned to Arianna, "I'm sorry that you had to find out this way. I don't know how she felt about your grandfather. She may have fallen in love with him with the same passion as she and I felt for each other. I just don't know. Please, don't think that I didn't love her. I still love her with the same intensity as the first time I saw her sitting on that river bank. She is the love of my life. When I heard that Prince Ellavorn had intended to marry you, I was celebrating inside for the both of you. At the same time, my heart broke as well because of what I had lost. Now, I know that I was correct in my feeling that your mother was my daughter. I never truly let go. I never spoke to your grandmother again, but I continued to watch her from afar. I followed her until the day that she died. That day, a part of my heart died as well."

Arianna swallowed. "I never knew."

Adasser shook his head. "No one did." He looked up into her eyes, tears brimming, and asked her, "Was she happy?"

Arianna nodded slightly. "I think so. She was always loving and caring. I don't remember her much. She died when I was young, before I got sick. But, I remember she always smiled."

He nodded, smiling himself. "Her smile could light up even the darkest moments. That memory is what has gotten me through the darkest of times."

Arianna shook her head, trying to absorb all of the information that was just given to her. "So, this means that I have elven blood?"

"Yes, it would appear so."

"That would explain the magic, and this symbol on my wrist. What does it mean?"

Adasser held out his hand and, hesitantly, she placed hers in his. He looked intently at it for a moment.

"This is our family crest. The bows and arrows represent our family skill. We are warriors, protectors. That is how our magic manifests itself. Each Elven family has a different kind of magic. Armen's family, however, is royalty. They pull from every kind of magic. The A on the tip is your first initial, just like mine. If you had a different first initial, it would be that."

"Why didn't this develop before? Wouldn't my mother have had magic as well?"

"Magic manifests itself when you are ready, or when it is necessary. When did your magic manifest?"

"A few days ago. The Dark Figure attacked Charlie. I threw my hands up, and these waves of white light came out and threw it across the room. I had no control over it. Then, the next day, someone threw a spear at me and again, I threw up my hands. The white light disintegrated that spear in front of my face. It wasn't until later that day that this appeared."

Armen nodded. "The crest appears when your magic manifests itself. It takes a little bit to appear. Your magic came to you because you needed it. Your mother probably possessed magic and never knew because she didn't need it."

"What about when she was attacked? She needed it then. Instead, she was killed!"

"I don't know why it wouldn't. That would have been a prime time for it to make its presence known. I don't have that answer. Armen?"

Armen shook his head, "I don't know the answer to that. Captain Oakford, you were there, did anything seem out of the ordinary?"

Joshua shook his head. "I don't think so. We were all so busy fighting off the attackers, that I wouldn't have noticed if there was. I do know that she put up a valiant fight, but I don't know any more than that."

Arianna sat in silence, listening to everything being said around her. The conflicting emotions inside of her were tearing her apart. On one hand, she had the memories of her grandfather. Or, the person who she thought was her grandfather. Memories that had brought her joy for so long. She still had the memories, but now she had to change her view of them in a way. This man wasn't really her grandfather, not biologically, at least. On the other hand, she had this man, this Elf, claiming that he was, indeed her grandfather. His story held so many parallels to her story with Ellavorn. She wasn't sure how she felt about all of this information.

"I need some air. Where is the closest balcony?"

Armen pointed in the direction. "Take as much time as you need."

Joshua made a move to escort her. She held up her hand.

"I need to be alone right now, please."

He looked hurt, but she ran off down the corridor.

Armen smiled a reassuring smile at him. "Don't let that hurt your feelings. She just needs some time. She'll be back.

Chapter 24

Arianna burst through the balcony doors, ran and threw herself against the railing and screamed, a long, loud, primal scream. She screamed until her throat burned and she felt that she couldn't scream anymore. She then sank to the floor, pulled her knees to her chest and began sobbing. Her entire family dynamic had been rocked to the core. She felt lost, alone and afraid. She no more understood the magic that coursed through her body, but she at least understood where it came from. She hated the information that she had just been given. She hated Adasser for what he told her. She even hated her grandmother for being a part of that story. She didn't want to believe it. She couldn't. She looked at her wrist, and the crest was still there, mockingly looking up at her, and making it impossible to deny that it was all true. At that moment, the doors creaked open slowly, and Adasser stepped out onto the balcony.

"What do you want?" Arianna asked, wiping her eyes.

"Are you ok?"

"No! No, I am not! How can what you told me possibly be true? All my life, I've only known one man to be my grandfather. Now, you're telling me that he's not. You're saying that all of my memories of my grandfather are a lie. How is it possible?"

Adasser sat down beside her and gently said, "I told you what happened. I wish that I could say that I would take it all back, but that would be a lie. I still love your grandmother more than anyone. Your memories are not a lie. That is who you knew as your grandfather. He will always be your grandfather. I wish that things were different and that you could have known the truth. I wish that I could have held your mother and you as babies and helped to raise you. But, you were raised by a man who loved you as your own."

"Do you think that he ever knew?"

"If he did, he never let on that he knew. I don't think that he did."

"Did you ever marry?"

"No. I gave my heart away completely. I have never met anyone who would ever compare to your grandmother. Although, you remind me an awful lot of her. I can see why the Prince would fall in love with you."

"I guess Elves and humans were not meant to marry at all. That makes two human/Elf relationships that were doomed."

"Your Majesty, they were only doomed because of our decisions. I wouldn't go to her parents out of fear. I loved her, but I just didn't know what to do. You pushed the Prince away because you were grieving. You had lost the two most important people in your life and you lashed out. We made those choices. We have to live with them."

"I know that all too well. There are so many similarities between your story and mine. Why didn't you ever say anything about this possibility?"

"I never knew for sure. Not until I saw your crest had revealed itself."

"I still miss him."

"I know. I still miss her."

Arianna smiled. "I know."

"Your Majesty –"

"I think under the circumstances, you should call me Arianna. Apparently, we're family."

Adasser smiled broadly. "Arianna, then. Arianna, you will always love him. Just like I will always love your grandmother. That fire will never go out."

"I have to marry. If I don't, my land will be cursed."

"Who will you marry?"

"Joshua."

"Captain Oakford?"

"Yes."

"Do you love him?"

"I do. Not like I love Ellavorn, but I do love him. I trust him. He has proven himself to be loyal, faithful, and he will make a great king."

Adasser nodded.

"When is the wedding?"

"We haven't set a date. We haven't even announced it to the kingdom yet." She started to twirl her engagement ring around her finger. Adasser noticed it for the first time.

"Your grandmother wore the same one."

"All of the engaged princesses and queens have. It's been in my family for centuries."

Adasser nodded again.

"Adasser, what does this mean for me now? Am I mortal? Am I immortal? It seems as though with every question that is answered, I have more that pop up. What about my children?"

Adasser smiled. "Your Elven blood will be passed on to them, no doubt. Aside from that, I don't know. Your mother was the first half Elf, half human ever born." His eyes grew wistful. "I wish that I could have met her."

It was Arianna's turn to smile. "You would have loved her. She was kind and loving and generous. You would have been proud of her."

"Thank you, Arianna. If it is ok with you, I would like to hear more about her. Perhaps when all of the evil has come to pass?"

"I would like that. It would seem that you are my only living relative now. It would be nice to get to know you."

"Thank you. It would be nice to know my granddaughter too. You are very much like your grandmother. She was also strong-willed, but put the needs of her people first. She was passionate and fierce in everything that she did and said. Yet, she was gentle and kind. You remind me of her."

Arianna smiled. She didn't want to say anymore. She didn't know if she could ever love him like she loved her grandfather, but she had meant it when she said that he was the only living relative that she had left. It would feel nice to have someone who shared her bloodline to talk to.

"What about my powers?"

"You will need to learn how to use them properly, not just sporadically."

"How do I do that?"

“Practice.”

“Meaning?”

“Meaning someone will be assigned to you to help you to master them completely. Since time is of the essence, I would think that Armen would assign you someone soon. Training will be intense. Most Elves start training when they are young, so they master their skills as they grow. You will be different. You will be put through some pretty rigorous training. I think that you can handle it.”

“I’m scared.”

“You should be. From what I hear, there is a very evil figure out there that wants you dead.”

Arianna gave a short laugh. “Oddly enough, that isn’t what scares me.”

“What scares you, Arianna?”

“Leaving my people unprotected. I can’t stay here long. They need me.”

“Of course, they do. But, that isn’t all that scares you, is it, child?”

She looked out into the distance, taking in the beautiful scenery. “No.”

“You can tell me what it is.”

“I’m afraid that I won’t be able to give Joshua everything that he needs. I still love Ellavorn. I think that I always will. But, I hurt him and he doesn’t want me anymore. I love Joshua, but I don’t love him like I do Ellavorn. I don’t know that I will ever be able to love him that intensely. He deserves that kind of love. He's a good man."

"I don't know Captain Oakford very well. But, if you say that he is a good man, then I will take your word on that. From what I saw in that room, he certainly loves you, Arianna. I have seen the look in his eyes when he looks at you and talks to you. It is the look of a man in love. You may not have those feelings as intensely as he does, but I don't think that it matters to him. You need to marry. He loves you. He will be good to you. In time, you will grow to have deeper feelings for him. However, you are right that you will never love him the same way that you loved Ellavorn."

"Well, that doesn't make me feel any better. I want to be in love with the man that I marry."

Adasser chuckled. "I didn't say that you won't love him, Arianna. You just won't love him the same way you love Ellavorn. They are two different individuals. With Ellavorn, you love the familiar. You've known him since you were a child. He saved your life and from that day forward, there has been a bond between the two of you. I saw it when you would meet in the meadow."

Arianna's head shot round, her eyes huge with surprise. "You saw us?"

"Of course I did. I patrol the perimeter of the Forest Glen. There was no way I would not have seen you meeting there."

"Were you spying on us?"

"Not at all. I never listened to your conversations. I only saw that you were meeting. As you heard, I know the need for privacy."

Arianna blushed. "We didn't need that much privacy."

Adasser laughed a hearty laugh. "I know."

"Joshua found Ellavorn. He did that for me. Ellavorn did not wish to return. That is how he came to possess the koutí profiteíavoun."

"Well, it sounds like he loves you even more than I thought. Arianna, any man who would go looking for the man that the woman he loves, loves is a good man. That could not have been easy for him to do."

"I hated asking him to do it. I didn't think that he would actually go himself, let alone be the one to find him. He is a good man, which is why I am so afraid. I don't want to hurt him."

"If Ellavorn came back into your life tomorrow, would you still take him as your husband?"

Arianna thought for a moment. She thought of all that she had shared with Ellavorn in the past, the good and the bad. She thought of how she had felt after she had broken off their engagement, and all of the pain that she had caused to the both of them. She still felt some of that pain, but most of it felt healed. She thought harder, and realized that it was because of Joshua that the pain had lessened. Joshua's face swam into her mind. She smiled a genuine smile and knew her answer.

"Honestly, I don't know definitely, but, I don't think that I would. I made a promise to Joshua to be his wife. I know that I had made that same promise to Ellavorn and broke it. The aftermath of that is still causing me pain. But, the pain has lessened. I have found friends, and I found a man who loves me. I know that I will probably never feel as intensely as I do for

Ellavorn, but I do love him. I will honor my promise to Joshua. No matter what."

Arianna thought of her grandmother, and how she must have had those same conflicting feelings.

As though Adasser was reading her mind, he said, "I wish that I could tell you what happened with your grandmother, but I never spoke to her again after our final meeting. I could never bring myself to go to her. I wish that I had been able to. I still can't bring myself to speak with her. I wish that I could tell you that everything was going to be ok, but I don't have those answers. Only you can answer those questions."

"But I don't have those answers either."

"Not yet. But you will."

"How?"

Adasser looked her straight in the eyes. "By living."

Chapter 25

Arianna and Adasser made their way back to the others. When they opened the door, Joshua sprang from his chair and ran to her, sweeping into a huge hug.

"Are you alright? I was worried about you."

Arianna pulled away to look him in the eye. "I will be. I just needed a moment to compose my thoughts and to start to process the information that was just given to me. It will take a while for it all to set in, though."

Joshua nodded. "Take your time."

He escorted her back to her chair with his arm around her waist.

Armen noticed the gesture, but chose not to mention it. "We need to discuss your training now."

"Your Highness, I cannot train here. I need to be with my people. How am I going to train and lead at the same time?"

"I will send someone to return with you, if it is alright with you. You need to learn to control your powers. You will also feel them grow with the proper training. There is much for you to learn in order to defeat this figure."

"I would appreciate that. Who will you send?"

"Adasser."

Both Adasser and Arianna startled at the suggestion.

"But, My King – "

"Adasser, you are my finest guardian and warrior. We need her to be well trained. There is no one better than you to do so. Besides," he turned to look at Arianna. "The two of you should really spend some time together. It will do you both some good."

"My King, who will protect you if I leave?"

"Adasser, your men are very well trained. You have done well for them. You now need to train your own flesh and blood." He clapped his hands onto Adasser's shoulders. "My friend, I have known about your love for Arianna's grandmother for decades. I know how much you love her. This is your chance to bond with the legacy that you have created. Arianna is your legacy."

Adasser looked flabbergasted. "You mean, you knew, but you never said anything?"

Armen nodded with a slight smile. "I did."

Arianna jumped out of her chair. "You knew and you never said anything?"

Armen shook his head sliently.

"You knew and never – wait, is that why you gave your blessing to a marriage between Ellavorn and myself?"

Armen sighed. "It was partly the reason, Arianna. I also knew that it was time for elves to broaden their horizons and to realize that it is acceptable to marry outside of our race. I knew that your marriage would be the first of its kind. I knew that there was already a coupling of an elf and a human, and like Adasser, I had a suspicion that your mother was his daughter. However, it is quite rude to make an inquiry of that nature. I had hoped to see what happened with your mother, but sadly, that would not be the case. She was a wonderful woman. It is tragic what befell your father and her. They were wonderful rulers, and, Arianna, I see you to be shaping up to be just like them. I am truly sorry that our kingdoms have not yet been brought together by marriage. Maybe in time they will."

Arianna gave a small smile. "King Armen, I feel it necessary to inform you that Captain Oakford has proposed and that I have accepted his proposal. We have not set a date as of yet, but the wedding should be soon."

Armen's smiled wavered. "I see. Well, congratulations to the both of you. I wish you a lifetime of happiness."

With that, he turned and walked out of the room. Arianna stood and went after him. She caught up to him in the hall.

"King Armen, please allow me to explain."

"Arianna, there is no explanation necessary. You are no longer engaged to my son. You are free to marry who you wish."

"We tried to find him. Joshua went himself. He was, actually, the one to find him. Ellavorn refused to come back. I am truly sorry for the pain that I have caused. I wish that I could earn forgiveness from all of you. I wish that I could turn back the clocks and take it all back. But, I can't. Joshua is a good man. He loves me. He will make a great king. I did not know it at the time, but if I do not marry within a year, a curse will befall my kingdom. We are already in danger. I cannot risk any more trouble coming to my people."

"Do you love him?"

"I do. Not as much as I love Ellavorn, but I do love him. He is a good man."

Armen looked at her kindly, sighed and said, "Then, you have my blessing and my forgiveness. You set out to find my son, and you did. What he chooses to do is not your responsibility. I hope that your marriage is a good one. However, I thought that you had to marry royalty? He is not royalty, Arianna."

"There is a stipulation. If I reject the royal suitors, I may choose someone of royal appointment. Joshua is the Captain of the Royal Guard, therefore, he is eligible. I didn't mean for this to happen. We became friends and it just sort of happened."

"I understand. Were the royal suitors really that terrible?"

Arianna chuckled. "Worse. Maybe one day I will be able to tell you about them."

Armen smiled and reached out to hug her. Arianna accepted the embrace for a moment.

"Do you really think that Adasser could train me well enough to defeat this dark figure?"

"I do. Adasser is the best warrior and protector that we have."

"Won't you need him?"

"Not as much as you do."

"There is no one else?"

"Are you trying to avoid getting to know your grandfather?"

"My grandfather is dead. The man in that room may share my blood, but I don't know that I could ever look at him as my grandfather."

"Arianna, he is very much your grandfather. He may not have been around for your entire life, but he is a good man and will stand by you. You must let go of your fears. It will be a good thing for you to get to know each other. You are more alike than you know."

He chuckled and walked away.

Arianna strolled back to the others. When she opened the door, Joshua and Adasser were arguing.

"You will not put my fiancée in danger!"

"She needs to train, Captain."

"Then you will find a way to train her that does not involve the chance of her getting hurt!"

"This figure is not going to go to battle without the intention of hurting her! It wants her dead. She needs to be able to defend herself. She needs to know how to control her powers. You need to stop treating her as a weak little child and allow her to become who she is supposed to be."

"How dare you? You know nothing of who she is, nor who she is supposed to be."

"I know the legends of my people," Adasser snarled. "I know that she is supposed to overcome this terrible evil and save all of us from its wrath."

"I will not allow this to happen. It is my sworn duty to protect her."

Arianna had had enough of the arguing. "Enough!" The room quieted down. "Joshua, I know that you want to protect me, but, Adasser is right. I do need to learn how to defend myself. I need the best training that I can get. That will involve me being in danger. He is right. This figure is going to fight dirty and stop at nothing until it gets what it wants, and that is me, dead."

"Arianna, you can't be serious? You want to train with him? He is going to be putting you into dangerous positions. I can't protect you in those positions."

"That is the point, Joshua. I need to learn to do this. I need to learn to use my powers, and grow them. I need to embrace that this is a part of me. I can't ignore it. I have to do this. I know that you want to protect me, and I am grateful for that, but you have to acknowledge that there are things that you can't protect me from. I have to do that on my own. I can only imagine how difficult that this is for you to hear, but, Joshua, this has to be done. I need to know what I am capable of. If this prophecy is correct, I am the only one who can defeat this dark figure that keeps threatening us. It will be ok. I have faith that Adasser won't harm me. Not intentionally, that is."

"Captain Oakford, Arianna is right. She needs to know how to work her powers. It is the only way that she can save not only your people, but mine as well."

Joshua collapsed onto a chair and buried his face in his hands. "I don't know how to let go of the protector in me. It's been ingrained in me since I joined the Royal Guard. Now, I am the Captain, the leader, and you are asking me to step aside and not protect the queen, of all people. Not just the queen, but my fiancée. How can I do that?"

Arianna knelt in front of him and took his hands into her own. "Joshua, I know that this is going to be difficult for you. I am not denying that. It will be hard for you to watch, if you choose to do so. But, this has to be done. You cannot stand in the way. Otherwise, you will be doing the exact opposite of protecting. You will be hindering our people. I cannot allow that. The training will be done. If you try to stop it, I will have no choice but to ban you from the training area."

Joshua's expression turned darker. "You can't do that, Arianna."

"I am the queen. I can do what I choose."

"You wouldn't ban me from the training area. I am your appointed guard, at least until our wedding."

"I will assign myself someone else during training sessions if need be. Joshua, you cannot interfere with this. It is vital to our victory."

Joshua stood directly in front of Arianna, his eyes boring into her's. "You can tell me all of this, but it will not make me like it any better. You are trying to force me to go against all of my training. I can't do that, Arianna. I won't do that."

"Then I will have to assign someone else for training duty. I'm sorry that you don't like it, but this is what needs to be done. I cannot allow some mysterious figure to constantly threaten my kingdom and myself simply because you feel that I can't protect myself. I am a lot stronger than you think, Joshua. I am also still your queen. You are not king yet."

With that, she turned on her heel and walked briskly from the room, leaving Joshua and Adasser staring after her with mouths hanging open in shock.

Chapter 26

Arianna slammed the door behind her and fought the urge to scream. She began pacing angrily in front of the door, muttering under her breath about the two men that she had just stormed out on when she heard a small, timid voice, "Your Majesty?"

She jumped to attention and realized that Charlie was sitting against the wall and had just seen her outburst.

"Oh, Charlie, you startled me. Are you ok?"

He nodded slowly. "Yes. I heard you yelling."

She walked over to him and sat next to him.

"Yes, sometimes people get mad and yell. It's ok, though, Charlie."

"Are you mad at Captain Oakford and the elf man?"

"I am."

"Why?"

Arianna sat for a moment, trying to think of a way to explain it to him. "Well, I have a very big task to fulfill, and they are arguing. While they do that, it's wasting time that I could use to train and become stronger. I know that Captain Oakford wants to protect me, but he can't always be there, and there are some things that he can't protect me from. I have to learn to do that on my own. Does that make sense?"

Charlie nodded. "He wants to protect you because he loves you."

Arianna smiled. "Yes, I know. But, sometimes, if you love someone, you have to let go a little bit to let them grow. Sort of how when you were learning to walk, your parents let you fall sometimes because if you didn't you wouldn't learn. It's sort of the same thing."

"But, I heard Captain Oakford say that what you want to learn is dangerous."

Arianna's eyes dropped. "Yes, it will be dangerous. But, it's something that I have to do in order to protect you and my kingdom."

Charlie nodded, but then burst into tears. "Your Majesty, I don't want you to do to this either. I love you too! I don't want you to get hurt."

Arianna gathered him into a hug. "Oh, Charlie, I know that you don't. I can't promise you that I will be ok, but I can promise you that I will try my best to be. I don't want to get hurt either. Can I tell you a secret?"

Charlie looked at her with tears in his eyes and nodded silently.

"I'm scared. I'm very, very scared. But, I know that I can do this. I have to do this. Do you understand why?"

Charlie shook his head.

"Well, I have to do this because I have to learn how to use my powers to defeat that dark figure that keeps appearing. I need to be able to protect my kingdom. Do you know why?"

Charlie shook his head again.

"Because I love you too, Charlie. I love you and everyone in my kingdom. Just like Captain Oakford loves me and wants to protect me. I have to protect my kingdom. That's what a queen does. She fights for her people. I have to fight for my people. I am going to do my best to win that fight. OK?"

Charlie threw himself into her arms again, clinging to her tightly while she held him. She rocked back & forth trying to comfort him while tears fell from her own eyes.

"Ari?"

Arianna looked up to see Abigail standing there. Her friend dropped down beside her, putting her arms around her and embracing her and Charlie both as the three of them sat crying together.

A few moments later, the door banged open again and Joshua marched down the hall, stopping momentarily to notice the three of them huddled on the floor together, comforting one another in their fears.

"We leave in ten minutes."

He then marched off to ready the caravan. A moment later, Adasser walked out of the room, nostrils flaring until he took notice of the trio sitting on the floor. He walked over to them and knelt in front of them.

"I know that you are all scared. It is normal to feel that way. Do not let anyone tell you differently. Even we Elves need to take a moment to fall apart at times." He looked from Charlie to Abigail. "She is going to need your help. Both of you. Are you both willing to help her to train?"

They both nodded in unison. Abigail spoke first, "What can we do?"

Adasser smiled. "The first thing that you can do is get up off of that dirty floor. Your moment is over. We need to get our things together and head back to Eumetadotos."

He turned to Arianna. "Is there a safe place for you to train? Somewhere where we can run drills and throw magic around without running the risk of hurting anyone?"

Charlie jumped up first. "The magic room! Oh, Your Highness, we can use the magic room!"

Arianna giggled at Charlie's quick change in demeanor. Adasser looked at them, confused. "You have a magic room?"

Arianna shook her head. "I guess you can call it that."

"It is a magic room! It's a room full of books with magic spells and all these drinks that you can't get to because there's this weird barrier around them, and I can light the candles!"

Adasser gave Arianna a confused look, and her giggled turned into a full on laugh.

"What Charlie means is that we found the room where the wizard probably stored all of his magic supplies. The drinks aren't actually drinks, but, we think that they are potion ingredients. There's a barrier around them, so we don't know for sure."

Adasser gasped. "You found the Odigós Domátio?"

"The what?" Charlie was confused.

"The Odigós Domátio. It is where the wizard practiced his magic when he was here. He would train his apprentices there as well. It was rumored to have been lost. The entrance was sealed when the wizard left this realm. No one has been able to find it."

“Well, they didn’t do a very good job of hiding it,” huffed Arianna. “The entrance is in the castle’s pantry. We found the key.”

Adasser looked shocked and excited at the same time. “From what I have heard, the Odigós Domάtio would be the perfect room in which to practice.”

Charlie began bouncing again. “I practice in there all the time. I’m getting good at magic.”

Adasser turned and eyed him curiously. “What do you mean you are getting good at magic? Surely, you cannot do spells? That is only for those of wizard blood.”

“I can so do spells! I’m getting really good at it too! I will show you when we get back to the castle.”

“No, young Charlie, I need you to show me now.”

Adasser ran to the room that he had just left and came back carrying a candle.

“You said that you can light candles. I thought you simply meant that you would light them with a match. Can you do that with magic?”

Charlie puffed out his chest. “Yes, I can! I can light it real good.”

Adasser tried hard not to smile at Charlie’s pride. “Please show me.”

Charlie stood back, cracked his knuckles, and yelled, “Diafotízos!” The flame crackled to life. He then extended his forefinger and raised it up. The flame grew in height. He lowered it back down and the flame followed suit. Abigail and Arianna both looked at him in awe.

"You're really improving, Charlie!" Arianna had genuine pride in her voice.

"Wow! I didn't know you had it in you, kid." Abigail was genuinely impressed.

"So, now we have a half human half Elf and a child somehow descended from the line of wizards. This is turning out to be an interesting meeting." Adasser shook his head in disbelief.

"Charlie, you will also need a teacher. We will have to figure out how to train you as well. Elves are not well versed in wizarding magic, so we will not be of much use to you." He looked at Arianna. "It would be wise to research the wizard's return as well. This dark figure is dangerous and every bit of help that we can find would be a good thing."

Arianna nodded in agreement.

"We should get going. The journey is not a long one, but it could be a dangerous one if that figure is lurking about."

They all turned to leave the castle. Arianna stopped for a moment to look around while the others went ahead. She closed her eyes and whispered aloud, "Good-bye, Ellavorn. I will always love you." She opened her eyes, turned on her heel and ran to catch up with her friends to begin the journey back to Eumetadotos.

Chapter 27

On the journey back, Arianna decided to get to know Adasser a little better. They would be working closely together while he was training her, and she wanted to know more about him. Joshua rode at the front of the line, obviously displeased with the turn of events. He would not as much as look in her direction unless it was absolutely necessary. Arianna and Adasser stayed at the back of the line.

"So, do you know much about the prophecy?"

"I know only as much as you do. Elves tend to keep their prophecies within our own race, and even then, it is mostly royalty that are aware of what is said. You are the first humans that I know of that have ever heard one. King Armen must have thought it was absolutely dire for you to hear it. Of course, you are no ordinary human."

"Right. I'm supposedly your granddaughter."

"Arianna, I have no doubt that you are my granddaughter. That mark on your wrist confirms it. It is my family's mark. Each family has a different mark that is passed down. The bow and arrow is a symbol of my family's warrior magic, as has been mentioned before. We are the best protectors in the realm."

"And ever so modest too," Arianna stated sarcastically.

"There is no need for modesty when it is the truth."

Arianna rolled her eyes at Adasser's vanity.

"You will see," he smiled.

"I'm sure that I will." She grimaced. "Can I ask you some things?"

Adasser sighed and gave a gesture of approval.

"Did you know the wizard and the story of his departure?"

Adasser stopped his horse.

"That was not what I was expecting."

"I really don't wish to hear any more of my grandmother's affair right now. No offense. It's kind of a lot to take in."

"I understand. Yes, I know of the wizard's plight. What would you like to know?"

"Everything."

Adasser laughed and nudged his horse forward. He told the tale as they rode. "Of course you do. You are so much like your grandmother it is unbelievable.

"The wizard left this realm over a century ago, as I am sure that you know. The country was in a state of peace, and the king did not feel that it was necessary to train any more apprentices. He wanted the wizard to enjoy the peace time. However, the wizard tried to warn the king that this was not a good idea. That he should be better prepared for something in the future. Peace can't last forever.

"The king, however, was foolish and refused to listen. The wizard pressed him to take measures, and eventually, the king grew tired of his insistence. He started to resent the wizard for not listening to him and laying down his magic. So, he started to think of a plan to get rid of the wizard.

"The wizard caught wind of his plot, and started to seal everything in the Odigós Domάtio away. He would spend hours in the chamber trying to secure it as best as he could. He was also doing research, unbeknownst to everyone, on how to travel to different realms. No one thought that this was possible. One day, the king had fully formed his plan to get rid of the wizard. He ordered his arrest. The wizard went along with it until he was brought before the crowd for sentencing. Once the king handed down the sentence, the wizard called out a final warning that there may be peace now, but if the kingdom did not heed his warning, the trouble coming would be devastating. He pointed his hands at the ground and hollered out an incantation that no one could understand. A portal opened beneath his feet, swallowed him whole and then vanished. No one has seen or heard from any wizards from that day forward."

He looked back at Charlie. "That is, until now. If the wizarding bloodline is appearing again, something dangerous is going to happen."

"Was there any clue as to where he went?"

"No one knows. The Odigós Domátio disappeared. The entrance sealed itself up and nothing was ever found to gain entry into that room again. Well, until now, if that is what you have, in fact, found."

"How do we know that it is what we think it is?"

"I will know," Adasser declared, with a slight air of arrogance.

Arianna rolled her eyes and changed the subject.

"So, you think that Charlie has wizarding blood?"

"It appears as though he may."

"How is that possible? If the wizard left this realm a century ago, wouldn't he have taken his family with him?"

Adasser gave her a look as if to ask, "Do you really need to ask that question?"

Arianna grimaced. "Right. But, Do you really think that it is possible that he just so happened to come to work in the castle?"

Adasser thought for a moment. "Not all wizards are directly related. Some people are just born with a special ability in their blood. Perhaps young Charlie has that ability."

"How would we find out?"

"Well, the only one who could recognize that would be a master wizard."

"And he's long gone?"

"And he's long gone."

"How do we go about bringing him back?"

Adasser looked at Arianna with utter confusion etched across his face. "Why would you want to do that?"

"Why would I not? If he can help –"

"But, would he? Arianna, this is not something to play around with foolishly. You are talking about a major feud between your direct line and his. I don't think that he would come back here too eagerly."

"Isn't it worth a try? Wouldn't he be helpful if he would come back? Even if only to train Charlie."

"He would be very instrumental in a fight, but only if he would come, which I doubt will happen. I do not want you to get your hopes up, Arianna. It would be best to leave this idea alone. I mean that."

"Can't we just –"

"No! I am serious about this. Let that idea go. We don't know where he went. We don't know where his bloodline resides now. We don't know what kind of hostility that they hold for your family. It would be safer to just leave it alone."

"Safer for who?"

"Safer for everyone."

"How do you know?"

"I just know," Adasser was growing irritated and frustrated by her increasingly difficult questions. "I knew the wizard. He was not a very – forgiving – man. I can only imagine that his bloodlines follow in that tradition. If he left this realm for another because he feared for his life, neither he nor his descendants would take too kindly from the reigning queen of Eumetadotos showing up and requesting that they return to the land from which they were exiled. Do you understand?"

Arianna grumbled, "Yes."

Adasser stopped their horses together and planted his horse in front of Lightning to impede their path forward. "Arianna, I have seen you rise to challenges and succeed. I have seen people tell you that something cannot be done, and you have done it. But, please, believe me when I tell you that this is a different story. This is a blood feud. It is not something that anyone takes lightly. Leave it alone."

Arianna puffed out her chest and sighed. "Fine."

Adasser moved his horse from her path, and stayed where he was for a moment. From the look on Arianna's face, he knew that she had just taken up a challenge that he had not meant to throw down. Knowing what he knew about her, she would not let anyone stand in her way to get what she wanted. He felt a knot form in his stomach and he wondered if he had done the right thing by telling her what he knew about the wizard. He figured that time would only tell and he hoped that she would heed his warning, but, in his heart, he knew that that hope was a foolish one. It seemed as though he had given her the next task, and she was going to complete it, no matter what.

He looked around the path around him and whispered, "Please let her make the right decision. The fate of this realm depends on it."

Chapter 28

The rest of the journey was made in silence. Finally, Joshua led the party into the castle gates and they all dismounted and made their way into the castle to get ready for dinner. Arianna sought out Adasser and introduced him to one of the guards, instructing the guard to guide Adasser to what would be his chambers. She then hurried to find Joshua. She found him on the stairs, making his way to his chambers.

"I know that you don't approve of my training, Joshua."

He froze. "No, I do not. Arianna, I have been trained from the first day to protect the royals. You are asking me to go against everything I have been trained for years to do. I won't apologize for not wanting you to do this. It feels wrong to me."

Arianna walked up to him. "Joshua, I will not apologize for agreeing to training. I have been taught from the day of my birth that the queen's sole purpose is to make sure that her people are safe. If I do not train and learn to use my powers, I will be failing in that duty. I respect that you have your duty to me. I respect your feelings, but I cannot fail in my duty to my people. They need me. My kingdom is more important to me than anything. I cannot apologize to you or anyone else for doing what I feel is best for them, nor should anyone expect me to. If I can find a way to defeat this dark figure, it is my responsibility to do so. Whether you like my decision or not, it is my decision. I do, however, ask that you respect that decision. If you stand in my way, I will have no choice but to have you banished from the training area."

"You cannot banish me. I am the Captain of the Royal Guard. I am also your fiancé."

"And I am the queen. We are not married yet. I will do what I have to do. You may attend those sessions if you do not do anything to prohibit my progress."

Joshua looked Arianna in the eye. "I will not allow you to injure yourself. It is vital that Eumetadotos has its queen in full health. You cannot expect me to just allow you to intentionally put yourself in a situation where you would be harmed. Arianna, this kingdom needs you. Why can't you understand this?"

"I do understand this. This is why I have to train! Our normal weapons will not work on this thing, Joshua! I need to learn to use these powers. If I don't, there will be no kingdom to need me. Why can't you understand that?"

The severity of Arianna's words seemed to hit Joshua then. He looked as though someone had punched him in the stomach, and he sank down to sit on the steps with his face buried in his hands. He looked defeated.

"You do not have to have me barred from the training area."

"Thank you. I know that it may be hard for you to watch –"

"No, I will not be in attendance. I cannot bear witness to you going through that training without wanting to rush in to help you."

The air seemed to rush from Arianna's lungs. "You mean that you will not be there?"

"No. I won't. I can't. I cannot watch you being attacked and not do something to stop it. If you must insist on doing this, then it will be without me. I won't watch."

Arianna's heart dropped. "You still don't approve."

"No, Arianna, I don't."

"Even knowing that I could be instrumental in helping to defeat this figure?"

"Not even then. It is not your job to fight the evil."

"It is my job, Joshua. You heard the prophecy."

"Prophecies don't always come true."

"This one seems to have come true. I have the violet eyes."

"So could someone else."

"Joshua, how many people have you ever met that have had violet eyes?"

"It could happen, Arianna."

Arianna sighed. "I have Elven powers."

"You could just not use them."

"No! This is a part of who I am. I know that it's a new part, but it is still a part of me. You can't tell me not to just stop being who I am."

"I just don't understand why it has to be you."

"I don't know either, but it does. You don't have to like it, but you have to accept that this is what I was born to do. I have to train. I have to save my people. I have to protect them." She stopped, took his face in her hands and looked deeply into his eyes. "I have to protect you this time."

Joshua snorted and turned his head.

"That's the issue, isn't it? You've never had to be protected. Your pride is getting in the way of your judgement."

"I don't need anyone to protect me, Arianna. I have always protected myself, and this family. I am not weak."

"And my family is?"

"I didn't mean that. I just meant that I have always had the ability to protect other people as well as myself."

"Well, you have never had to protect anyone from a magical being before. This is different. I cannot stand back and watch my kingdom fall and not do anything, and that is exactly what will happen if I do not train. The decision is not yours to make, Joshua. It is mine and mine alone. I will be training with or without your approval. I wish that you felt differently and I wish that you would help me with it, but I cannot force you to do this. I will command you to loan me some of your guards."

Joshua snorted again. "Do you really think that I would allow my guards to participate in such an activity?"

"I will give a royal command."

"I will not obey."

An incredulous look spread across Arianna's face. "Then I would have no choice but to have you thrown into the dungeon."

Joshua looked stunned by her words. "I am your fiancé. I am the Captain of the Royal Guard. I –"

"You are interfering with something vital to the safety and protection of Eumetadotos. You are being a hindrance to my training."

Joshua looked infuriated by what she said. His voice started to rise. "I cannot believe that you would do that to me."

Arianna's voice started to rise to match his. "I cannot believe that you are acting like a spoiled child!"

"I'm acting like a spoiled child?"

"Yes! You are!"

They began screaming at each other back and forth until Abigail came running.

"What is going on here? Why are the two of you screaming at each other?"

Joshua jumped in first. "She will not listen to reason. She wants to go and battle these dark forces without any protection. She wants to train and put herself in danger. Now, she wants me to allow my guards to help with this task."

"I have to train, Joshua. I need to develop these powers. You will not be able to protect me with physical weapons alone! I need to know what I am doing. I have a kingdom to think about. This is what must be done. I cannot force you to be a part of it, but I need you to help me in some way. I can force you to provide me the manpower that I need in order to make this work."

Abigail looked from Arianna to Joshua and back again. "Captain Oakford, Ari's right. She has to do this. You heard the prophecy. This is her destiny. You cannot stop her from doing this any more than you can stop the rain from falling. What you are doing is dangerous. Ari's right. You don't have to like it, but she needs your support. I know that you want to protect her. We all do. But, the best protection that you can give her is the freedom to train the way that she needs to. She has not done anything to flaunt her abilities in front of you. She has been respectful of your feelings. But, you have not returned that respect to her. You say that you love her. Is that true?"

"Of course I love her! But –"

"Then, you have to trust in her. She's stronger than you think she is. She can do this. I have faith in her, as does the kingdom. You should too. If you really love her, you must give her the freedom to grow. You may not like what she has to do, but you have to respect what she has to do. She has already said that she will not force you to participate or even watch, but you must stand behind her."

Abigail turned on her heel and started to walk away. She looked over her shoulder and yelled to Joshua, "I swear, if we all die because of you, I will find you and kill you again!"

Arianna beamed after her friend. She turned slowly to Joshua in order to let her smile fade a little and not to gloat. "Don't you see, Joshua, this is what I have to do. Even Abigail sides with me on this one. You don't have to like it, but you have to support me in this."

"Fine. I will allow two of my men to help. Arianna, if you get hurt, I will never forgive you."

"That is why I need to train, so that I don't get hurt. I have to be able to defend myself. I need to do this. I need to protect my people. They need me."

"Whatever. I will not be coming to dinner. I will see you in the morning." Joshua huffed away to his chambers and slammed his door behind him.

Chapter 29

Dinner that night was an uncomfortable affair. Arianna had Adasser escort her to the dining room, which causes ripples of whispers throughout the staff. When she addressed the room, she introduced him and invited him to sit in Joshua's seat for the night. She did not mention her familial ties to him, nor mention that her powers were Elven. She was tired and did not care to deal with the questions at the moment. So, she sat and ate her dinner in silence.

"Are we not being joined by Captain Oakford, Arianna?"

Arianna snapped to attention. "Oh, no, he decided not to come to dinner tonight."

"Why?" Adasser knew the answer. He had heard them arguing in the stairwell, but he did not want Arianna to think that he had been spying on her.

"He does not approve of my training. He feels that he could protect me, and that I am putting myself in harm's way by doing this."

"Well, he is correct that in training you could get hurt, you know."

"How will I learn if I don't train?"

Adasser smiled broadly. "That was the answer I hoped that you would give."

Arianna gave a weak smile. "I sure didn't make him too happy with agreeing to train."

"Child, you cannot please everyone. There comes a time in life where you must let go of caring what people think of you and you must decide to do the right thing. You cannot allow people to manipulate you into doing what they want you to do. You are doing the right thing. You cannot allow him to stand in the way of that. Your powers are a gift. They are something that should be encouraged, not hidden. You must train in order to defend yourself and your kingdom. A few melted spears are not going to save your kingdom. There are other techniques that you must learn. You must also learn to attack. It is not an easy thing to think about, taking the life of another. But, in the end, it will be necessary for you to do so. This dark figure will not stop until you do. It is unpleasant, but it is necessary. I will help you as much as I can, but when we are on a battlefield, you will need to be able to fight on your own. I cannot be there for you all of the time. No one can. I can only help you to realize your full potential and to meet it. It is my honor to help you, Arianna. You have been very brave so far."

"I don't feel very brave."

"By standing up to the man whom you will marry, that is brave. Too often, we cave into our loved ones. We know that they love us and that they have the best intentions for us, but sometimes, they let their love blind their judgement. They know deep in their hearts that the dangerous path is the right one to choose, but the consequences could be painful for them. Captain Oakford is speaking from a place of fear and of love, but mostly fear. He fears losing you. It is a valid fear. That could very well happen. You do understand that, don't you?"

"Yes, I do understand that, but I have to take that risk to ensure the safety of my people. I need to know that I have done everything that I can to make sure that they are protected in every way possible. I don't understand how he can't see that."

"He does. He just doesn't like that it has to be you that does the protecting. That is all. It has been ingrained in him, just as it has been in me, to protect our royal family. When one of them is required to do something dangerous, it is very hard to change your perception of your duty."

Arianna nodded slightly, still not consoled.

"Maybe my engagement to Joshua is a mistake. Maybe I should call it off. It would make things easier on him."

Adasser's eyes grew wide with shock and fear.

"No, Arianna. I have seen the way he looks at you. He is in love with you. He probably has been for years and never spoke up because he knew of your affections for Prince Ellavorn."

Her breath caught at his name.

"I still miss him so much."

"I know that you do. I can imagine that he misses you as well, since he will not return. You wounded his pride, Arianna. Elves do not handle that very well. He is worse than most. He is fairly young still, by Elven standards. There is a lot still for him to learn. One day, he will learn his lessons and come back to us. Of that, I can be sure."

"But, not in my lifetime," Arianna added miserably.

Adasser gave her a look of sympathy. "That, I do not know. Although, you have Elven blood. We do not know what your lifetime will be. It could be a very, very long time."

Arianna looked confused. "Do you mean I might be immortal?"

Adasser shrugged his shoulders. "I don't know. But, if you are, you are welcome."

Arianna scoffed at his returned arrogance. She could not figure this Elf out. One minute, he was kind and caring, the next he was arrogant and aloof. She didn't understand the constant change. He confused her, yet, she found him oddly comforting.

"Why do you do that?"

"Do what?"

"Change in an instant. One minute, we could be having a substantial conversation, and you will be contributing something useful, and the next moment, you put up your guard again and only allow your arrogance to show. I don't understand it."

"I contribute what I feel is useful. I have no need for pondering of things I don't have the answers to. Time is a precious commodity, and not one that should be squandered with pointless idle chit chat. No amount of talking will change who you are, or what you are. We can only wait and see what happens."

Arianna gave a frustrated cry. "You are so frustrating!"

Adasser's jaw dropped. "I have only been told that by one other person."

Arianna simply glared at him.

"Your grandmother used to tell me that all the time. It was, by far, one of my most favorite saying of hers. You even say it the same way that she did."

"Please, I do not wish to speak of my grandmother's affair right now."

Adasser nodded his ascent. "Understood."

"When do we start training?"

"I was hoping in the morning."

"Good. The sooner we start, the better. We shall begin after breakfast."

With that, she pushed away from the table and hurried out of the dining room up to her chambers, got ready for bed and fell into a deep sleep.

Chapter 30

The following morning, Joshua escorted Arianna to breakfast and they ate in silence. Arianna was nervous to begin her training, and Joshua was still angry from the day before. Everything Arianna ate tasted bland and she soon gave up trying to eat anything. After the only people left in the dining hall were Arianna, Joshua, Adasser, Abigail, Charlie and the two guards that Joshua had assigned to training duty, Adasser approached Arianna.

"Are you ready to begin?"

Arianna took a deep breath and tried to steady her shaking hands. "I am."

"Then please show me the room that you believe to be the Odigós Domátio."

Arianna stepped forward, and was stopped by Joshua clearing his throat.

"Aren't you even going to say good bye to me?"

"I didn't realize that you wanted me to speak to you."

Joshua looked around. "May we have a moment, please?"

The others left the room and stood outside the closed doors.

"Arianna, I still do not approve of what you are doing. I cannot watch you put yourself through this. But, if you insist on doing this, Abigail is right, I will have to respect that decision and trust you. I will still argue with you about it if you bring it up. I still do not support it, but if you feel that this is what you must do, then I will not stand in your way. Just, please, do not get hurt."

"Thank you, Joshua. I will try not to get hurt. I can't guarantee that, though. I have to be put into a situation where I can learn. I respect that you do not wish to be a part of this and I will not ask you to be. But, please, trust me."

They embraced for a moment before Arianna told him, "Now, I have to go." She leaned up and kissed him before turning and running out.

The group moved into the pantry, where Arianna took out the key. Adasser gasped.

"I haven't seen that key in over a century. It is still as beautiful as I remember."

Arianna pushed the key into place and the spiral staircase once again began to set itself into place. She made sure to look at Adasser's bewildered face as he watched what was happening. When the staircase had set itself, they all began to descend the stairs. Once again, the torches on the wall lit as they walked past.

"I don't think I will ever get used to that, Ari," said Abigail as they made their way down.

"I don't think I will either." They laughed together.

When they reached the bottom of the stairs, Arianna made a motion for Charlie to light the candles for more light.

Charlie grinned from ear to ear, threw out his hand, and yelled, "Diafotízos!" A small fireball erupted and made its way around the room, lighting all of the candles before extinguishing itself.

Adasser looked around the room in bewilderment. "I can't believe I am standing in the Odigós Domátio once again. The wizard made every effort to preserve everything about it."

He moved around the shelves with the books. “It is a bit dustier in here, but it is exactly the same.”

He walked over to the different liquids and was stopped by the force field. “The wise old man put up a pedío dynámeon spell to protect the potion ingredients. There are probably some dangerous liquids in there. Without the proper training, it is best to stay away from them.”

Arianna noticed Charlie’ face fall at that declaration.

“It’s ok, Charlie. You can still work on the spells that you’ve been learning.”

Adasser turned and knelt in front of the boy. “It is vital that you work on those spells, young Charlie. You can help with the queen’s training.”

Charlie’ eyes lit up with the possibility of having such an important task.

“Of course! Anything to help the queen!”

Adasser grimaced. “You may not like what I will ask you to do.”

Both Charlie and Arianna gulped at the same time.

“Charlie, I need you to learn attack spells. Arianna is going to be facing some powerful dark magic. She needs to be able to counter attack those spells. Can you do that for me?”

The color drained from Charlie’ face. “I don’t know. I couldn’t do anything to hurt her. She’s my friend.”

Adasser gave him a reassuring smile. “It’s ok. She will still be your friend. But, she needs to train. Do you understand?”

Charlie grumbled, “Yes, sir.”

“Good, let’s find a book of attack spells for you to study.”

Charlie shuffled over to the bookcases. Abigail followed behind him. “I will help you, Charlie.”

He seemed to brighten a little at her suggestion and they made their way around the book shelves trying to find a book of attack spells.

Adasser turned to Arianna.

“Now, it is your turn to start training.”

She drew in a shaky breath.

“Ok, where do we start.”

“First of all, you need to concentrate. Do not allow your thoughts to stray to anything except the task at hand. Understood?”

“Yes.”

“Good.” He motioned for one of the guards to step forward.

“I am going to give the signal for him to throw a spear at you. You must concentrate on dissolving that spear before it leaves his hand.”

“How am I supposed to do that?”

“Concentrate. Reach down inside yourself, Arianna. Feel the magic in there and bring it to the surface. Allow it to flow through you.”

Adasser stood behind her.

"How will I know when he is ready to throw?"

"You won't." He gave the signal.

"But, then, how will I – OW!"

The spear grazed her arm.

Adasser ran over to her. "You weren't concentrating. This is why I told you to concentrate. Your enemy will look for any distraction at all. It will even cause a distraction in order to call your attention away. You must concentrate. You're lucky that wasn't any worse. It's just a flesh wound. No need for any medical treatment."

Arianna shot Adasser a filthy look. "Maybe we should have a medical professional down here while we are training."

"If you wish. It wouldn't hurt. Now, let's get back to the task at hand, please?" He gave the signal again, but Arianna saw it, and was able to dive out of the way.

"You were supposed to use your magic."

"I didn't have time."

"You won't have time to think in battle either. Your magic is your best chance."

"This is so frustrating."

"Focus!"

"Fine!"

Arianna stood, facing the guard again, who by this time, was looking rather nervous. He had thrown his spear at his queen twice, once striking her. He knew that Joshua was not going to be happy with him.

Adasser gave the order again. The guard threw the spear, and Arianna's hands went up, dissolving the spear in mid-air.

"Better. But, you have to dissolve it before it is released."

Adasser tossed a new spear to the guard, who took his place again.

Arianna stood in place, closed her eyes, took a deep breath, and started to feel something stirring inside of her. She concentrated on the guard, and he raised his hand again. She threw her hands up and the spear left his hand, but only made it about a foot before disintegrating into thin air."

"Better. Try again."

This went on and on for two hours before Arianna turned to Adasser, begging for a break.

"We have been at this for hours. I need some water and food. I didn't realize how exhausting using magic could be."

"In battle, you will not be able to take a break, Arianna."

"I know that, but we're not doing battle right now, Adasser. We are training. It is my first session. I need to take a break."

Adasser nodded his consent. "Take a break. I should find young Charlie and check on his progress in locating an appropriate spell book."

Arianna sat down and the guard who had been spectating brought her some water.

Adasser searched the bookshelves, looking for Charlie and Abigail. He finally found them, poring over book after book.

"I still don't know how you can read this, kid. It's all foreign to me."

"It doesn't look foreign to me. It's easy to read."

"I guess that's why you're the magical one and I'm not, huh?"

"I guess so. Abigail, do you think I will be good at this?"

"Honey, you already are. You're getting better and better every day. Now, you'll have something new to learn, and you can help Arianna train. Isn't that exciting?"

"Yes," Charlie said flatly. "I guess so."

"You don't seem too happy about that, kid."

"What if I throw a spell at her and it hurts her? I don't want to hurt her."

Abigail knelt in front of him and took his hands in her own. "Charlie, I know that you are nervous about this, but Ari needs you. She needs you to learn how to attack. In a battle, you will be able to help by throwing those same attack spells at the enemy. I don't think that Adasser will let her get too hurt. But, if neither of you trains properly, when it comes time to do battle, you will both get hurt, and badly."

Charlie swallowed. "I guess you're right, Abigail."

"Of course she is right, young Charlie," Adasser made his presence known.

He knelt in front of the boy. "I give you my solemn promise that I will not allow any of the spells that you throw at her to harm her too badly. We will start off with easy spells for you both." Charlie grinned. "I will also have her throwing spells at you as well. You need to learn to protect yourself too." The grin turned to a worried look, and Adasser couldn't help but laugh.

"Don't worry, I won't let her harm you either. But, you both do need to train in both aspects." Charlie nodded. Adasser pulled a book off of the shelf next to him. He held it away from Abigail and Charlie and blew the dust off of the black cover. The golden letters glittered in the light, "The Volume of Umbral Magus."

Adasser flipped open the pages and smiled. "This, young Charlie, is what we were looking for. I want you to start learning these spells. They will be quite useful."

Charlie took the book from him, and looked over the spells. "These are all spells to do in battle?"

"They are some. It's a good start."

Charlie nodded and went to sit at the table to start studying. Abigail followed him.

Adasser went to get Arianna up again and the training session resumed.

Chapter 31

The next few weeks passed quickly with both Charlie and Arianna making great strides in their progress. Adasser, while still aloof, turned out to be a highly qualified instructor for both of them. He seemed to regard Arianna with a mixture of curiosity and indifference. Arianna was starting to tire of having him begin to open up only to clam up again. One day, she had had enough and decided to sit down next to him and confront him about it during a break in training.

"Adasser, are you happy here, training me?"

"It has its perks, Arianna."

"That isn't an answer. Why do you do that? It is so frustrating. I want to know you. You're supposed to be my blood relative. My only living blood relative, and you act as though you couldn't care less."

Adasser snapped to attention. "I care."

"This is what I mean! I'm trying to talk to you and you give me short answers. You act as though I am a burden and you don't wish to know me."

Adasser turned to look her in the eyes. "Arianna, you should try to understand my situation as well. I only found out a few weeks ago that I had a daughter. A daughter who was murdered. I never got to know her. You have had months to grieve. I have had days. Yes, I have a granddaughter now, but I would have liked to have known my daughter too. Even if she did not know that I was her father. So, you see, it is not that I don't care. I care very deeply. My heart is broken. I lost your grandmother to my foolish pride, and, it turns out that I also lost my child as well. It is not easy for me to face that fact. I enjoy our time together. I honestly do. However, it makes me yearn for the opportunity to know my child as well."

Arianna's chin trembled. "I miss her every day. She was my best friend. I would give anything to have her back, if even for just a moment. She was wonderful. You would have loved her."

Adasser smiled a sad smile. "I am sure that I would have. I am getting to know you, and that should give me a glimpse of her. She raised you. A person's upbringing shines through in the person that they become as an adult. You are a good person, Arianna. That teaches me that your parents were good people. But, it still does not alleviate the pain that I feel knowing that I could have known her firsthand. Do you understand?"

"Yes," she whispered.

"Are you happy here?"

Arianna's head whipped round to look at him, confused. "Of course I am happy here. This is my home. It's my kingdom. I love it here."

"What about Captain Oakford? Are you happy with him?"

Arianna looked down at the floor and started picking at a thumbnail. She stayed silent.

"Arianna?"

"I don't know."

"Why is that?"

"Well, he claims that he loves me, but he is against my training."

"Still?"

"Yes. We argue every time I come here."

"And yet you still come?"

Arianna looked up at Adasser, eyes wide. "Of course. My kingdom needs me to be here."

Adasser smiled and nodded.

Arianna continued. "I don't know. I guess I just think that if he really loved me, that he would allow me to grow. But, then I think that he loves me and doesn't want to see me get hurt. I know that it is ingrained in him to protect me at all costs, but he can't be around forever and he can't protect me from what I suppose is my destiny."

"No, he can't protect you forever. He has to allow you to grow and discover your talents."

"But he doesn't see it that way. He thinks that I am being stubborn and pig-headed."

"Aren't you?"

Adasser burst into laughter at the shocked face Arianna made.

"Those things aren't bad qualities, Arianna, so long as they are used in the correct manner, such as this. I have learned over the last few weeks that you rise to a challenge. You are made of stronger material than you think you are. I have watched you over the last few weeks embrace your powers and grow them. You have overcome a lot in the last few months. Your training has shown me that you can take care of yourself. Captain Oakford is trained to protect you. He is doing his job. I understand that, but, he also needs to understand your desire to do what you are doing. When are you to be married?"

"We haven't discussed a date yet. I guess we should start doing that. I have to be married before the one year anniversary of when I became queen. Otherwise, a curse will befall my kingdom."

"A curse? What kind of curse?"

"I don't know. I was reading the law books of Eumetadotos, and it only says a curse."

Adasser nodded his head. "I will try to look into that for you."

"Thank you!"

"I cannot promise that I will be able to help. Many of your laws were written before my kind came to live here. I may be hard-pressed to find someone who lived then, or someone who knows anything about your laws."

"I would appreciate any answers that you can find."

"Of course. Now, I think that we should get back to training."

Arianna jumped up, and immediately stumbled back to the ground.

"Arianna!" Adasser fell to his knees in front of her, checking her all over.

Arianna pushed his hands away. "I'm ok. I just feel light headed. I need to rest for a moment." She moved to get up more slowly, and fell again.

"Arianna, you are not ok. Guards! I need help!"

The guards rushed over with Charlie and Abigail right on their heels.

"She's light headed and fallen twice. We need to get her up to her chambers immediately."

"I'm fine! I –" Arianna fainted.

Adasser caught her, and one of the guards lifted her up, carrying her out of the Odigós Domátio. All of them raced up the stairs, where Joshua sat, waiting for training to be over. He jumped up when he saw Arianna lying in the guard's arms.

"What happened?" He raced over and started yelling at Adasser

"What did you do to her?"

"I did nothing! We were getting up from our break, and she felt lightheaded and fell. I summoned the guards over, and she fainted. We need to get her to her chambers and in her bed immediately."

With that, a wind blew in, and they heard the cackling of the Dark Figure.

"No!" Joshua cried and pulled his sword.

"Oh, yes, Lover Boy with the Big Sword! I warned you that I would take what I want. Your queen will die!"

"What did you do to her?" Adasser asked as he jumped in front of Joshua to prevent him from racing towards the Dark Figure and probably sending himself to his own grave.

"I cursed her and anyone who would stand in my way of ruling this kingdom."

Adasser raised his chin, and growled out dangerously, "Which curse did you use, beast?"

The Dark Figure cackled its shrill laugh again. "A beast, am I? I am no beast! She is the beast! She and her family."

Joshua cried, "What did she ever do to you?"

"Do you not know, you sword-wielding monkey?"

Adasser held his arm up to stop Joshua from charging at it again, which led to Joshua becoming enraged.

Adasser whispered over his shoulder, "Be still." Joshua became even more livid as Adasser confronted the Dark Figure again.

"What curse did you use?"

The cackling came again. "The last breath, you will take, but hell, your life will be made. You will fall, in pain and agony. No relief may you find. Death, to you, will not be kind."

The color blanched from Adasser's face. "The Argós Thάnatos. Why?"

"The bitch must pay."

Joshua looked bewildered. "What is going on?"

Adasser put his hands up and shot a light of pure white, much like Arianna's at the figure, who evaporated before them, cackling once more.

Adasser turned to Joshua. "Get her to her chambers immediately. I will go back down and see if I can find something to reverse this curse. There must be something that we can do."

Joshua looked confused, but took Arianna from the guard's arms and fled to her chambers with her. Adasser went back down to the Odigós Domátio frantically. Charlie and Abigail followed him. He started searching the room in a frenzy.

"Adasser, what happened to Queen Arianna?" Charlie asked, frightened.

Adasser stopped and bowed his head before looking up and directly at two of Arianna's best friends.

"Argós Thánatos. It is the curse of the slow death. The Dark Figure cursed her to die a slow, painful death. I must find a way to reverse it."

He began scrambling through papers, trying to find a spell that would help to counteract the curse, but came up with nothing. He hung his head in shame, ready to begin weeping when Abigail's voice rang out loud and clear, jolting him from his emotions.

"Finally! There is a book that I can read! Is it really so hard to put things in a language for people to understand them? Sheesh!"

Adasser and Charlie looked at each other in disbelief, then turned to see a jubilant Abigail racing up the aisle, book raised in her hand. She gave the book, named *Dreambinder Epitome Of Lost Hope*, to Adasser and stuck her tongue out at Charlie, who returned the favor.

Adasser looked at her in bewilderment. "This book should not make sense to you. It is a potion book. The recipes are top secret. Only the highest level wizard or an Elf could understand this. How is it possible that you can read it? Charlie, can you read this?"

Charlie looked at the book and screwed up his face. "No, it's a bunch of scribbles on the page."

Abigail beamed proudly. "Guess you're not the only one with magical abilities, huh, kid?"

Charlie stuck his tongue out at her again.

Adasser shook his head. "Now is not the time to argue. Time is of the essence. We need to get into those shelves to find the ingredients for this potion."

Abigail and Adasser flipped through the book and found a potion marked "Apokatástasi." Hope glimmered slightly in Adasser's eyes.

"This is a relief potion! It may not lift the curse, but it may counter act some of her pain and buy her more time."

He laid it on the altar to read the ingredients. Adasser looked up from the book at the liquid ingredients encased within the pedío dynámeon spell, pondering how to drop the spell to get the ingredients that he needed. He was trying to determine whether it would be quicker to ride back to the Forest Glen and retrieve the ingredients from Armen or to search the books, trying to find a counter spell when Charlie spoke.

"Adasser, sir, maybe the spell to get through the barrier is in one of my books. I didn't look in them yet."

They flipped through *The Volume of Umbral Magus* and *The Thaumaturgy of Magus*, to no avail. Charlie looked defeated, but Adasser put his hand on his shoulder.

"Don't fret, son. It was a good suggestion. I will send word to the Forest Glen immediately to request the ingredients that we need."

"But, won't that take time? You just said that we don't have much time."

Adasser smiled and pulled a pouch from his pocket. He sprinkled some powder on the altar, and blew on it. It formed a figure of Armen and Adasser began speaking.

"Armen, we urgently need your help. The Dark Figure has cursed Queen Arianna with the Argós Thάnatos. We need the ingredients for a relief potion named Apokatástasi. I know that it will not counter act the curse, but it just might help her. It is urgent."

The figure nodded and said, "I will send them immediately. Stay where you are." The figure disappeared. The trio stood, staring at the spot for a moment. Soon, the altar began to glow, and smoke began to swirl. A flash of light burst into the room, and what had been an empty altar, now displayed all of the necessary ingredients for the potion.

"Woah!" Abigail and Charlie exclaimed in unison.

Adasser told Abigail to start measuring out ingredients, and they instructed Charlie on what to gather from around the room.

"It is very strange," Adasser said, looking up from mashing herbs with the mortar and pestle that had materialized with the ingredients.

"What is?" asked Abigail.

"Usually, someone with wizarding blood can read both potions and magic. It is strange that Charlie can only read spells and you, only potions. I wonder how that can be."

"I have no idea. I'm just glad that I can be of some use in this mission." She glanced at the shelves of potions and continued. "I wish I could have found something that could drop that barrier."

"Do not concern yourself with that. It is a barrier that only the wizard or his next living kin can infiltrate. I fear that we may have to heed Arianna's wishes to find the wizard's relatives and bring them back."

"Why would that be a bad thing, Adasser?"

"As I explained to Arianna, the wizard fled this realm in fear of his life. He left because the king wanted to put him to death and he saw no other choice, but to escape and find a new realm completely to call his home. I would not think that his next in line would take too kindly to being asked to come back to help the very same line that all but banished his family from their home. It will probably be a fool's errand."

"I hate to say this, but what about kidnapping?" Abigail gave him a mischievous grin and Adasser stopped with a look of horror on his face, as though she had been reading his thoughts.

"I hate to entertain your ideas, but it may be the only way to convince them to help."

Abigail looked around again. "Adasser, what would happen if the Dark Figure appeared down here? It could get its hands on these books, and maybe even those potions. Wouldn't that be catastrophic?"

"It can't get in here. The Odigós Domátio is spelled so that no one with an evil heart can enter, no matter how they try to enter. They would be expelled immediately. It is quite ancient magic. The first wizard asked the Elves to cast that spell, and it has stayed to this very day. I feel it when I pass through."

"I don't feel anything when we come down. Why is that?"

"You don't know what to feel for. Most humans do not. If you had been trained under a wizard, you would probably have an inkling."

"Does it hurt?"

"No. It is more like feeling the wind inside of you. No need to worry, child. Nothing evil will get into this room. Now, we are ready to mix the potion."

They gathered the ingredients, and Abigail read them off to Adasser as he put them in one by one, following the instructions exactly. After he added the last ingredient and stirred, there was a small poof, and the red potion began to illuminate and sparkle."

Abigail looked at it, wide-eyed. "Wow! It's beautiful."

"Yes, it is. It is also important that we get this to Arianna immediately." He poured it into a flask, and said, "Let's go!"

Abigail, Charlie and Adasser raced up the stairs and through the corridors until they reached the hall where Arianna's chambers were located. They turned and heard horrible shrieking coming from her chambers. The screaming spurred them on, and the three of them burst into the room.

The scene that they encountered was eerily reminiscent of the one nine years prior when Ellavorn and Arianna met for the first time. Arianna lay on her bed, thrashing with a fever, pale as the dead, screaming and riving in pain. Charlie began to cry and Abigail pulled him back into the hallway away from the commotion.

Adasser rushed to her side, across from where Joshua sat, holding her hand, looking helpless with a single tear making its way down his cheek. Adasser made a noise and Joshua looked up at him, a glimmer of hope in his eyes.

"Captain Oakford, you must hold her still so that I can administer this potion to her."

"What is it?"

"The Elixir of Apokatástasi. It is a restoration potion."

"Will it work?"

"I don't know. If it does, I do not know how long the effects will last."

"And if it doesn't work? What then?"

"She will be in the same state that you see her in now."

Joshua climbed onto the bed, straddling Arianna's body and as gently as he could, held her shoulders down on the bed. Arianna opened her eyes and screamed loudly.

"Ari, you have to lie still. We have something that might work."

Arianna screamed again.

"Please, Ari, please, listen. You have to drink this."

Adasser moved over and put the flask to her lips. She started shaking her head violently.

Adasser yelled, hoping that his raised voice would get through to her. "Arianna! Stop! You must take this. Your life and the fate of your kingdom depends on it."

Arianna's body calmed a little. She was still pale and sweating profusely, but the violent thrashing had stopped. Adasser put the flask to her lips and this time, she drank some of the potion. I bright white light started to glow around her, startling Joshua. He leaped off the bed.

"What was that?"

The light grew brighter.

"The restoration powers of the potion," Adasser explained. "This is a good sign. The white light will, in essence, burn away the darkness. It may not be a permanent fix, but it will give us more time to figure out what to do next." Joshua nodded.

The light started to shrink until it was a small ball of light, which plunged itself into Arianna's chest, into her heart. She gasped, opened her eyes and looked around.

"What happened to me? What did that thing do to me?"

Adasser looked her in the eyes and said, "The war has begun."

Chapter 32

Joshua had ordered the chef to bring Arianna soup to help her regain her strength. He lifted the bowl and brought the spoon to her lips. She pushed it away.

"Please, Joshua, I don't need soup right now. I need to plan our next move." She turned to Adasser. "What do you suggest?"

Adasser was seated in the chair across the room from her. He put his head in his hands and sighed.

"I was hoping that it would not come to this, but I think that our only option now is to find the wizard and bring him back."

Arianna set her jaw and swatted Joshua's hand away again as he tried to feed her another spoonful of soup. She shot him a look of fury and he dropped the spoon back into the bowl and walked out of the room with his head hung down sadly.

"Arianna, he is trying to help you. You need to eat to get your strength back."

"I am not hungry right now."

Adasser stood and walked over to her bed and sat beside her.

"Captain Oakford and I do not get along, that is true, but even I can see that he is trying, Ari. He is lost as to what to do. Don't be so hard on him right now."

Arianna looked at the door and frowned.

"He loves you. I saw that when I walked in that door. Arianna, I saw a man who was at his most vulnerable. Do not be so hard on him right now. Let him care for you. How are you feeling?"

"I feel strange. I don't feel the pain anymore, but I feel as though something is there, inside me."

"Just as I suspected. The potion is only a temporary fix. We have to find a way to break this curse."

"We need the wizard for that."

"It would seem so. We cannot get into the potions ingredients."

"How did you get the ingredients for my potion?"

Adasser smiled. "I sent word to Armen. He teleported them."

"You can do that?"

"Elves can." He saw the look on her face, and continued. "We cannot teleport living beings. It has never been done. It is too dangerous."

"Wait, no one has ever tried it?"

Adasser's face went ashen as he realized where her train of thought was going.

"No! I will not teleport you anywhere. It is dangerous. I refuse to do it."

"Adasser, it could be the answer to our problem."

"No, Arianna, I will not do it. No Elf will ever dare to teleport a living creature. Ever."

Arianna leaned back on the bed and sighed.

"Ellavorn would not do it, either," Adasser said softly, reading her mind. "No amount of cajoling on your part would have changed his mind either. The risk is way too great."

She nodded. “We do need to figure out how we are going to open a portal to that realm, Adasser. How are we going to do that?”

Adasser shook his head slightly. “I don’t know. I can check with King Armen as to what he knows about traveling between realms. As far as we know, the wizard was the only one to ever do so.”

“Maybe there is a spell in one of his books?”

Adasser shrugged. “There may be, but it will take us months to go through all of them. I will return to the Forest Glen in the morning to consult with Armen. For now, you must rest.”

Arianna lay back down and Adasser left.

She turned on her side so that she was looking out her window and her mind started to wander to Ellavorn. She started to wonder where he was, what he was doing, and if he was thinking of her. Silent tears slipped out of her eyes and over her nose, dropping onto the pillow. Her heart ached for him. She couldn’t help but wonder if he were here, would this still be happening? She drifted off to sleep and the dreams started.

Ellavorn was standing before her, on the deck of a ship. He was watching the ocean churn below, each wave slapping together and then getting lost under the bow of the ship.

“Ellavorn!” Ellavorn closed his eyes, sighed and turned to face the man with the harsh voice. He met the jet black eyes of a man who looked as though he had seen quite a few battles. The man had jet black hair and was dressed in head to toe black with the exception of an iron belt, the buckle in the shape of a horrid demon. Arianna gasped. She knew who he was in an instant. The most deadly pirate who ever lived. His name would strike fear into the hearts of the bravest of men.

"Captain Iron Demon," Ellavorn addressed him.

Iron Demon nodded and clapped a hand on his shoulder. "Aye, Elf. How much further to this kingdom that you have told me about? I am looking forward to raiding this castle and doing away with this queen that you spoke of. I will even let you drive the dagger into her heart. She broke your heart, you may break her's."

The air in Arianna's lungs rushed out. "Captain, I appreciate that offer, but, as you know, Elves cannot kill another living creature unless in defense."

"Pity. It feels so good to crush someone who has wronged you. Revenge is a wonderful thing, Elf." Ellavorn clenched his teeth in apparent annoyance as Iron Demon's lack of respect to his title. He simply stared at the vile man.

Iron Demon moved closer to Ellavorn and started speaking again, "What would happen if you killed her?"

"My powers would cease to be. I would become mortal."

"Ahhhhh, mortality, it is a thorn in the side, is it not?"

Ellavorn gave him an amused look. "I wouldn't know, and I don't intend to find out."

Iron Demon gave a hearty laugh. "Ahhhh, Elf, this is why I like you. You have spunk. It really is a pity that you won't kill her. It really is a wonderful feeling. Maybe I will cut her heart out for you and present it to you to do what you wish."

Ellavorn swallowed. "I do not wish to look upon her heart."

The pirate grinned and said, "As you wish, Elf. Now, tell me, how much further?"

Ellavorn seemed to turn to look at Arianna directly and said, "Four days' time."

Arianna awoke from the dream, screaming.

Chapter 33

Arianna screamed so loudly that Joshua, Abigail, Adasser and Charlie all came bursting into the room to see what was going on. Adasser held another vial of the Elixir of Apokatástasi in his hand, ready to administer it to her if necessary.

"Arianna, what happened?" Joshua rushed to her side, grabbing her hand.

Arianna had stopped screaming and was breathing heavily from fear.

"Ellavorn. Dream. Iron Demon."

Everyone looked around at each other, confused.

Adasser stepped forward and knelt beside the bed. "Arianna, you must calm down. Tell us what happened."

"I fell asleep and I saw Ellavorn. He is aboard Iron Demon's ship. They're planning on coming here to kill me and take over Eumetadotos."

Joshua relaxed and said, "Ari, it was just a dream. You're ok. Everyone is ok."

"No, it was so real, like I was standing on the deck of the ship. I could feel the wind on my face. Ellavorn saw me. He spoke to me at the end. They're coming."

Joshua and Adasser looked at each other. Adasser stood and broke the silence. "What did he say?"

"They will be here in four days' time."

"He spoke directly to you?"

"Well, no. He was speaking with Iron Demon, and when he asked Ellavorn when they would arrive, Ellavorn looked at me and said, 'In four days' time.' They're coming."

Joshua took her hand again. "Ari, it was a dream. It's not real."

Arianna shook her head as if to clear it. "It seemed so real."

Joshua gathered her in his arms and held her tight to his chest. "It's ok, Ari. That is my area of expertise in protection. I can protect you from that threat, if it's real."

"Captain Oakford is right. It is just a dream. Even if they show up here, his guards are strong. But, I doubt that my prince would betray you in so vile a manner. No matter what, he still loves you. He would not do anything to hurt you. I would not place much value in that dream."

Arianna leaned back against the pillows and fell silent. She looked to Abigail and Charlie, both of whom were leaning sleepily against the doorframe. They nodded their agreement with Adasser and Joshua. She turned her head to look out the window.

"Fine, maybe it is just a dream. But, what harm can come from being prepared?"

"I will have two guards outside of your door and at your side at all times, if that will put your mind at ease."

Arianna nodded.

"I will issue the order immediately. Now, let's all go back to our rooms. We all need some sleep."

Arianna turned on her side again while everyone except Adasser left the room. He approached Arianna's bed.

"Arianna?"

"I don't wish to speak to anyone right now. None of you believe me, yet, I feel in my heart that this was no mere dream."

"Are you familiar with telepathy?"

"You mean like reading someone's mind?"

Adasser smiled. "Sort of, but not quite. You see, Elves have the ability to communicate through different means. Prince Ellavorn is especially talented in this ability. He may have unknowingly opened a connection to you."

"So, wait, you believe me, yet you made me look like a fool in front of the others?"

"I believe you, but it is a skill that very few humans know that we possess. I cannot let our secrets out, not even to your friends. I ask you to do the same. I know that you have not been brought up by Elven standards, but we are your brethren. I am your blood, this is why I can share this with you. Do I have your word?"

"I will not say anything to my friends. I promise. Does this mean that what I saw is true?"

"I don't know. I'm saying that it is possible. If Ellavorn opened that connection, he must have done so accidentally. He does not know of your powers."

"Do you think Armen may have told him? I mean, if Elves can communicate in this manner, wouldn't he do so?"

"The prince would not allow him to make a connection. It is possible that that may have changed, but I have not heard anything from Armen about that."

"So, he may have made that connection by accident?"

"It is possible."

"Would he have seen me?"

"Yes. When we connect telepathically, it is as though we are standing in front of each other. We can see each other clearly."

"Would anyone else have seen me?" Arianna grew fearful of the thought of Iron Demon.

"No. Especially not a human who does not possess telepathic abilities."

She breathed a sigh of relief.

"How do I connect to him again?"

"I don't know that you will be able to do so. It is possible to block the communication if you so wish to do so. You are also new to your powers. I am going to ask you a personal question now. What were you thinking of when you fell asleep?"

Arianna looked away from him. "I was thinking of him. I miss him so much, Adasser. I just keep wondering if this would all be happening if I hadn't acted so impulsively. We would be married by now, you know."

"Yes, I know. You cannot dwell on what might have been. You must focus on what is. It is the only way that you will be able to win this war."

"You keep saying 'war.' Why?"

"We are at war. We are all at war with this Dark Figure. It may not have a physical army, but, believe me, its dark magic is all the army that it needs. It is powerful, that is for sure. We must find a way to defeat it. If Prince Ellavorn was making a connection to you, we have more to worry about. I suggest extra training for your guards, if Captain Oakford will allow it."

Arianna nodded. "Do you really think that he would kill me?"

"Who? Iron Demon or my prince?"

"Ellavorn. He looked so angry."

"Elves cannot harm another living being unless it is to defend themselves or their kingdom. To do so would demand forfeit on their immortality. If there is one thing that my prince, like most elves, values over almost anything, it is his immortality. I do not think he will harm you."

"That is what Ellavorn told him. But, what about Iron Demon?"

"The pirate is a different matter. He is pure evil. I have seen the things that he can do. None of which are good. The man was born of hatred, and with hatred, he lives. They say that his father is the devil himself. It would explain a lot."

"That does not make me feel any better."

"Arianna, you are well protected. Between your guards and myself, you should have nothing to fear."

"Except Ellavorn. He is working with him, Adasser."

"That, I cannot explain. I would be shocked if my prince were working with this pirate."

"That is exactly what it looked like. He was on his ship. He gave him the name of my kingdom, and told him our story. Iron Demon even offered to allow him to kill me! When he refused, he offered to cut out my heart and allow him to stab it. It was awful."

"Time will tell. For now, get some rest. We will come up

with another plan in the morning. Good night."

"Good night, Adasser."

Adasser walked to the door and turned back, looking at her laying in the moonlight. He felt a tug at his heart looking at the woman who was his granddaughter, and made a silent wish that everything would turn out the right way. He hated seeing her in so much pain, emotional and physical. They needed to find answers to their dilemmas and quickly.

Chapter 34

The next morning, Arianna woke up feeling as though she hadn't slept a wink. Every time she closed her eyes, visions of Iron Demon holding her heart haunted her. She got out of bed when Abigail knocked on the door to get her ready for the day.

Abigail poked her head in and asked, "Did you have any more dreams?"

Arianna shook her head. "No, nothing like that. It felt so real."

She was honoring her word to Adasser and not discussing this new ability with anyone. If he felt that the secret needed to be kept, then there must be a good reason for it.

"I have dreams like that too. Mostly about my parents."

Arianna looked at her friend, who wore a sad expression on her face.

"You don't speak of them often."

"I was young when they died. I don't have many memories of them."

"What were they like?"

Abigail smiled. "My mother was kind and so beautiful. She loved to sing and her voice was like that of a songbird. She always wore a smile and I never heard her say a mean word against anyone."

"She sounds lovely. What about your father?"

Abigail tipped her head to the side. "I don't remember much of my father. He was a farmer, so he was out tending the fields most of the day and would come in later at night. But, I remember he was kind. They loved each other so much. You could see it in the way that they would look at each other."

"Abigail, what happened to them?"

"My father woke up in the middle of the night. The barn was on fire. He ran out to save the cows and the horses, and my mother ran out to help him. They saved a few of the animals, but when they went back in, the barn collapsed. They were trapped inside."

Arianna gasped. "Oh, Abigail, that is awful!"

"I slept through it all. The sheriff came into the house looking for me. They feared that I had gone out to help. They found me, asleep in my bed. I was sent to live with my aunt. She was not too pleased with the idea of raising a child. So, she had me take on all of the house cleaning duties. She met a man who she intended to marry and I was forced to leave the house. It's how I came to work here."

"I am so sorry that you have lived through that. But, I will be honest. I am glad that you are here."

Abigail smiled. "I feel as though you are the sister I never had, Ari. I feel as though I am home here in the castle. I don't remember much about the farm house. But, I never felt at home with my aunt. Here, I have found where I fit in and where I feel as though people actually care about me."

Arianna took Abigail's hand in her own. "We do care for you. You are cared for a great deal."

"Thank you. Now, let's get you ready to start the day. Adasser said he wants to help to train me as well. In what, I don't know since we can't get to those potion ingredients. I'm just glad that I can help in some way, other than helping to dress you and do your hair."

Arianna laughed and they got to work.

A short while later, there was another knock on the door. When Arianna opened it, both Adasser and Joshua were standing outside. Both were ready to escort her to the dining hall, and neither was willing to look the other in the eye and concede.

"It seems as though I have a choice as to who escorts me today." Arianna could barely contain her amused smile.

The men shuffled in place, awaiting her choice.

"I think that both of you should escort me today."

They finally made eye contact and exchanged an astonished look.

"Listen, Joshua, you are my fiancé. Adasser, I am coming to accept that you are my grandfather. That makes you both important to me. I care about both of you, and I want the two of you to try and get past your foolish pride and make peace with each other."

She held out both of her arms to them, and they awkwardly took them and the all walked down the hall together to the dining hall, where they all sat and ate together.

After breakfast, they made their way to the throne room in the same manner. The tension between the men was palpable. Once inside the throne room, Arianna took her place and the two men took their places at the table. Abigail and Charlie sat as well as a few guards.

Arianna addressed the room. "Now, some of you may know that a curse was put upon me by the Dark Figure. Adasser, Abigail and Charlie figured out a temporary solution, but we do not know how long it will last. I have been training, and progressing well, but I still need more time, which we do not have much of. It is now vital that we find out which realm the wizard escaped to and to find a way to open a portal to find his descendants and try to talk them into coming back."

Everyone around the table nodded their ascent.

"I also want security to be amped up. I have an unsettling feeling, and I would like to be well prepared in case of an attack."

Joshua looked at her in disbelief, and started to say something as he stood up. Arianna interrupted. "Joshua, I have to trust my gut on this. I want extra security not only in the castle, but around the kingdom as well. At least for another week. If nothing happens, fine, but I want to be prepared in case something does happen."

Joshua sat down and glared at her, unhappy that she did not discuss this with him before her announcement.

"Is there any other business that anyone would like to discuss further before we retire for training?"

No one said anything.

"Ok, good. Then we shall adjourn and meet again tomorrow. You all know where we will be in case you need us."

They started to dismiss and Joshua went over to her and grabbed her arm.

"How dare you execute an order on my guards without discussing it with me first."

"Excuse me? If I had discussed it with you, you would have

told me that I was overreacting. I feel it in my gut that something is going to happen, and I want to be prepared. I will not allow you to minimize my authority any longer. Fiancé or not, I am still the queen and I still make the rules."

Joshua was dumbfounded. He stood there looking at her with his mouth opening and closing like a fish out of the water.

"Arianna, I do not minimize your authority."

"You absolutely do. You have been doing it from almost the beginning of this whole ordeal. I cannot stand it any longer. I need you to listen to me and to support my decisions whether you agree with them or not. You would never have undermined my parents in this manner. I have tolerated your attitude up to this point, but I am at my limit. I am not asking you to participate in or even to attend my training, but when I tell you that I want something done, you need to respect that and follow my orders."

"You are not your parents. You are behaving foolishly. You want to run off and fight this creature that you know nothing about –"

Arianna interrupted. "No, I do not want to run off anywhere. It brought the battle to me. I am training to be able to fight it. I now know that I possess a magic that can help to defeat it. Why wouldn't I want to do that to defend my kingdom? I didn't ask for any of this, Joshua. I would trade it all back in a heartbeat if it meant that I could have my parents back."

"And your prince too."

Arianna took a step back in shock. "What?"

"Oh, please, it is obvious. You are still in love with him. What are you going to do if your feeling is correct and he comes back here to kill you? What then?"

"Ellavorn would not kill me. I have never denied that I still love him. I have never once said that I don't love him anymore. I think that was pretty self-evident when I had you send your men out to look for him. If I didn't still love him, I would not have had you do that."

"You claim you love me as well. How can you possibly love two men at the same time?"

"Joshua, I do love you. I would not lie about that. But, I love you differently than I love Ellavorn. Your own jealousy is getting in the way of seeing that."

"Jealousy? You claim that you have seen him plotting to kill you, yet you still love him. He left you without a trace, and, yet, you still care for him. You are a fool, Arianna. I wouldn't leave you."

"You did!"

"Excuse me?"

"You did leave me. You left me to help try to find Ellavorn. You left me because you were jealous. You were angry with me because of the love I have for him, and the fact that I will not let it go. Ever. I have been honest with you from the start. I have not lied to you. What I shared with Ellavorn was very different than what I share with you. I have known him most of my life. You can't erase that overnight. Believe me, I have tried. I tried to not love him anymore. I tried to let him go. But, those feelings and those memories will remain. Always. If you can't handle that, then maybe we should not get married."

It was Joshua's turn to be shocked. "You don't mean that."

"Yes, I do. I cannot spend my life with someone who I have been nothing but honest with, and who still tries to make me pay for it over and over. I cannot spend my life with someone who wants to keep me in a bubble when I was born to step out of that bubble and do greater things. I cannot share my life with you, Joshua, if this is the way it is going to be."

"You have to marry within a year of your coronation. It's already been three months."

"I will find a way to handle that. But, I cannot share my life with someone who will not stand behind me when I need them to. I need someone to understand that I am not as delicate as you seem to think that I am. If you cannot do that, then we cannot marry. This was one of the issues that arose when my parents were trying to find me a suitor. Mostly because I wanted Ellavorn, but also, because I knew that a marriage to any of those men would condemn me to a life that felt like a prison sentence. I cannot have someone who puts restrictions on my growth. I need to marry someone who will allow the light to shine on me and let me grow to my fullest potential."

Joshua scoffed. "Adasser has been filling your head with nonsense. Kings and queens do not fight. That is the job of the guards. You rule the kingdom. You make the laws and are the ultimate judge of what happens. My guards and I are here to uphold those laws. That is the way that it works. You cannot change a system that has been in place for hundreds of years."

Arianna held his gaze and defiantly pulled her ring off, placed it in her pocket and ground out, "Just watch me." She then turned and stormed out of the throne room, slamming the door behind her and leaving Joshua staring at the door in complete disbelief.

Chapter 35

Abigail heard the door slam and ran over to her friend. "Arianna, what happened?"

"I'm pretty sure I just broke off my engagement to Joshua."

Abigail's jaw dropped. "Why?"

"Abigail, I know that you want me to marry him. But, I cannot marry someone who tries to restrict everything I do. I need to be able to make decisions regarding my kingdom without someone telling me that I am wrong at every turn. He has been doing just that all along. It's – suffocating me."

Abigail nodded. "I have noticed that he has been acting quite possessive lately. You're right, Ari. You are the queen and you have to do what is best for the kingdom. If that means that you have to break off your engagement to Captain Oakford, then so be it. You know that I will stand by you in your decisions."

Arianna looked relieved. She had been expecting a fight from her friend. She grabbed Abigail and hugged her tightly. "Thank you. You don't know how much that means to me."

Abigail hugged her back. "I know that this is not the right time to bring it up, but what are you going to do about the curse if you are not married?"

Arianna gave her a defeated look. "Let's handle one curse at a time. Let's get to the Odigós Domátio to begin our training." They began walking towards their training room.

"How are you feeling? Adasser is worried that the potion won't last forever."

"I feel strange. I'm not feeling the pain, but it's like

something has invaded my body and is lurking in the background. I hope that we can break this curse soon. I don't like feeling like this."

"Well, we will find a way to break it. I will be poring over those books until I can find one that I can read and I will find a potion."

Arianna laughed. "If there is a potion that will help. Regardless, I know that you will put all of your efforts into finding something. I do not doubt that. Abigail, you have been a true and loyal friend to me from the beginning. Thank you."

"You're welcome. You have been a great friend to me too. I've never really had a friend before. Growing up, I wasn't allowed to socialize much. Here, everyone is wonderful, but they're all busy with their own tasks. It doesn't leave much time for friendships. Not that I am complaining about the time I work. I love it here."

Arianna put her hand up. "I understand what you mean. We all have our own duties to worry about. Right now, our duties are to train, and find a way to open a portal to the realm to which the wizard fled. After that, we will need to find a way to break this curse."

That plan seemed to steel Abigail's resolve and she marched on, determined to accomplish all of that.

"Abigail, you do know that we will not be able to do all of this in one day, right?"

"Arianna, I am not one to back down from a challenge. Let's go." She grabbed her friend's wrist and both raced off to the Odigós Domátio.

When they arrived at the bottom of the stairs, Adasser was

barking orders as though he were the Captain of the Royal Guard.

"Charlie, fetch me any book that you can on healing! I need them immediately. Oh, good, you two decided to join us. Abigail, gather any potion book that you can find. We must find a way to open that portal to bring the wizards back to break this curse once and for all. Arianna, you begin training with the guards. Guards, do not show her any mercy. She needs to be able to combat anything that comes at her."

Arianna and Abigail exchanged surprised looks. Adasser had always been a bit abrasive, but never quite so authoritative before. They were equally scared and impressed.

Arianna began disintegrating lances, spears and arrows while Charlie and Abigail searched the books. Adasser watched Arianna intently, ready to spring at the first sign that the potion was wearing off. After an hour, he instructed the guards to stop and let her rest.

"Arianna, how are you feeling?"

"I feel strange still. I still feel as though there is something lurking in my body, but I am not in pain. Do you know what it is?"

"I can only surmise that it is the curse. It has been subdued, but I don't know for how long. I think that it would be best if you took another dose of the Elixir."

"What will it do?"

"It will not hurt you. The curse seems to be bound, but only temporarily. If it begins to free itself, you could wind up in the same state that you were in yesterday. I would rather not observe that again."

"I would rather not experience that again," she answered as he passed her the vial of Elixir.

"I have several of those in my possession at all times. I suggest that you carry one on yourself as well just in case we get separated." He passed her a vial and she tucked it into her pocket next to her ring.

"Thank you, Adasser, for all that you have done for me."

"You are welcome, child. Now, let's get back to training."

The rest of the day passed quickly with Arianna picking up new skills, but Charlie and Abigail having no luck in finding anything that would open any portals.

Arianna was not about to give up hope. "Wherever he hid this spell, he hid it well. We will find it."

The rest of them just nodded their heads, unsure if they actually believed what she was saying. They were beginning to become discouraged.

As the rounded to corner to the hall where Arianna's chambers were located, they noticed Joshua sitting on the floor by her door. He looked as though he had been crying.

Arianna took a deep breath and motioned for the rest of them to give her a few moments with him. She walked over and opened her door.

"Joshua, please come in and talk to me."

He stood silently and followed her into her chambers and sat in the corner. She left the door open and sat across from him, on the bed.

"Please talk to me."

"I don't know what to say, Arianna."

"You look terrible."

"My fiancée just broke off our engagement. How am I supposed to look?"

"Your fiancée broke off your engagement because she is the queen of a kingdom in danger and you were interfering with her plans to keep it safe. Joshua, my first priority is to my people and their safety. I have to think about what is best for them. If that includes my training and fighting in a battle, then that is what must be done. I know that you don't like it, but you have to accept that. I've told you this countless times. If you cannot accept that and support me in doing this, then I cannot marry you."

Joshua looked her in the eyes for the first time. It scared her. She had never seen such a broken expression in anyone's eyes before.

"Arianna, I cannot accept you putting your life in danger. I will not support it. You are the queen. It is my sworn duty to protect you. You are asking me to break that oath. You are asking me to ignore the fact that you are putting your life on the line. You are asking me to allow you to sacrifice yourself."

"Yes, I am. This war is different than any other in our history. Never before has there knowingly been a ruler with Elven blood. Never before has there ever been a magical battle waged upon us. It so happens that both are happening at the same time. I am that ruler, Joshua. I have to protect my people. You cannot do it this time.

"You are a wonderful guard, and an even better Captain. You can fight in a physical battle very well. You are wonderful with a sword and any other weapon. If we were under attack by any kind of soldiers, you are the first person I would want to defend me. But, you do not possess magic. This is a magical war. To fight magic, you need magic. I have that ability. I am getting stronger with it every day. It is necessary for me to hone those skills in order to be able to protect my kingdom. I need someone to understand that. If you don't, then I cannot have you rule with me. If you can let go of what is traditional and open your mind, we have a chance. But, Joshua, you cannot try to prevent me from fulfilling this destiny. No matter what. Do you understand?"

"I know what you are saying. I don't like it and I don't agree with it. This will become a big issue if you keep training. I cannot have my queen – my fiancée – in danger like this. It reflects as a failure on myself."

"No, what reflects as a failure is your inability to see that things are not the same as they were three months ago. My family was destroyed. My life was turned upside down. This was all thrust upon me and I am still figuring it all out. You say that you love me, but you do not accept me for who I am. Joshua, that is not love."

"How can you say that I don't love you? You know nothing of what I feel." Joshua jumped out of the chair and made his way over to Arianna. He grabbed her by her shoulders and picked her up so that she was staring him in the eye.

"Arianna, I do love you, but you are right, I cannot accept this suicide mission that you have decided to take on. I will not be engaged to someone who does not value her own life." He released her hard and she fell back onto the bed. He stormed out of her chambers, slamming the door behind him. It was Arianna's turn to stare at the door in shock.

Chapter 36

Arianna sat on her bed staring at the door for what seemed like an eternity. Finally, someone pushed the door open and Abigail popped in.

"Is it safe to come in?"

Arianna nodded and looked away.

"Ari, what happened?"

She took a deep breath before answering.

"Joshua and I had a fight. He stormed out. If I wasn't sure before, I am now that the engagement is off."

Abigail pulled a chair over and sat in front of her. She clasped Arianna's hands in her own.

"I'm sorry. He has been acting differently towards you since he arrived back. I'm sorry to say it, Ari, but I think that this is a good thing. He wasn't very supportive of you at all."

"I know," she whispered. "I just didn't expect him to be so angry with me. I didn't ask for this. It was just thrust upon me. I don't know how to go about saving the realm. It seems like an impossible task. Abigail, I don't even know where to start looking for the wizard. I feel so lost."

"I know you do. But, that is why the rest of us are here…to help. We'll figure this out together. We'll find the wizard and convince him to come back. We have to. The rest of us are in this with you, all the way. Forget Joshua. We don't need him."

"But, we might, Abigail. He is a skilled fighter. He's the best, which is why he was made Captain of the Royal Guard. You don't attain that title with mediocre skills. We will need him at some point. I just hope that he is still there."

"You don't think that he would abandon you, do you?"

"I don't know. He was pretty angry."

"Well, he better not. I'll teach him a lesson if he does."

Arianna smiled a small smile. "Oh, really? What would you do?"

"Haven't you heard? I'm a potions master now! I'll turn him into a frog!"

Arianna's smile widened at her friend's attempt to cheer her up.

"That, I would love to see."

"Magic, even potions should only be used for light. It is very easy to be seduced by the darkness that can come from the power you will feel by wielding it."

"Oh, lighten up, Adasser," Abigail said. "I wouldn't really turn him into a frog. I was just trying to cheer up Arianna."

Adasser looked from one girl to the other, trying to figure out how that could cheer her up. "I don't understand. Would exacting revenge on someone really bring you such joy?"

Arianna smiled again. "No. We would never actually do anything to harm anyone. Abigail was just trying to cheer me up. I'm pretty sure that Joshua and I are no longer engaged. We had a terrible fight and he stormed out. Sometimes, it will make someone feel better to think about how to get revenge on the person who hurt you. We would never act on it."

"I still don't understand. Why would you want to inflict pain on someone else?"

"We don't want to. We're not going to. I promise. Haven't you ever fantasized about something, or day dreamed?"

"Arianna, I am the Head Protector. I do not have time for such nonsense."

"Well, we humans do it a lot. It makes us feel better without actually hurting anyone. We just play out a scenario, and then forget about it, like it never happened."

"Humans are strange."

"So are Elves," said Arianna.

Adasser looked surprised at her quick comeback, and Arianna and Abigail burst into giggles. Adasser simply shook his head in confusion at the two young women.

"I shall escort you to dinner this evening, if that is acceptable."

"Of course. I would be honored. I would like for all of us to sit together and try to come up with a plan to find a way to open this portal and find the wizard."

Arianna and Abigail each took one of Adasser's arms and they set off for the dining room.

Once they arrived and were seated, Arianna couldn't wait to get the conversation started. "How do we know which realm the wizard escaped to?"

"I have looked for clues, but I cannot find any," Adasser said.

"Well, then how do we know where to look?" Arianna sounded desperate.

"Isn't there a spell or a potion that we can use to find him, or his descendants?" Abigail chimed in.

Adasser stopped and looked at her. "There is a locator spell, but I do not know if it will span realms. I would need Armen's assistance in the spell as well. It is quite complicated."

"Armen is always welcome here at the castle. Please, send him an invitation immediately."

"It is not that simple, Arianna. The spell is quite complicated. It will need a lot of work from both of us as well as some potion work as well." He looked at Abigail. "Are you willing to help?"

"Of course! I am willing to do anything in order to save the kingdom!"

"I need you and Charlie to go to the Odigós Domátio and see if you can find anything in regards to locator spells, and potions. Also, see if you can find anything on crossing realms. If you are finished, go now. I have some things to discuss with Arianna."

Abigail and Charlie nodded their ascent and dashed out the door.

Adasser turned to Arianna. "I will send for Armen. He will know if it can be done."

"Will he help us, Adasser?" Arianna sounded unsure.

"Armen will help if he deems it beneficial for our realm. Given our circumstances, I can be sure that he will help. He would be a fool not to. The prophecy has deemed you the one who can save this realm. Armen knows that you cannot do it alone. You need help from the Elves. He knows that our survival, as well as your own, depends on your victory."

"And what of Iron Demon? How do we handle that situation?"

"You need to convince Captain Oakford of the danger there. If this dream was, in fact, a premonition, you have three days' time to do that."

Arianna's head hung. "He won't trust me on this. I don't know why he won't listen to me. I don't understand why he is so insistent that it was just a dream. I just don't understand him anymore."

"Captain Oakford does not understand because he has never known this life, Arianna."

"I have never known this life, Adasser. Well, not until a few weeks ago."

"You understand better because you have been around Elves. You have made a connection with one yourself. In fact, you are one."

"But I didn't know that until recently."

"It doesn't matter if you knew. What matters is that it is true."

"Abigail and Charlie don't seem to have any problems with the truth. In fact, Joshua is the only person that is having this particular issue."

"Arianna, I have said it before. He loves you. He worries about you because he does not wish to see you hurt. He has told you himself, he has sworn an oath to protect you and your family. Now, things have changed and you are planning to go into a battle that he has no chance of winning on sheer manpower. He does not understand magic. Your people have been sheltered from it for too long. Humans fear the unknown. Actually, everyone fears the unknown."

Arianna huffed. "Elves don't seem to fear anything."

"No?"

"No. You all seem to have the answers all of the time. There is no unknown to you."

"Sure there is."

Arianna gave him a confused look. "I don't understand."

"Elves do not understand death. We do not understand the mourning process, and all that goes with it. It is very rare that one of our own is killed. We tend to stay out of battle and live in peace. We fight when we must, but there is rarely any need for it. So, we know little about death. It is a mystery to us. It is probably one reason why most Elves tend to not mate with humans."

Arianna looked thoughtful for a moment. "I always thought that it was because Elves did not wish to taint their blood with mortality."

Adasser chuckled, startling Arianna. It was a very rare sound, one that wasn't unpleasant. She didn't know that she would ever get used to the stern Elf's laughter. "You sound like the Prince. He would say things like that often."

Arianna blushed. "That's where I heard it."

"I figured. He is right, but only to a point. We do not hate humans. Well, most of us do not. Prince Ellavorn is still very young by our standards. But, he is correct. Most Elves do not mate with humans because they fear the unknown. They fear to fall in love with someone only to lose them. They fear to watch their loved ones die before their eyes. Prince Ellavorn sees mortality as a curse. I think that it is the opposite. I believe that immortality is the curse."

Arianna looked confused. "I thought that Elves cherished their immortality."

Adasser chuckled again. "I think that we have established that I am not like most Elves."

Arianna smiled. "No, you definitely are not. So, would you give up your immortality if you could?"

Adasser's eyes took on a far off look, and he sighed. "I think that I would. But, we have digressed from our original topic of conversation. How are we to convince Captain Oakford of the urgency without giving away our secret?"

"That is what I have been trying to figure out. He will not listen to me anymore. He is so stubborn. I don't know how to convince him that we need to do this."

"You are the queen. You can issue a royal decree."

"I know. I was hoping not to do that. I was hoping that he would listen to me and realize the urgency that this situation puts us into."

"It is hard when the person you love does not agree with you. I know that much. But, Arianna, you are the queen. You have to think about your kingdom first. Not everyone is going to like every decision that you make. That includes your friends. If Captain Oakford is not listening to you, you must make him listen."

Arianna nodded. "You're right. I will make the decree today."

"I will summon Armen and request his help in locating the wizard. Now, we should summon Abigail and young Charlie to meet in the throne room to go over strategies."

Adasser started to stand up, but Arianna grabbed his arm, stilling him. "Thank you, Adasser. Your guidance is greatly appreciated."

Adasser smiled a small smile at her, and said, "You are most welcome."

Chapter 37

Arianna entered the throne room and was met by an icy glare from Joshua, who stood in the far corner. She shuddered and made her way to the throne, feeling his eyes follow her as she crossed the room. She sat on the throne and turned to meet his gaze.

"Captain Oakford, are you going to join in this meeting, or are you going to lurk in the corner the entire time?"

Without a word, he trudged over to the table that was set up every morning and sat in the seat farthest away from Arianna.

"Is this how it is going to be? You cannot avoid speaking with me forever. I am the Queen. You are the Captain of the Royal Guard. We have to speak at some point."

She was met by another glare. "I will speak to you only when necessary. I don't feel that it is necessary to have a conversation at this point in time."

Arianna shook her head in disbelief. "Fine. I cannot force you to speak to me."

They sat in an uncomfortable silence for a few moments before the guards, Abigail, Charlie and Adasser came into the room to begin their daily meeting.

Arianna started. "As most of you know, I had a dream the other night that we are going to be attacked by Iron Demon and his pirates."

Joshua groaned from the back. "Here we go with this again."

Arianna ignored his comment and continued. "I am ordering security be heightened in the castle and throughout the kingdom."

Joshua's head jerked up in surprise. "You can't possibly think that I will allow this."

"You have no choice. That is an order, Captain Oakford. I will not have you question my judgement any longer."

Joshua gritted his teeth and ground out, "Yes, Your Majesty."

Arianna glared at his insolence, but decided not to say anything more on the matter.

"I want guards in the village at all times, and I want heightened security in the castle as well. Any slightest hint of trouble, and I expect to be notified at once."

The guards all nodded their ascent. Joshua continued to shoot icy glares in her direction. Arianna was hurt by this, but she was determined not to let her disappointment in him be known. She carried on as though she did not notice.

"Adasser," Arianna nodded her head in his direction, "will summon Armen. He feels that Armen will be able to help us locate the realm to which the wizard fled and possibly open the portal."

Again, Joshua made another disgruntled sound.

"Is there a problem, Captain Oakford?"

Joshua made a face, and said coldly, "No, Your Majesty. Whatever you wish, Your Majesty."

Arianna was growing tired of his antics. "Captain Oakford, I would like a word with you after this meeting is over." "Whatever you wish, Your Majesty," he said again.

The meeting went on the much the same manner. Arianna would set a plan and Joshua would make retorts in a mocking tone. Soon, Arianna dismissed everyone. As the rest of the attendees got up to leave the room, Joshua made to follow them, despite a direct order to stay. Arianna grabbed his arm and pulled him back into the room. Her eyes were glittering in anger.

"How dare you undermine my authority in front of everyone!"

"I wouldn't undermine your authority if you weren't making foolish decisions."

"I don't care if you think that they are foolish. I am the queen. You are under my rule. You are not to question my judgement in matters like this."

"Matters like this are matters of protection. That falls under my domain, Your Majesty. You are being foolish to believe a dream. This is a fool's errand."

"So, now I am a fool?"

"Those are your words. If you feel that they apply, who am I to argue?"

"I do not feel that they apply," Arianna growled at him. She was beginning to lose her patience. "I feel that you are being insubordinate and quite insolent as well. You are undermining my authority every chance that you get, and I do not appreciate it one bit."

Joshua snorted in derision. "I am being insolent and undermining your authority? You just demanded that I increase security in the entire kingdom because of a dream that you had one night."

"I demanded it because you will not listen! I am the queen, Joshua! I don't like to use that in order to get my way, but if I must, I will. I am doing what I feel is right for my people. I am protecting them the best way that I know how."

"By undermining *my* authority."

"I cannot apologize to you for this. I have to trust my instincts here. I just wish that you would see it that way too. If you cannot understand what I am trying to do and that it is what I believe to be the best thing for our kingdom, then I think it is best that we have called our engagement off. You are the Captain of the Royal Guard. You are not the king. You do not make the rules. I do. You may not agree with everything that I do, but it is your duty to implement the safety demands that I deem necessary."

Joshua looked livid. "Well, Your Majesty, maybe I will resign as the Captain of the Royal Guard. Then you can appoint someone who will be your little puppet."

"I don't want you to resign. There is no one who possesses the skills you do. You are the best choice for that position. I have never doubted that. However, I do not appreciate the disrespect that you have now shown to me on numerous occasions. I am quite capable of making decisions that I determine are the best course of action. In this instance, yes, I want extra security in the kingdom. I would rather be prepared than be caught off-guard."

"You speak of my disrespecting you, but you have shown me disrespect on multiple occasions as well."

Arianna was stunned by his words. "How have I shown you disrespect?"

"You sent me to look for your ex-fiancé, knowing how I feel about you."

"I did not send you. I asked you to send your men to look for him. I never once hid my feelings for Ellavorn from you. You volunteered to take that task on yourself. Do not put the blame for that on me. You did that of your own volition."

"No," he scoffed, "you're right, you have never hidden your feelings about him. You have only made him out to be perfect."

"I have never said that Ellavorn was perfect. He has his flaws. I have always been honest with you about my feelings for him. I have always tried to show you the utmost respect when it came to matters concerning him. How have I shown you disrespect? If being honest and open with you is disrespectful, then you have an argument. However, I do not see it that way. I have always tried to take your feelings into consideration, Captain Oakford. That is a courtesy that you have not returned to me lately."

"Feelings have nothing to do with my lack of enthusiasm for your actions. I will not be like the others and follow your lead like a sheep follows its shepherd."

Arianna felt the sting of his words. "How dare you! They are following orders from their queen. We are trying to ensure the safety of our people. Have you forgotten that I have a curse on me? Have you forgotten that I could die at any moment because of that curse? You say that feelings have nothing to do with anything, however, before magic resurfaced, there were no issues between us. You are afraid of magic. That is why you are lashing out at me in this way. You fear what you don't know, and now, that includes me. Captain Oakford, if you fear me so much, then resign. I do not wish you to leave, but if you cannot fulfill your duty, then I will have no choice but to accept your resignation."

"Then, Your Majesty, consider this my resignation." With that, Joshua pushed past her, knocking into her shoulder, and left.

Chapter 38

"I cannot believe that he left!" Arianna had made her way to the Odigós Domάtio and was pacing the floor furiously.

"He really told you that you showed him disrespect?" Abigail asked, timidly.

"Can you believe it? I have never been anything but honest with him! I always made it known that I wanted to find Ellavorn. Joshua knew that. I never asked him to go himself to look for him. He chose to do that on his own." Arianna flopped down next to Abigail, exhausted and dejected. "I don't know what to do, Abigail," she whispered to her friend, who wrapped her arms around her to console her.

"I will tell you what to do," a deep voice said from above her. Arianna looked up into Adasser's eyes. They were full of warmth and kindness. "You will get up off that floor and you will practice your skills. You will not allow Captain Oakford's doubt cloud your judgment. You will be the queen that you are meant to be and save your people. That is what you are going to do."

Arianna smiled, a genuine smile at him. She realized that he was right. She was beginning to let Joshua's doubt cloud her mind. She knew that, in order to succeed, she had to push those doubts away. She pushed herself up from the floor and said, "OK, I am ready. Let's train."

Adasser threw tougher and tougher obstacles at her, and, one by one, she was able to defeat them. Her skills had been getting better and better, but now, she felt more confident than ever. She was feeling so relaxed, that she let her guard down, when Adasser threw an attack spell at her, hitting her in the arm.

"Ow! What was that for?"

Adasser's face was serious. "Arianna, you must always be on your guard. Do not let it down until your enemy is defeated completely. You are getting better. It is ok to be confident in your abilities. You need to be in order to fight. But, you cannot let the confidence take over. You must be in control at all times."

Arianna nodded, humbled by the experience. There was, however, one thing that she wanted to know. "Adasser, you have been training me with blocking and defending. When am I going to learn to attack back? I can't win a battle by just deflecting spells."

"You are correct. I think that the time has come for you to learn the attack spells. We shall start with a simple one now."

Arianna grew excited. She hoped that she would never have to use these spells, but she knew that the time was drawing nearer when she would have no choice but to do just that.

"The simplest of the attack spells is *epíthesi.*"

Arianna repeated the word over and over until she was able to pronounce it correctly.

"Perfect. Now, put your hands up, and throw the spell at that training dummy over in the corner."

Arianna looked at the training dummies that had been erected against a wall and was confused. "Where did those come from?"

Adasser smiled. "A little bit of Elf Magic." He leaned down and whispered, "I had the guards put them together while we were sparring."

Arianna smiled and gave a quiet laugh. "OK, let's get started."

Adasser showed her how to position her hand. "Your right hand must be held up, bent at the elbow. Position your fingers like this." He held his fingers as though he were holding a baseball. "Now, whisper your spell. You want to try to catch your opponent off guard. And throw."

Arianna held her hand up the way that Adasser showed her, whispered the word, "Epíthesi," and a bright white ball of energy appeared. She threw it at the dummy with a direct hit. The dummy exploded in front of her eyes. She looked up at Adasser, whose eyes were wide with surprise.

"Not a bad start," he said. "Not bad at all."

Arianna beamed.

"Now, try it again. I want all of those dummies destroyed."

Arianna looked around there were about ten dummies scattered around.

"That seems easy enough."

"Don't be so sure. You will be defending yourself as well as attacking."

Arianna's face fell, and she felt panic rising up. "What do you mean?"

"Well, you can't expect to be in a battle and have your opponent just allow you to attack. It doesn't work like that. They are out to destroy you, not to give you equal playing ground. You have to be able to defend yourself and attack at the same time."

She took a deep breath and said, "OK, let's do it."

Adasser walked to the other side of the room and hid behind one of the dummies. Arianna held her hand up, ready to throw the spell, when a ball of white light came soaring at her. She changed the position of her hand and easily deflected the spell.

She recovered quickly and threw a spell at one of the dummies, exploding it easily. Another spell came flying towards her. By the time she saw it, it was too late to throw a defensive spell, so she dropped into a roll on the floor. The spell that she had just dodged hit the wall, exploding and causing some of the stone to explode with it.

Adasser's voice echoed through the room. "Good move. Be on your guard."

Arianna scrambled to her feet and held her arm up again to throw another spell. As she readied herself, another spell came hurtling towards her. She threw her hand up to deflect the spell at the same time as throwing the spell that she had just conjured. She deflected the spell and heard the unmistakable sound of a dummy exploding. She heard Adasser yelp as well.

"That was excellent, Arianna," his voice once again echoed around the room.

Arianna was getting a little disconcerted by the echoing voice, but she focused on the next target. She held her hand up and threw her spell. The dummy exploded, and she saw another spell coming her way from the corner of her eye. Once again, she dropped to the ground, avoiding impact. However, this time, the spell turned in midair and made its way towards her once again. Arianna held her hands up in the defensive position and was able to disintegrate the spell.

"You are doing very well, Arianna."

The false battle went on and on with spells being thrown and dummies exploding for what seemed like hours. Finally, the last dummy exploded, revealing Adasser standing behind it, smiling at his student.

"You have fought very, very well, Arianna. You are not ready for a true battle just yet, but you have proven that you are a very skilled warrior. That will end our training for the day. You should get something to eat. You need your strength."

"Adasser, how can I eat when I have so far to go? I need to train more. I need to be able to defend my people."

Adasser walked over to her and put both hands on her shoulders, turning her to look him in the eye.

"You need your strength. You cannot learn everything in one day. I admire your ambition, Arianna. However, you need to take care of yourself as well. If you are not in good health, then you are not going to be able to properly defend yourself or your people."

"Fine. But, after I eat, we need to train some more."

"No, you need to rest. I need to rest as well. Besides, you must start interviewing for a new Captain of the Royal Guard. I also need to send a message to Armen requesting his help. If we are to find which realm the wizard escaped to, I will need his assistance."

Arianna sighed, thinking of the task of replacing Joshua. It was not going to be an easy feat. "OK. I admit that we need to get working on finding the wizard. But, training shall resume tomorrow."

"I accept those terms."

As Arianna and the others left the Odigós Domάtio, Adasser watched her leave. She had come so far in her training and grown a lot in general as a person. He could not help but feel some pride for his granddaughter as she moved up the stairs.

He sighed, thinking about her grandmother. When he was sure that everyone was gone, he pulled a chain around his neck that he kept hidden from everyone. On the chain was a locket with a beautiful design on the front. He opened it to reveal a picture of Arianna's grandmother and looked at it longingly.

"I wish I had known sooner. You would be so proud of the woman that our granddaughter has become. She will win this war. I promise, I will give my last breath, if I must, to make sure of that."

Chapter 39

Arianna sat at the table, picking at her food. Abigail noticed that her friend seemed a bit distant tonight.

"Ari, what's wrong?"

"I have to find a new Captain of the Royal Guard. Abigail, how am I going to replace Joshua? He is the best of the best. I don't know who will measure up."

"When do you have to make a decision?"

"As soon as possible. We need a leader to protect the city. Especially with this new threat looming. I have called all of the guards to an emergency meeting for after lunch."

"Are you sure that Iron Demon is really coming?"

"Yes. I can't explain it, but I know he is. He means to destroy my kingdom. I cannot allow him to do that."

"Are you sure that Joshua will not return?"

"I don't think so. He was pretty angry at me when he left."

"I'm sorry, Ari. I know that you care for him." All of the sudden, Abigail looked at her as a realization set in. "Ari, what about the curse? You have to be married before your coronation date of one year!"

Arianna buried her face in her hands. "Abigail, can we work on one curse at a time? I think the threat of the Dark Figure is the bigger threat at this time. We need to defeat it."

"You're right. We do. But, we also can't forget about this one, either, ok?"

"I know this. I will figure it out. I promise."

"Is there anyone else?"

Arianna looked sad. "If I must, I will marry one of the other suitors. I hope it doesn't come to that, but I will. Abigail, I will figure this out. I promise. But, right now, I need to focus on appointing a new Captain."

They got up from the table and walked to the throne room. Arianna couldn't help but notice the empty chair where Joshua normally sat. A hollow feeling wormed its way into her stomach. She sat at the head of the table and waited for everyone to take their seats. Once everyone was present, she began the meeting.

"As most of you may know, Captain Oakford has resigned his position as Captain of the Royal Guard, effective immediately." She swallowed a lump that was forming in her throat. "I must fill this position immediately in order to properly protect Eumetadotos."

The room was filled with the din of chatter among everyone present.

"Do I have anyone who would be interested in the position? If so, please step forward."

Three guards stepped forward. This first stood almost seven feet tall. He was extremely brawny. His jet black hair was cropped close to his head. His dark brown eyes shone with ferocity, with an underlying kindness to them. Arianna liked him instantly. He made her feel safe.

The second guard was shorter by at least a foot. He looked as though he had seen his share of battles judging by the scars running down his biceps and forearms. His light brown hair was a little longer than the first guard, but still short. His blue eyes seemed to have been made of ice. He made Arianna a little uneasy.

The third guard was the shortest of the three, barely making it to six feet tall. He looked very new to his position. He had blonde hair that fell to his shoulders and blue eyes that sparkled. Arianna almost pitied him. She didn't think he would last a single round in the tournament.

"May I have your names, please?"

The first guard answered, "Dustin Granitious." Arianna took notice of his physique again. His biceps bulged. She wondered why he had not been appointed Captain before based on his appearance. He dwarfed every other guard in height and brawn.

The second guard answered, "Garrett Diamonte." Arianna looked him over again. While he was not as big as Dustin, he still seemed to be able to handle himself in a crisis situation, based on the scars. His eyes seemed to bore into her soul. She shivered slightly before moving on.

The third guard answered, "Wyatt Redwood." Arianna tried not to let the pity that she felt towards him show in her eyes. She knew that she should wait to see what the man could do, but she just couldn't help but picture him going up against either of his competitors. They were both huge.

"Very well. Dustin Granitious, Garret Diamonte and Wyatt Redwood are our candidates for the position of Captain of the Royal Guard.

"In accordance with the tradition of Eumetadotos, they must complete a quest. They must venture into the forest and save a maiden from kidnappers. She will be hidden deep in the forest. It will not be an easy task to find her. She will be hidden by the elves. The terrain is dangerous. There are no trails where you will need to go. You will need to rely on your bravery, strength, wisdom and endurance. The first one to make it back will be the winner and the new Captain of the Royal Guard. The elves are not to be harmed. This is not a real kidnapping. Your quest will begin in an hour's time."

The three contestants looked at each other in disbelief of the lack of warning.

"You may pack any necessary supplies and report to the courtyard. The kitchen is preparing rations for you to take with you. They will be given to you in the courtyard. If any of you wish to reconsider, now is the time."

Arianna dismissed them and Abigail turned to her and asked, "Who has been kidnapped?"

Arianna smiled at her friend apologetically. "Well, you will be."

Abigail's face blanched. "What?"

Arianna giggled. "Don't worry. Adasser has assigned one of his men to take you into the woods. You will be perfectly safe. He will not leave your side."

"Well, I don't know if he will, but I certainly won't." A female voice echoed into the room.

Arianna's head snapped round and she came eye to eye with a female elf. She had long, auburn hair that went to her waist and brown eyes that warned that she was not someone to be crossed. She was heavily armed with two swords crossed and strapped to her back. Arianna also noticed three daggers attached to her belt as well. She didn't want to imagine what else this elf had on her body.

Arianna raised her eyebrows in surprise. "You're a female."

"My name is Tanelia. And, yes, I am a female. Were you expecting a male?" Tanelia did not look happy with the exchange.

"I'm sorry, I didn't mean to offend you. It's just that we've never had a female guard here in Eumetadotos. It just took me by surprise."

"I assure you, Your Majesty that I can do just as good of a job, if not better than any male."

"I don't doubt that you can. I trust Adasser and his judgement. If he chose you then you must be the best choice."

"Well, I am his second in command. I would say I would be the best choice. Now, if we are through with the idle chitchat, I would like to get on with my mission."

Abigail looked at Arianna with a fear in her eyes. Tanelia did not seem like she wanted this task. She wasn't so sure that she could trust her.

Arianna put her hands on her shoulders. "Abigail, I promise you, you will be fine. Trust me. If Adasser trusts her, than I do too."

Abigail looked at Arianna with a pleading look.

"I really don't want to go into that forest. With or without protection. It's not a nice place."

"I know that it isn't. I don't disagree with you. But, you have the best elf there with you."

"No, I don't. Adasser is here. I have the second best elf." Abigail pouted.

Arianna smiled. “Will you please help me? It won’t be long. It’s just until one of the guards finds you and returns you.”

“OK, fine. I will do it. But, I won’t like it.”

“Noted,” Arianna said with a grin. “Now, you have to get going if you’re going to get ahead of the guards.”

Abigail nodded. Arianna embraced her friend and watched as she turned and left with Tanelia, who did not so much as look in Arianna’s direction. Arianna thought this to be odd and decided to ask Adasser about it. In the meantime, she had to prepare for the big send off.

Chapter 40

After Tanelia and Abigail left, Arianna went to find Adasser. She found him in the Odigós Domátio. He was poring over books.

"Still looking for a way to locate the wizard?"

Adasser jumped.

"Yes. I think I may have found something."

Arianna rushed over to his side to take a look at what he was reading.

"How do you know that this is the right one?"

"I don't, but it looks like it is. The spine of the book is cracked slightly and this page is slightly more weathered than the rest. It looks as though he was studying it for a while. The spell looks like it is the one that we are looking for. I can only be sure when Armen looks it over."

"Do you really think that this will work?"

Adasser looked her straight in the eye.

"I sincerely hope so."

He marked the page and they left the Odigós Domátio to go out for the contestants' send off. They stopped in the kitchens to make sure that the rations had been prepared and went into the courtyard.

The contestants were lined up, packed and ready to accept their rations to head off into the woods. Arianna stood in the middle of the courtyard and began handing out the ration bags before stepping up onto a platform to deliver her speech.

"Ladies and gentlemen, thank you for coming to see these brave men off."

All of the sudden, there came a loud clattering noise from the gate. All heads turned to see Joshua with Abigail riding on the back of his horse. They were riding at break-neck speed, and Abigail looked sick. Tanelia came running behind them just a second later. Arianna wasn't sure which surprised her more, seeing Joshua or seeing the elf keep pace with him on foot.

Arianna jumped off the platform and ran over to them.

"Abigail, Tanelia, Captain – I mean, Joshua, what is going on?"

Joshua stepped forward, looking very upset. He dropped to his knees and looked up at her.

"Arianna, please, forgive me. I am so sorry that I doubted you. I came as quickly as I could to warn you. You were right. Iron Demon's crew is heading this way. We need to secure the kingdom. Close the gates and prepare for the attack."

The wind seemed to rush from Arianna's lungs. She had hoped that the vision had just been a dream. Now, it seemed, it was not.

"Thank you, Joshua."

She turned to the guards. "We must cancel the quest and prepare the kingdom for attack. Iron Demon and his crew are heading this way! Secure all entries into Eumetadotos. Evacuate as many people from the kingdom as possible."

All of the guards turned to leave except Wyatt. He sat on his horse, smirking at Arianna.

"Wyatt, go! You must secure the people."

"No. I must complete my mission."

"Your mission has been canceled."

Joshua turned to look at who Arianna was speaking to.

"Your Majesty, who is that?"

Arianna's head whipped round, looking Joshua in the eyes. "Wyatt Redwood? He's one of the guards who stepped forward to compete for the title of Captain of the Royal Guard."

Joshua's eyes grew large and he shook his head.

"He is not one of my men. I have never seen him before this moment."

Arianna felt dizzy for a moment.

"What do you mean?"

"I mean, he is an imposter."

They both turned to Wyatt again, who was still mounted on his horse and he began to laugh.

"So, you have figured out that I am not a guard? Well, I shouldn't say I'm not a guard. I am. I am just not one of your guards."

Arianna set her jaw and said firmly, "Who do you guard?"

"I think you know, little queenie. It sent me here to infiltrate your guards. It seems as though your fickle boyfriend foiled that plan."

Wyatt raised his hand and they began to glow black. He made

as if to throw the spell at Joshua, but Arianna leaped in front of him, throwing her white magic at him. Her spell blasted straight through his and hit him square in the chest. Wyatt fell to the ground.

Arianna and Joshua raced over to his side, where he lay motionless. He was still alive, but barely. Joshua lifted his head, and Arianna spoke.

"Did the Dark Figure send you?"

Wyatt's broken body began to shake with laughter.

"Of course. And now I have the highest honor to die for my master."

With that, he drew a shuddering breath and went still. Arianna stood in shock, staring at him. Joshua dropped Wyatt's head back to the ground, and quickly was at her side, embracing her, he picked her up and carried her back to the castle, where she started screaming.

Adasser came running around the corner, followed by Charlie. They both looked from Joshua to Arianna and back, trying to figure out what had happened. Abigail and Tanelia came running into the castle behind them.

"Tanelia, what has happened?" Adasser could not hide the concern in his voice.

"Sir, I was taking the human to the designated hiding place, when the former captain stumbled upon us, racing back this way. He informed me that the pirate is heading this way. We put the human on the back of his horse and we came back as quickly as we could. We found that the queen had already started getting the guards together to send out on their quest. When she issued the order to secure the kingdom, one of the contestants revealed himself to be a traitor. He is a guard to the Dark Figure. He tried to attack the former captain and the queen fired a spell back. Quite impressively, it not only hit the spell, but went straight through and knocked the traitor off of the horse, and killed him."

Adasser was at Arianna's side instantly, trying to take her out of Joshua's arms. They started arguing as to who was going to take care of her.

Meanwhile, Abigail sidled up to Tanelia and grumbled, "We all have names, you know, you could use them."

Tanelia gave her a look of disgust. "Why bother? You're all going to die anyway. After that, no one will remember your name in a few decades."

Tanelia walked away, trying to pull Adasser away. "Sir, I need my next set of orders."

"Tanelia, I am busy right now. Wait for me in the courtyard."

Tanelia seemed surprised by his response. "Since when do you care so much about humans?"

Adasser stopped, turned and looked her dead on. "Since I found out that she is my granddaughter. Now, go!"

Tanelia's stunned reaction told him that Armen had not broken the news that Arianna had elven blood as of yet. He wasn't sure whether that was a good tactic or not. On one hand, it might help to spur the elves into action to come to the aid of Eumetadotos. On the other hand, it could cause them to doubt the truth and question whether it was true or it was just a tactic to get them to help.

Adasser turned back to Joshua and instructed him to take Arianna to her room. Abigail and Charlie followed Joshua. Adasser then turned and went out to speak with Tanelia.

He met her out in the courtyard. She was standing in the middle, looking angrier than he had ever seen her.

"You mated with a human?"

"Her grandmother. I was in love with her. I am still in love with her to this day. She became pregnant before her wedding. I never knew that Alexandra was mine. I don't know if she even knew. I never spoke to her again after her wedding."

Tanelia looked livid.

"How could you? You could have had an elf who would have given you children who would not die. Now, you have tainted your bloodline and will have to watch all of your descendants die. Adasser, how could you have been so foolish?"

"I was not foolish, Tanelia. I love that woman still. I always will. You should know how it feels to watch the one you love to pledge to marry another."

Tanelia turned away.

"Do not speak of him. He turned me away to marry a human, only to have that human reject him. Now, he has joined that disgusting pirate. I saw him, Adasser. He's leading them right here. Why would he do that? Does he hate her that much?"

Adasser looked surprised at that development.

"I don't know. I don't understand this at all."

"She broke his heart. He's probably going to exact his revenge on her. I don't understand. Why would he do that? If he killed her, he would forfeit his immortality. Do you think that he's going to have Iron Demon try to kill her?"

"Tanelia, I have no idea what his plans are."

"I just don't understand why he would join forces with that vile human."

Adasser gave her a look to silence her.

"I do not know what Ellavorn's plans are, Tanelia. I do know that we have to protect Eumetadotos. But first, I must tend to my granddaughter."

Tanelia laughed coldly. "I never thought I would hear you say those words, Adasser."

"Well, now you have. I expect you to either help here or return to the Forest Glen. Either way, I do not wish to hear you make any more disparaging comments in regards to my family. If you do decide to return to the Glen, I expect you to not say anything about what you have learned here."

"You expect me to keep all of this a secret from Armen and our people?"

"Armen knows. He will decide when is the appropriate time to tell everyone else. Do you understand?"

Tanelia clenched her jaw tightly. "I understand. Against my better judgement, I will not say anything on my return."

Adasser nodded and turned to go back into the castle. He was surprised to notice Tanelia follow him.

"So, you will be staying?"

"I don't have much of a choice. One of our own is in danger."

Adasser smiled. Tanelia may be a strong warrior, but she was extremely loyal to her people. He was glad to see that the loyalty extended to those who were not pure-blooded elves.

Chapter 41

Adasser and Tanelia turned the corner of the corridor leading to Arianna's chambers. They could hear her screaming as soon as they turned.

"The queen needs to gain control."

Adasser gave her an incredulous look.

"It was the first casualty at her hands. I remember the first time you killed, Tanelia. You were not that far off from where she is now. From what I remember, both of you killed accidentally."

Tanelia fell silent and followed Adasser into Arianna's room.

Holding her hands, Adasser spoke to her kindly.

"Arianna, look at me."

She looked at Adasser and started wailing again.

"I killed him, Adasser! I killed him! How am I any different than those bandits that killed my parents? I took a life!"

Before Adasser could say anything, another voice answered.

"You had to. He was going to kill your friend. You saved your friend's life. I saw the whole thing, Your Majesty. You did what you had to do."

Arianna relaxed slightly, "But I still killed a person."

Tanelia knelt beside her. "You killed in a battle. It was a life or death situation. You killed saving the life of someone good. You took out part of the evil in the world. You have nothing to feel badly about."

"How can I not feel badly?"

"Your Majesty, from what I have gathered, you are at war. With whom, I do not yet know. But, it is a war all the same. You cannot mourn evil. You will not survive if you do."

Arianna looked into the eyes of this elf who seemed to hate her from the very core of her being. She couldn't understand why she was being kind to her.

"Why do you care how I feel? You seemed to hate me on sight."

Tanelia stood and walked to Arianna's window. She stood looking out as though her eyes were searching for something.

"No, I hated you before I saw you."

Understanding hit Arianna hard.

"You hate humans."

Tanelia blew out a puff of air.

"I do and I will not apologize for that."

Arianna shot a steely glance at her.

"Why?"

Tanelia met Arianna's gaze with one just as steely.

"Why wouldn't I? Your kind is an infestation. You bring with you your wars and your violence. This leaves many dead in the process. Then, you start the entire cycle again. It's sickening. You all die in the end anyway. Why bother getting close to you at all?"

"Because not all of us are bad. Not all of us want war. I want to live peacefully. I don't want to go to war. This was thrust upon me. All of this. I would love to go back to being a princess and not having all of this responsibility on my shoulders. I would love for my parents to be back with me. I did not ask for this. I did not ask to be born human."

"Or a three quarters human as it may be?"

"You know?"

"A human could not have produced that spell. Not many elves could produce a spell that powerful. I figured it out before Adasser confirmed that he was your grandfather. I just didn't know whose lineage you followed."

Arianna fell silent. She looked at Adasser. She knew that there were no laws against elves and humans mating. She just didn't know how deeply the prejudices in the Elven race ran. She was contemplating what implications this meant for him.

"I'm not going to tell Adasser's secret, if that's what you're thinking. I'm not a fool. He's the best warrior elf that we have. We need him."

"Armen knows. He said that there are no laws against elves mating with humans."

"No written ones. Adasser knows the hatred that we hold for humans. He would be labeled an outcast should the rest of the elves find out."

"It is a small price to pay, Tanelia."

"Wait, elves would disown one of their own should they fall in love with a human?"

"Yes."

"No matter who the elf is?"

Tanelia looked her straight in the eyes and said, "No matter who it may be."

Arianna looked at Adasser, who would not meet her gaze.

"But, it's not a law!"

Tanelia scoffed. "What do you not understand? Most elves hate humans. Your precious prince was no different not that long ago. He didn't even want to save your life. He begged Armen to let you die."

"Tanelia! That is quite enough!"

"Why? Do you not want to hurt her feelings? Don't you think that she deserves to know?"

"I already knew."

"What?"

"You see, Ellavorn and I never kept secrets from each other. He told me how he used to hate humans. He told me how he didn't want to save my life. How he wanted me to die. He hated me without even knowing me. I don't know what happened that day, but it changed his heart. I am glad for that. I have been glad for that every day since. I just never knew how deeply rooted the hatred was with your race. Just because we are different from you, you hate us? It makes no sense."

"I explained it to you. Humans are violent. They destroy, that's what they do. Why would we want to pair ourselves with such vile creatures?"

"Because not all humans are like that. Some are quite kind. The people in this room are prime examples. You have not witnessed how they have been trying so hard to find a way to fight this figure that keeps threatening my kingdom. We've been trying to put a stop to it."

"Why should elves care about that?"

Adasser stepped forward. "Because, Tanelia, if we do not help them, this figure could come after us next."

"Adasser, do you really think that we would not be able to defeat this figure?"

"No, I don't, and neither does Armen. Eumetadotos is in danger. Like it or not, we have lived in peace with them for centuries. We are allies. You know it, and so does every other elf in the Glen."

"It still doesn't mean that we should have to help them."

Arianna spoke up. "Which part are you not understanding? Allies means that we defend each other."

Tanelia sneered at Arianna and put her hand on one of the daggers. "You may be part elf, but you are still mostly human. I would not have any problems ridding the world of more human blood."

Arianna put her hands up and they started glowing white. "You are welcome to try. But, you saw what my magic can do back in the courtyard."

Tanelia smirked at her. "Now, you are speaking like a warrior."

Arianna looked confused. "All of this was to get me to act like a warrior?"

"No. I do hate humans. That part will never change.

However, you do have to think and act like a warrior if you plan to win this battle."

Adasser sat on the bed, looking extremely frustrated.

"Tanelia, if you are going to be of any help to us, you must put your prejudice aside. Not all humans are bad. Some are actually quite good."

"But, Adasser –"

"Need I remind you that not all elves are good, either?"

Tanelia stopped talking immediately and looked annoyed. "I need no reminders," she said sharply.

"They need our help, Tanelia. Just like some others needed mine at one point in time. Do I need to remind you?"

Tanelia drew her dagger quickly. Arianna was surprised at the speed with which she moved. Just as quickly, Arianna threw a spell. The magic hit the dagger, disintegrating it immediately.

Tanelia sneered at her again.

"That was my favorite dagger!"

"You shouldn't have pulled it out."

Tanelia gave her a threatening look and turned back to Adasser.

"I told you before, I need no reminders."

Tanelia turned and stormed out of the room, slamming the door behind her.

Chapter 42

Arianna looked at Adasser. "What was that all about?"

"I need to go after her."

"Fine, I will have someone get her chambers ready if she wishes to stay."

Adasser nodded and left the room.

Arianna sat down on the chair and looked up at Joshua, who had stayed quiet the whole time.

"You came back."

Joshua looked at the floor. In his civilian clothes, he didn't look as commanding as he did in his guards' armor. He looked sheepishly at the floor.

"I had to. I couldn't leave without warning you of the danger."

"Thank you for coming back. Is this a temporary stay or will it be more permanent? Because we could use your help. You are the best fighter that I have ever seen. If you want your job back, it is yours."

Joshua looked at Arianna and took a deep breath. He looked around at Abigail and Charlie, who were looking at him, awaiting his response.

"Could we have a little privacy, please?"

Abigail and Charlie both nodded hesitantly and started to head towards the door. Abigail turned back to Arianna and said, "If you need us, we're right outside the door."

"Thank you."

They left and closed the door behind them.

"Your Majesty, I am sorry for leaving the way that I did."

"Joshua, please, titles aren't necessary between us."

His eyes fell to the ground.

"I am no longer the captain, I am no longer your fiancé. I acted foolishly. I do not deserve your kindness."

"Everyone deserves kindness. You have not answered my question."

Joshua looked up at her with sad eyes.

"I would like very much to come back as Captain, although, I do not deserve it."

Arianna smiled.

"There is no one more deserving of the title."

Joshua gave a faltering smile.

"I am sorry for leaving."

"Why did you leave?"

Joshua ran his hand through his hair.

"I don't know. I was so angry. You know I do not approve of magic, yet, I have been sworn to protect that very thing which I despise. I feel genuinely conflicted. And again, I have feelings for you, yet, you can conjure magic. Is it possible to love someone and yet hate them at the same time?"

"You hate me?" Arianna looked wounded.

"I don't hate you. I shouldn't have said that. I hate that you do magic. I could never bring myself to hate you."

"But, magic is part of who I am now, Joshua. I cannot change that. Things will not go back to the way that they were after we win this war. I know more about my bloodline now and I cannot change that, nor do I want to."

Joshua nodded.

Arianna continued. "I want you to come back as Captain. You are the best person for the job. I need you to come back."

"And what about our engagement?"

"That, we can discuss later. I am not in a position to plan a wedding in the first place. We have to prepare for an attack and a war. I also have to figure out how to locate the wizard's descendants to help with this war. That will involve using magic. I need you to accept that."

"I understand. I will do what I can. I will defend Eumetadotos by any means."

"Thank you. Let's make the announcement and find Adasser and Tanelia."

"I don't like her. I don't like her at all. How can we trust her? She hates humans. Why would she agree to help us when she hates us?"

"I don't know. It does seem suspicious to me as well. Do you think that she could be a spy?"

"No, I don't think so. Adasser trusts her completely. She's been his second in command for a very long time."

"You are too trusting."

"Adasser has not given me any reason to doubt his judgement. Besides, I am his flesh and blood. Do you think that he would want to hurt me?"

"You are also part human."

"And he is the reason that I have elven blood running through my veins. He and my grandmother had an affair. Do you not remember Tanelia saying that elves will label those who have an affair with humans as outcasts? He has more to lose than we do by acknowledging me as his descendant."

"How do you know that she won't go back to the Forest Glen and announce it?"

"I don't. But, I trust Adasser. If he trusts her, that is good enough for me."

Joshua shook his head.

"If that is how you want it, so be it."

Arianna looked at him suspiciously.

"You're not going to argue with me?"

"I want to. I want to wholeheartedly, but you have been right all along. I have to learn to trust you. I don't know how you knew that the threat of Iron Demon's attack is real, but you were right. You were right about a lot of things. I haven't been supportive of you and your…gifts. I have to learn to listen to you and to trust you. I will try to do that. I promise."

Arianna looked at him suspiciously again.

"You have come around too easily. You are usually more

stubborn than this."

Joshua smiled an eerie smile at her. A cloud of black smoke swirled around him. Arianna screamed, alerting Abigail and Charlie that something was wrong. They both crashed through the door as the smoke settled and the Dark Figure stood before them, cackling. Behind it was Joshua's unconscious body. Arianna screamed again, unsure if he was dead or alive.

The Figure's cackling quieted down.

"Don't worry, little queenie. He's still alive…for now. I'm surprised to say the same about you. I would have thought that my curse would have killed you by now. Did your elf friend save you again? He won't be able to keep you alive forever. Not like the last time."

"What do you mean, the last time?"

Arianna's eyes darted from Joshua to the Figure, trying to get a look under the hood, but it kept slinking away just far enough that she couldn't see who was under it.

"Haven't you figured it out yet? I tried to kill you before, when you were a child."

Flashbacks of the pain that she felt during that fever rushed through Arianna's mind. Her unexplained illness finally had an explanation.

"You? You cursed me?"

The Figure cackled again.

"It took you long enough to figure it out. Too bad your elf prince isn't here to help you out this time."

"You orchestrated this whole thing to get Ellavorn to leave so that you could try to kill me and get the throne?"

It cackled once again.

"You're figuring it out, queenie."

"Let Joshua go."

Another cackle.

"Why would I do that?"

"He has nothing to do with any of this."

"Oh, but he does. You still love him. He will be very useful."

"No! Let him go!" Arianna's eyes began to fill with tears. "Please! Let him go!"

Adasser and Tanelia came crashing into the door. A flash of white soared past Arianna, hitting the Figure in the left shoulder. The cackling finally stopped, replaced by a scream.

"You will regret that!"

It turned to Joshua. Arianna screamed again, running to throw herself between Joshua and whatever the Figure was going to throw at him. She threw her hands out and magic soared at the figure, hitting it in the same shoulder. A howl erupted.

It was now flanked with Arianna to its front, blocking Joshua's body, and Adasser and Tanelia behind it. Seeing that it had no other choice, it disappeared in a cloud of smoke, leaving Joshua behind.

Arianna threw herself on top of Joshua's body, sobbing. She grabbed his shirt and began to shake him.

"Wake up! Please, Joshua, wake up!"

Adasser and Tanelia were next to her a second later, followed by Abigail and Charlie. Adasser lifted her off of Joshua and placed her on the bed.

"Stay here!"

"I want to see what is going on! I want to help!"

"You can help by staying here. Abigail, Charlie, make sure that she stays here."

They both went and sat on either side of her, holding her hands.

All three of them watched as Adasser and Tanelia whispered back and forth over Joshua's body, shaking their heads.

"Tanelia, you have to save him. You don't understand. It will destroy her if he dies. We need her to be in her best state of mind. It is the only way to win this war."

"Adasser, we can't. We are warriors, protectors. There is only one elf that can heal him and from the sounds of it, he will not be willing to help. Without him, he's lost to us."

Adasser's eyes glazed with tears, a sight that is so uncommon that Tanelia gasped.

"Please don't tell me that you have grown to care for this human as well?"

"Tanelia, he is a good man. You cannot understand this yet, but I hope as you get to know them, you will have a change of heart. They are not the despicable creatures that the elves make them out to be. These humans are kind. They want peace."

"I can't believe this, Adasser."

Adasser put his hand affectionately on Tanelia's shoulder.

"I do not expect you to understand just now. But, I hope that you will in time. For now, we must move his body to his room."

Adasser grabbed Joshua under his armpits and Tanelia grabbed his waist. They began to move him to his chambers. Arianna saw this and began to sob uncontrollably. After Joshua was moved, both elves came back into her chambers. Adasser sat next to her and embraced her lovingly. Tanelia looked on in stony silence.

"Arianna, I know that you are distraught over Captain Oakford. But, I need you to settle down. He is not dead, merely sleeping."

"Like a sleeping curse?"

"Yes. It is a powerful one. This figure knows what it is doing."

"There has to be a way that I can help!"

"Yes, you can help by focusing on defeating this figure. If you defeat it, you will break the curses on you and Captain Oakford. There is only one other way to help him, but it looks hopeless."

"Adasser, what is it? I will do anything to help him."

"Ellavorn."

Arianna stilled. "What do you mean?"

"Ellavorn is the most powerful healer that has ever lived. If we don't defeat this figure, only his power will help."

Arianna felt as though she had been hit in the stomach. Her

breath rushed from her lungs.

"But, he is with Iron Demon."

"Yes."

"Do you think that he has other plans, Adasser?" Arianna asked hopefully.

"I do not know, Arianna. But, I sincerely hope so."

Chapter 43

Arianna cracked the door to Joshua's room. She pulled up a chair and took in the surroundings. The room was practically empty, due to his leaving, but a few remnants remained here and there. His armor was in the corner. His helmet was sitting on the bureau. She walked over and picked it up and hugged it. It still smelled of him. She let the tears flow freely, and sat back down, leaving the helmet on her lap.

She leaned over and grasped his hand. She leaned in and whispered in his ear.

"Joshua, if you can hear me, please, come back to us. Don't let go. We need you. Please, hold on."

She knew that she wouldn't get a response, but she still felt disappointed when nothing happened.

"I will fix this, Joshua. I promise. I will bring you back, if it's the last thing I do."

Arianna stood up, put the helmet on the chair and made her way down to the dining hall.

After dinner, Arianna and her friends made their way to the Odigós Domátio to plan their next course of action.

Tanelia looked around the room in awe.

"This can't possibly be—"

"Oh, but it is, Tanelia."

"That's impossible. It was sealed, Adasser. Only the one from the prophesy –"

"I know, Tanelia. Arianna was the one to open it."

Tanelia looked at Arianna in shock.

"That isn't possible! You're a human!"

"So was the wizard, Tanelia," Adasser pointed out. "This is the wizard's lair, need I remind you? It would make sense that a human would be the one to open it. Especially if that human is the child born with violet eyes."

Tanelia turned in surprise. She looked at Arianna's eyes and gasped. In all of the commotion, she had forgotten of the rumor that the queen had eyes the color of the midnight sky. She hadn't thought to look.

Arianna felt uncomfortable with her staring at her. She shifted her feet and her eyes darted to Adasser.

"Adasser, have you sent for Armen?" Arianna asked.

"I have. He will be here at any moment. He believes that we have located the appropriate spell."

Tanelia looked confused. "What spell have you located that you are planning on performing?"

"We have found the spell to locate which realm to which the wizard escaped."

Tanelia's eyebrows rose in surprise.

"And you are going to locate him? He's long dead by now."

"But, his descendants will be able to help, Tanelia," said Adasser.

"Why would they? After the way that they were treated, you would be lucky if they didn't kill you on sight."

"We can hope for the best, Tanelia."

"And if that hope fails?"

"We will have to decide another course of action."

"But, you think that finding someone who was banished over a century ago will help? Do you really think that he would be so quick to forgive? He was banished."

"We can try. Tanelia, I don't think that you realize how dire the circumstances are."

"Yes, you have told me. It could be the end of Eumetadotos." She leaned over to look at the spell that Adasser had open on the altar. She smirked. "There still stands another problem. It says that a human must perform this part here. You don't have any humans to perform that part."

Adasser gave her an amused smile. "Oh, but we do." He indicated Abigail and Charlie.

Tanelia gave him a look of disbelief. "What do you mean? Can these humans perform magic as well? Did you father them too?"

Adasser's eyes grew furious. "That is quite enough, Tanelia. No, they are not my kin. They do, however, possess magical abilities. Young Charlie can read all of the spell books in this room. Miss Abigail can read a few as well. Mostly the Alchemy books. She will be preparing the potion, and Charlie will assist Armen and me with the spell."

Tanelia looked over at Abigail and Charlie, still not believing what she was hearing.

"I don't believe it. The wizard left no descendants here. It is impossible."

"You know as well as I do that some humans possess magical abilities. The wizard could detect the magic within them. That is who he would decide who to train. It did not have to be his own kin. Young Charlie has grown quite good at casting spells."

"I'll believe it when I see it."

Adasser smiled, whispered something to Charlie and said, "Go ahead, show her."

Charlie looked unsure. He took in Tanelia's sleek body and remembered how quickly she moved. There was no doubt in his mind that she could kill him without a second glance.

"I knew that he couldn't do it," Tanelia sneered.

Adasser put a hand on Charlie's shoulder. "Go ahead, Charlie. She will not hurt you. I promise."

Tanelia gave them an uneasy look.

Charlie held up his hand and said shakily, "Siopí!"

Tanelia tried to laugh, but no noise came out. Her face grew surprised, then dangerous. Charlie ran behind Adasser.

"Tanelia! Enough! You wanted him to demonstrate. I told him the spell to use. I am growing weary of your comments. Leave the boy alone. The spell should only last an hour. Now, I must go and wait for Armen. You are free to join me, if you wish."

Tanelia shot a look full of daggers at Charlie, who ran to hide behind Arianna this time. Adasser chuckled and took Tanelia's arm, leading her back up the stairs. Tanelia turned to look at the group one more time and gave Charlie another murderous look.

He ducked behind Arianna again. Arianna couldn't help but suppress a smile.

Once Adasser and Tanelia were up the stairs, Charlie stepped from behind Arianna and gave her a fearful look.

"Your Majesty, she's going to kill me! She's not happy. She's scary!"

Arianna knelt before him.

"Charlie, she will not harm a hair on your head. I will not allow it, and neither will Adasser. He promised. He has not broken any promises yet, has he?"

"N-n-n-no."

"Do not fear Tanelia. I have no doubt that she is lethal on the battlefield, but something tells me that she is not so fierce with her allies."

"But, she hates humans!"

"Many elves do. But, they have never attacked us, correct?"

Charlie thought about this for a moment then looked up with a radiant smile on his face.

"No!"

"I'm sure that Tanelia does not wish to be known as the first elf to do so."

"Maybe not, Ari, but I think that Charlie is right. I think that we should be extra careful around her," Abigail interjected.

Arianna thought about it for a moment.

"Maybe you are both right. We will be extra careful. But, I

don't think we have anything to worry about. Remember, an elf cannot harm a living creature without forfeiting his or her immortality. She hates humans because of our mortality. Why would she sacrifice that which she values over all else to become that which she despises most?"

"You make a good point," Abigail said, "but, it still wouldn't hurt to be more vigilant."

Arianna stood and looked her friend in the eye. "It is always a good idea to be more vigilant, especially in these times, Abigail."

Arianna crossed the room and sat with her back against the wall. She felt sad, scared and more tired than she had ever felt in her life.

Abigail sat next to her. "Did you see Joshua before you came down?"

Arianna simply nodded.

"Was there any change?"

Arianna shook her head. She was afraid that if she spoke, that she would start crying.

Abigail put her arm around her friend and pulled her in close.

"We are going to save him, Ari. We have to."

"I have to go to the next realm, Abigail. I have to go and help to find the wizard's descendants."

"I will go with you."

"No, Abigail. You must stay here."

"Arianna! I can't stay here while you go off to some unknown land."

"You have to. I can't have anything happen to you."

"Ari, I would never forgive myself if something happened to you and I wasn't there to try to help."

"I need you to promise me something."

"Anything, Ari."

"I need you to look after Eumetadotos while I am gone, especially Joshua. Please, Abigail. I trust you more than anyone else."

Abigail gulped. "You want me to be queen?"

Arianna realized what her friend thought she was asking.

"No, I would not pass this curse onto you. You will be the acting queen. You will not take the vows to pass complete authority onto you. I will keep the curse."

"You're sure?"

Arianna nodded. "Yes. The title is cursed, not the person. I will keep the title. You will not have to deal with this."

"Ok. I promise. I will do my best to keep everyone safe. I will visit Joshua every day and I will do my best to keep him safe too."

"Thank you, Abigail. I knew that I could count on you."

"Forever and always, Ari."

Chapter 44

Arianna heard laughter coming down the stairs. She looked up and saw Adasser leading Armen and Tanelia back down the stairs. Armen kept looking at Tanelia and laughing, side-splitting laughter. Tanelia had the most murderous look on her face.

"Oh, I cannot wait to see young Charlie again and shake his hand. It is not often that we see Tanelia so quiet."

He received another dagger-filled glance, which set off another round of laughter.

"Oh, Tanelia, what is wrong? Are you at a loss for words?"

At this, he received a sneering glance, which caused even more laughter.

"I am sorry. It's just that I am not accustomed to you being so quiet. It is quite humorous to me that you cannot speak your mind and tell us all what is wrong with our plans. Maybe this will teach you to listen from time to time."

Tanelia looked incredulous.

"Don't look at me like that. You know that it is true. You tend to disregard what anyone else says in favor of your own opinion. You are very intelligent, Tanelia. You are very skilled, but you are not always correct. No one is. Now, let me look around the Odigós Domátio. It has been so long since I have been in here."

Adasser quickly walked down the rest of the stairs, looking around in awe.

"I never thought that I would see it again. It is as wonderful as the last time I saw it."

He stopped before the barrier by the potions.

"This is new. I have not seen this before. The wizard must have had some powerful potions in here. I do not recognize some of these potions."

He held up his hand, but was met by the barrier. It wavered slightly, but then stilled. Arianna looked surprised.

"It hasn't done that before."

Armen smiled. "It was reacting to my presence. I have been in this room before. My presence was felt in here when this barrier was erected."

"Does that mean that you can break it down?"

"No. This is powerful magic. It detects the wizard's bloodline. Only the heir will be able to drop this barrier."

"So, in order to get to these potions, we have to find the wizard's descendant and bring him back?"

"Yes. I'm afraid so. These potions will likely be the key to defeating this Dark Figure."

Arianna let the news sink in. She had been hoping that Armen would be able to drop the barrier and would give her news that the travel to another realm would not be necessary.

"Ok. How do we get there?"

Armen smiled. "You are just as determined as ever. That is a good thing. It will help you to accomplish this goal and, ultimately, to win this war."

Arianna just stared at Armen. She still didn't want to fight this war. She still wanted to go back in time when her parents were still alive and she was happy.

"I know what you are thinking, Arianna. I would like nothing more than to tell you that you do not have to do this. I would like to promise you that we will come out victorious. I would like to tell you that everything will go back to the way it was before this war.

"The truth is, I don't know the outcome. I can tell you that things will never be the same again. You will never be the same again. With the passage of time comes knowledge. Don't ever wish for that knowledge to be taken away from you. I don't know everything, but I do know that you are the only one with the chance to defeat this being. You are stronger than you think you are. We will do everything that we can to help you."

"Thank you, Armen. I just wish that my parents were here to help me."

Armen nodded.

"Come with me."

They walked to the altar. Armen looked at the rest of the group.

"Will you all please take leave for a moment and give us some privacy?"

They all made to leave.

"Adasser, you stay too."

Adasser looked confused, but walked back to the altar.

"My Lord?"

Armen smiled at him.

When the rest of the group had left, Armen gathered a few ingredients from the wizard's cabinets, still in awe at how the passage of time had seemed to spare everything in the room.

When he got when he needed, he laid the ingredients on the altar.

Adasser looked confused.

"My Lord? What is this for?"

"There is a well-kept secret of Elven Royals."

Armen began combining the ingredients in a bowl. When he had mashed everything into a paste, he poured in some liquid and motioned Arianna and Adasser to step closer.

"Now, I need both of you to put one of your hands the liquid together."

They both looked at him, and he smiled.

"Please, trust me."

They put their hands together and plunged them into the bowl. The air in front of them seemed to swirl. It got faster and faster. When it stopped swirling, in front of them stood smaller versions of King Jasper, Queen Alexandra and Arianna's grandmother, Elfreda.

Arianna gasped. Adasser stopped breathing for a moment.

Arianna found her voice first. "Is it really you?"

Alexandra smiled. "It is, Love."

Jasper spoke next. "We are so proud of you."

"But, I have made a mess of everything."

Alexandra looked sad. "No, Love, you haven't. You made some mistakes. But, you have worked to make amends. You are doing a wonderful job. We are so proud. We wish that we could be there with you in person to help you on your journey, Arianna, but we are with you always. We love you."

Arianna realized that tears were streaming down her face.

"I miss you both so much. It hurts so badly."

"We miss you too, Love."

Alexandra's hand moved to touch her daughter's face, but neither felt the contact, which disappointed them both.

Jasper stepped forward. "Arianna, we have always known that you are a strong woman. You can do this. This is your destiny. You must save Eumetadotos. This is what you were born to do. We love you."

Elfreda moved forward now, looking straight at Adasser, who had not taken his eyes off of her from the moment she appeared.

"Well, now, isn't this a pleasant surprise?" Elfreda said with a smile. "It took you long enough to come see me. I didn't know I had to wait until I was dead and gone for you to do so."

"Elfreda," Adasser said her name for the first time in decades.

"Yes, that is me."

"Did you know?"

"Know what, Darling?"

"Did you know that Alexandra was mine?"

Elfreda's eyes fell. "Yes."

"Why didn't you ever tell me?"

"How could I? Adasser, you were nowhere to be found. I was the queen. Do you realize what would have happened to both of us? You would have been cast out. I would have been publicly humiliated by the scandal. It would have put my kingdom at war. I could not chance that. I wanted to tell you. I could never find you. I went to our place numerous times. You never came."

"I couldn't. It hurt too much."

"You haven't been there since that night." It wasn't a question.

"No. I will not return to that spot."

Elfreda nodded. "I understand."

"I still love you."

"And I, you. I never stopped loving you. I never will, even in death, Darling."

Adasser let a single tear slid down his cheek. "I never thought I'd hear you say that again."

Elfreda smiled. She kissed him on the cheek, but like Alexandra and Arianna, neither of them felt the contact.

Elfreda turned to Arianna.

"My lovely granddaughter, I am sorry that I never told you or your mother the truth. You deserved to know. I did love your grandfather, just in a different way, and never as much as my true love. We had a wonderful life together. Please don't ever doubt that."

"Grandma, I am in a dilemma much like yours. What do I

do?"

"Child, I cannot answer that question for you. You have to follow your heart. I know that you love them both. I have seen that. The love that both of them have for you is pure as well. Whoever you choose will be a good choice."

"Grandma, it says that if I do not marry within a year, a curse will befall the kingdom. What will happen?"

Elfreda grew serious. "Child, that curse is nothing compared to what you are facing now. The kingdom will fall into a famine and drought if you are unmarried after a year. If you do not win this war, none of that will matter. Save your kingdom before you go making choices of the heart. Your kingdom is more important. Oh, and Arianna,"

"Yes, Grandma?"

"Please do not choose that awful Prince Ethan, or that Blubbering Buffoon." Elfreda smiled.

Alexandra stepped forward. "Thank you, Adasser for taking care of her. We must go now. Our time is done. We love you, Arianna."

With that, all three figures vanished.

"No, Mother! Wait!"

Arianna reached out for her mother once more, but she had gone. She collapsed in a heap, sobbing uncontrollably. Adasser slid next to her, and pulled her to him and the two cried together.

Chapter 45

Armen gave the two a few minutes to pull themselves together before saying, gently.

"Come, now, it is time to start working on this spell."

As Adasser and Arianna stood, and composed themselves, Armen ascended the stairs to call the rest of the group back down.

"Arianna, are you ok?"

"Yes. Are you?"

"I think so. I had no idea that Royals could do that."

Arianna smiled. "I guess there are secrets that even you don't know."

"I have never doubted that," Adasser smiled back at her. "Did this help you?"

"I think it did. I know that my parents are proud of me now."

"Why wouldn't they be proud of you, Arianna?"

"Well, I have made so many mistakes from the beginning."

"Everyone makes mistakes. I have never seen someone try so hard to correct them. Your parents are correct. If anyone can do this, it is you."

"Thank you, Adasser." Arianna hugged him.

"Well, look at that. You really are a human lover."

"Well, look who has her voice back. Careful, Tanelia, I will have Young Charlie silence you again."

Tanelia closed her mouth.

Armen smiled, but did not laugh this time. It seemed that even he was a bit fearful of Tanelia.

"Let us get to work on this spell. I read the directions. It seems as though this is one of the few spells that elves cannot do on their own. The potion must be made by human hands. There is also a part of the spell that must be said by a human. I can work on the other part of the spell."

A look of concern crossed Arianna's face. "How will we get back?"

Everyone turned and looked at her. Everyone had been so concerned with getting to the other realm that no one thought of the return trip.

"Well? How will we get back? It will not do any good to us if we find the descendant, but cannot get back."

"Arianna makes an excellent point," Armen said. "Have not one of you thought of the return trip?"

They all looked at each other. He sighed.

"We do not know if magic works in this realm. This means that Abigail, Charlie and I must stay behind."

"Abigail was staying anyway. She is to take care of Eumetadotos while I am gone."

Armen nodded. "I will see that this is how it is carried out."

"You also know that I will not be crossing realms today. Captain Iron Demon shall be arriving tomorrow. I cannot leave my kingdom with the threat of an imminent attack. We have to figure out how to cross the realm and I will go after the battle."

Armen nodded in understanding.

“A wise choice. Now, we must figure out how to get you back.”

Charlie spoke up. “Can you do the spell any number of times?”

Armen looked at him. “Yes. You can do any spell as many times as you want, so long as you have the ingredients for it.”

“Well, why don’t we just do the spell every day? They can come back to the place where they transport and we can just do the spell, and they come through?”

Armen chuckled. “Such a simple solution, yet, it is the perfect solution. Young Charlie, you are quite intelligent.”

Charlie beamed.

“Now, we must first locate the wizard’s realm.”

Armen pulled out several bottles.

“Armen,” Arianna broke the silence this time.

“Yes?”

“Why doesn’t anyone refer to the wizard by his name?”

Armen froze. “It had been forbidden to say his name for so long. I don’t know that many would remember his name.”

“Do you?”

“Yes, I would never forget the name of one of my closest friends.”

“What is his name?”

Armen smiled, indicating that he was not going to tell that secret just yet.

He stood, combining bottles and mixing potions and dry ingredients. When he finished, he had a beautiful purple potion sitting in front of him. He moved to the back of the room and came back with a cloak.

"What is that?" Arianna asked. The cloak was a beautiful sky blue with gold around the collar and sleeves. It looked as though it were made of silk, but the way the fabric shimmered, she couldn't be sure.

"This is the wizard's cloak."

"Where did you find that? We've been all over this room. We never found that."

Armen smiled brightly. "Arianna, you forget that I spent many hours in this very room. I know most of its secrets."

Armen laid the cloak on the altar and dripped a few drops of the purple potion onto the fabric. It glimmered a beautiful silver color. Armen smiled.

"It will work."

"What will work?"

"The locator potion. Now, Abigail, you need to make the transport potion."

Armen stood with her and instructed her carefully how to make it, helping to clear up any instructions that didn't make sense. Soon, the potion was complete. Abigail looked down at the blue liquid.

"That is what is going to get them to another realm?"

"Yes, it is."

Armen picked up the cloak and placed it carefully on the floor, and indicated for Abigail to pour some of the liquid on the cloak.

"Now, Charlie, come here."

Charlie stepped forward.

"You must read this part of the spell. I will finish it. Then, we must both speak together the spell, 'Anoichtí Pýli.' It is very important that we speak those words together."

"What happens if we don't?"

Armen looked at him sheepishly. "We could make the room explode."

Charlie gulped.

"Together?"

"Together."

They completed the spell, and together, they yelled, "Anoichtí Pýli!"

The air over the cloak seemed to shimmer, then swirl. Suddenly, a portal opened up. On the other side, they could see buildings. They seemed to be houses, but they were all connected. There were also roads, but they were paved in what seemed like a single, black stone with yellow and white lines painted on them. It seemed to be a strange place.

"What is that place?" Arianna wondered out loud.

"That is where he traveled. Now, we have to figure out the name of his descendant."

"How do we do that?"

Armen pulled out another flask of liquid. He poured a few drops onto the cloak and said, "Find the living descendant of Aldore."

"Aldore?"

Armen smiled. "Yes, that was his name."

A silver mist swirled next to the portal. It opened what looked like a looking glass. There was no sound to the scene, but it showed the face of an old man. He looked kind. He was smiling at someone. The scene panned out and there were twin teenagers, a boy and a girl. They were throwing brightly colored orbs that seemed to be filled with water at each other. As the orbs burst, they were laughing. The man's head threw back in a silent chuckle.

The mist closed the picture and swirled around Armen's head. He smiled and nodded.

"You need to find Magus."

Chapter 46

Arianna spent the night in Joshua's chambers, sitting in the chair. She dozed off a few times, but never for long. She was anticipating the next day. Iron Demon's crew was scheduled to arrive that day.

Arianna heard a sound outside. It sounded like hundreds of marching feet and something being rolled down the road. She looked out the window of Joshua's chambers and saw that Iron Demon and his crew were, indeed, preparing for an attack on the castle. They had rolled the cannons through the kingdom, and they were now preparing to send cannonballs flying towards the castle.

She tore away from her window, screaming. She raced through the hallways, banging on doors, trying to get everyone up. Abigail, Charlie, Tanelia, Adasser and Armen all bolted from their rooms at the sound of the urgency in her voice.

Abigail saw the fear in her eyes first. "Ari, what's wrong? What's happened?"

"Iron Demon is here. He's preparing for an attack. We must get everyone who is left out of the castle without him knowing!"

"Ok, how do we get everyone out?"

"Run! Alert everyone that you can. Do not sound the alarms. It will let them know that we know that they are here. If we can get everyone out, we might be able to surprise them with a counter attack. Get them all out through the tunnels under the castle. He won't be able to track them. When we get everyone out, we all meet in the dining area with all of the guards."

Everyone agreed and set off running in different directions, yelling and banging on doors. Arianna fled down a hallway, and had gathered many of the kitchen staff. She was leading them through the Grand Hall when the first cannonball hit the side of the castle. No damage had been done inside, but it shook the castle, and she knew that another blast like that would blow a hole in the wall.

"Run! Quickly! Follow me!"

She took off running as fast as she could towards one of the tunnels. She knew that this one would lead them far from the castle and to safety.

The servants followed closely behind her, eager to get out, but concerned for their queen as well.

They finally reached the tunnel, and Arianna opened the entrance. ""Go quickly. This will lead you out to the woods surrounding Eumetadotos. Stay there. Set up camp until I send someone to alert you that it is safe to return."

"Your Majesty, what if no one comes?" It was the master chef who had looked at her with such disdain that day in the library. That day, she could feel the animosity towards her rolling off of him in waves. Today, he looked scared. Whatever ill feelings that he held toward her on that day were gone, replaced by a trust in his queen and a fear for his life.

"Wait for two days. If no one comes, then you make your way to Polýtimos and make them aware of the situation. Tell them that you need sanctuary. They are our allies. They will help."

He stepped forward. He came directly in front of her and put his hands up to touch her, but thought again and dropped his hands and instead, dropped to a genuflect in front of her.

"Thank you, Your Majesty. It has been an honor to serve in the castle under you. I hope to return quickly and to serve you for many more years to come."

He then turned and started ushering people into the tunnel and to safety. "Your Majesty, please, run. Do what you need to do to save yourself and all of us."

Arianna made several trips to several of the tunnels with different groups of servants. Once she was sure that everyone was safe and knew where to go, she began to make her way to the dining hall to meet with the rest of the group. There, they would devise a plan.

Arianna rushed through the Great Hall on her way to check one of the tunnels. She was about to turn the corner when the door crashed open, and she felt a tingling sensation go down her spine. She stopped dead in her tracks and hesitated before she turned around. When she did, her heart dropped to her feet. In front of her, dressed in pirate garb, stood Ellavorn.

He was staring at her with a look of amusement on his face. She couldn't tell what amused him, and she didn't want to break the silence, so she began circling him, and they continued their staring contest for a moment longer. Arianna finally gathered her strength and found the courage to speak.

"So, you've come to – do what, Ellavorn?"

Ellavorn smiled at her. It wasn't a friendly smile, but it wasn't a menacing smile either. For the first time, Arianna had no idea what to expect from him. It scared her.

"Do you mean to exact your revenge on me? If so, why go to this length? Why hurt my people? They have done you no wrong."

Ellavorn's face wavered a little, betraying his emotions. It only lasted a second.

"I do not wish revenge."

"Then what? Why would you go and join a pirate's crew – and Iron Demon of all pirates?"

"My reasons are my own."

"You Elves with your riddles! What do you mean to do with me? I'm sure that Iron Demon has plans. But, Ellavorn, please, I must get my people to safety. They are helpless right now."

"My orders, along with the rest of the crew are to find you and bring you to Iron Demon."

"Ellavorn, please, let me save my people."

Ellavorn's head turned slightly, as though he were listening to someone approach. He turned his face back to Arianna's and urgently said, "Run!"

Arianna didn't think twice. She turned and raced around the corner. She didn't get very far when she ran straight into a big, burly pirate. He grinned a menacing grin and grabbed her around the waist.

He hauled her back into the Great Hall, where Ellavorn had been joined by Iron Demon and a few of his crew. They turned to see who had entered the room, and, simultaneously, Iron Demon's face broke into a smile of triumph, and Ellavorn's fell slightly in despair.

The pirate placed Arianna on her feet in front of the treacherous captain and Iron Demon looked her over. A stabbing pain began to develop in Arianna's stomach. She had waited too long to take the elixir today. She tried not to wince, but Iron Demon saw it and mistook her pain for fear.

He laughed a maniacal laugh and began to walk in circles around her, looking her up and down as one would a horse at auction.

"So, this is the queen? Such a little waif. It should be easy to kill you."

Arianna's back stiffened, and she glanced at Ellavorn. His face gave away nothing as to what he was feeling.

Iron Demon continued to circle her, assessing how easy this kill would be.

"Why do you want to kill me?" Arianna's voice sounded regal, with no hint of the fear she was feeling.

"Why, so that I can take your throne, little queen."

"My throne? Why would you want to rule this kingdom?"

Iron Demon stopped behind her and pressed himself against her back. He hissed into her ear, "Wealth. Eumetadotos is very wealthy. I want that wealth. I am a pirate. I collect it. Haven't you heard?"

He slinked back a little and continued circling her again. He finally decided that he had played with his prey enough and stopped, looked at the pirate who had caught her and said, "Kill her."

A plan formed in Arianna's head immediately.

"Wait!" Arianna exclaimed. "If you want to rule Eumetadotos, you can't simply kill me. I must abdicate the throne to you. You cannot simply kill me and take it. The throne has certain rules that come with it."

Ellavorn gave her an incredulous look, trying to figure out

how she could so easily abdicate her throne to this monster. He simply shook his head in disgust.

Iron Demon sauntered over to her again. "Why should I believe you? You could just be saying this in order for me to spare your life."

Arianna looked at him. "Who says that I'm not? However, if I do not dictate to whom I abdicate my throne, it will automatically set itself on the next living member of my family. I have heard awful stories of this man. I do not wish to allow him to rule my kingdom."

Iron Demon burst out laughing. "Could he possibly be more horrible than I?"

"I have heard stories of you as well. You are quite treacherous. However, this man makes you look like a bunny rabbit."

Iron Demon's face began to turn bright red in anger. "How dare you! I should kill you now with my own blade!" He drew his sword and swung it at her, stopping short of her neck.

"Would you chance that? You want to be king of my kingdom, don't you? Would you risk what I am saying to be a lie?"

Arianna could see the struggle in Iron Demon's eyes. He lowered his sword and grabbed her arm.

"Fine. Go on, then, abdicate your throne."

"Not so fast. It can't be done here. Besides, you're right. I do wish to spare my own life. As well as anyone who is left in this castle. If I abdicate my throne to you. You must give me your word as a pirate that you will spare us all."

"You want me to just let you walk out of the castle, free?"

"Yes," Arianna's eyes glittered in defiance.

"You're not as stupid as you look, girl."

"Is that a promise?"

"Yes, yes, I give you my word, as a pirate, that I will allow anyone in the castle today to walk free after you abdicate your throne to me."

"Then I will show you where we must go. But, first, we must stop and gather my friends. They have an instrumental part to play in this ceremony." Arianna headed off to the dining area with Iron Demon close behind, followed by Ellavorn, and the rest of the pirate crew.

They opened the doors to the dining room and the group jumped to their feet, ready to attack. Arianna held her hands up, and they all looked at her, surprised. The pain laced its way through her stomach again, and she grimaced.

She was quick to recover and said, "I have decided to abdicate my throne to Iron Demon in exchange for our lives."

Everyone in the room began to argue at once. Arianna held up her hand to stop them from talking.

"We must go to the Odigós Domátio at once for the ceremony."

She turned to Iron Demon and said, "I must speak to Adasser and Armen in private before we begin."

"Get on with it, queenie."

Arianna motioned for Adasser and Armen to come forward.

"I have a plan. Please, just follow my lead. I promise you, this is not what you think. Adasser, have the elixir ready, but only a half of a dose."

The Elves nodded and made to follow her. At that moment, Iron Demon moved to the side a step, and Armen caught his first sight of his son. He looked shaken at his appearance.

"Ellavorn!"

"Father." Ellavorn refused to meet his father's eyes.

"Ellavorn, what have you done? How could you betray us like this?"

Ellavorn looked at his father, his eyes cold.

"There are things that even you would not understand, Father," he sneered.

"My son, I am very disappointed in you."

"Armen, I know that you have a lot to say to Ellavorn. I do too. But, we must get going if we are to honor our promise and stay alive."

Armen gave a one last look of disgust to his son and stormed off in the direction of the Odigós Domátio. Everyone followed until they reached the pantry. Arianna placed the key in the hole, and the stairs appeared. The pirates all looked at her in fear. Ellavorn looked at her in shock.

"Now, in order for this ceremony to happen, your pirates must stay here, aside from Ellavorn. He may attend, since he is an Elf. My guards shall stand watch at the top of the stairs to prevent anyone else from coming in. Now, follow me."

"Hold on. Ellavorn, you follow the queen to make sure that

she isn't playing some game."

"I assure you that this is no game."

Ellavorn stepped behind her. "Go on. Lead the way."

Arianna shot him a look that could curdle milk. She hated that he thought that he could just barge right back into her life and start ordering her around. But, she also knew that this was not the time to argue with him. Without saying a word, she began her descent. Everyone else followed behind.

Ellavorn started hissing at her the entire way down the steps. "What are you thinking, Arianna? Iron Demon will destroy this kingdom. I thought that you had more common sense than this. I can't believe you would do this."

Arianna turned her head slightly and hissed back, "What I do is no longer your business, pirate."

The retort seemed to stun Ellavorn and he stopped berating her. When they reached the bottom, he looked around in wonder. "No, this can't be…is this…the Odigós Domάtio?"

Arianna looked at him defiantly. "Yes, it is."

"That's impossible."

"I am beginning to find more and more that things aren't impossible."

"Yes, yes, a lover's reunion. You may make up all you like after I become king and you get out of my castle. Let's get on with this, shall we?"

A pain went up Arianna's stomach again. This time, she couldn't hide the wince from the pain.

“Regretting your decision? Getting cold feet? Don’t back out on me now, queenie.”

“I don’t intend to.” Arianna composed herself, and nodded to Adasser and Armen to come over.

“We must join hands so that I can state my intentions.”

Iron Demon rolled his eyes and sneered before taking her hand. He looked at it and chuckled.

“Your hands are soft. You might just make a good wife. Maybe I’ll force your hand in marriage once I become king. You’ll be the queen after all.”

Arianna’s first instinct was to jerk her hand back, but she knew that she had to stick to her plan, so she ignored the remark.

“I, Arianna of Eumetadotos, abdicate my throne, and my title to the pirate, Iron Demon. He shall now rule the Kingdom of Eumetadotos in my stead.”

As she said the words, a swirling dark gray mist emerged from her stomach, and swirled around Iron Demon. It plunged itself into his stomach and was gone. The pain that Arianna had been beginning to feel was completely gone. She smiled a triumphant smile and looked at Iron Demon, whose face had gone ashen.

“What have you done to me?” He gasped as he clutched his stomach in pain, screamed loudly and then passed out.

“Adasser, the elixir. Just enough that he stays alive.”

Adasser raced over and put a few drops of the elixir on Iron Demon’s tongue. The pirate’s breathing began to even out, but he was still unconscious.

“Tanelia, have the guards take him to the dungeon and lock

him up."

Tanelia looked at her in complete awe and nodded. "How will I explain this to his pirates upstairs?

Ellavorn stepped forward. "He tried to attack her, you stepped in and knocked him out. I saw it with my own eyes. They will justify you imprisoning him since he broke his word. You might want to hit him in the head in order to make it believable." As he said it, he hit Iron Demon over the back of the head with a candlestick that he had grabbed from the altar.

Everyone gave Ellavorn incredulous looks. None more so than Arianna. He looked around at all of the faces and shrugged. "What? It has to be believable, or those men will kill you."

"You never came here to hurt me, or anyone, did you, Ellavorn?"

Ellavorn looked at her and his face softened. "Arianna, I could never harm you."

"I know. Elves don't harm living creatures."

"No, we don't. But, really, don't you know, or do you still need to be hit over the head with a brick, little – well, I guess I should call you little queen now," he gave a small, quiet laugh.

Arianna looked at him, her eyes brimming with tears of joy. She closed the few steps between them and threw her arms around him, squeezing tightly. Ellavorn recovered from the attack and hugged her back.

Armen cleared his throat. "Now is not the time for reunions. My son, I am sorry that I doubted your intentions. We need to fill you in on what is going on. First, let us get Iron Demon to the dungeon."

The group ascended the stairs. They were met by angry stares of the pirates when they saw Iron Demon's body. They gave a murderous roar. Ellavorn held up his hands. "Traitor!" They yelled.

"No! Iron Demon is the traitor. He gave his word that if he abdicated the throne, he would allow them all to leave. He drew his blade and attacked the queen before they could make the vow. Tanelia stopped him from attacking the queen. Now, he must pay for his crime in the dungeon. Do you not believe me? Check his head. It is where the she hit him."

The pirates all strained their necks to look. They all caught sight of the lump and began to talk amongst themselves.

The burly pirate who had caught Arianna earlier spoke up. "Captain Iron Demon has never broken pirate code before. Why should we believe you?"

Ellavorn's eyes took on a murderous glare. "Are you calling me a liar?"

"Well, no, Elf, no. I was just wondering is all."

"I don't know what Iron Demon's intentions were. I just know what he did. I assure you, that he was not harmed without just cause."

"What do we do now?"

"Go back to the ship. Appoint a new captain and go about your lives. Iron Demon shall be here for a very, very long time."

The pirates looked uneasy, but they shuffled out of the castle and left the kingdom, pulling their cannons behind them.

Arianna looked at Ellavorn when they had all left. "How did

you know that would work?"

"Pirates are stupid. What really happened to Iron Demon?"

"We'll explain on the way to the dungeon. We need to get him behind bars."

On the way to the dungeon, Arianna explained, "A Dark Figure has brought magic back to Eumetadotos. He put a curse on me. It's a slow death curse. It is extremely painful. Adasser has been making an elixir to help keep it at bay.

"I was on my way back from getting people out through the tunnels when you came in. I thought for certain that you were going to turn me in. Then, you let me go. Once I was caught by the other pirate, I had to come up with a plan.

"Once I found out that Iron Demon wanted the throne, I knew exactly what I had to do. I had to allow him to take on the curse. Therefore, I would be free to go look for the wizard in the other realm without worrying about the elixir and whether or not I had enough. It was the perfect solution.

"The only problem with that plan would have been you. I didn't know what your intentions were. I didn't know why you were here and if you were truly on his side."

"Arianna, I could never hurt you. I told you that. I love you. When you broke off our engagement, my heart was shattered. I took off.

"In my travels, I found the koutí profiteíavoun. I gave it to Captain Oakford when I met up with him on the road one day. He explained that you were looking for me, and that my father no longer considered you an ally. I thought, correctly, I see, that if I gave you this, it would mend that rift. I couldn't return at that point. I had heard that Iron Demon was looking to conquer a kingdom, and there was a rumor that it was Eumetadotos. I had to find him and make sure that I did everything in my power to keep him from hurting you.

"I didn't come back because I didn't love you anymore. I came back because I was trying to protect you from him."

Arianna looked deeply into his eyes, and saw that he was telling her the truth. She had never been so relieved in her life.

"Well, Adasser, Armen, Charlie and Abigail found a way to locate the realm to which the wizard escaped. We were going to open the portal before the attack. We must get back and start the spell."

The group headed back to the Odigós Domάtio, where Armen had been busy gathering the necessary ingredients for the portal. Once he had everything in order, they motioned for Abigail and Charlie to join them. Armen poured a few drops of his locator potion o the cloak, and then Abigail made the potion and poured that onto the cloak as well. Together, Armen and Charlie began to summon the portal to open.

At their last words, there was a wavering of the air on the wall. It grew bigger and began to swirl. It finally stopped growing, and held fast, waiting for them to step through. The group moved over and looked at Arianna and Ellavorn, waiting to see what they would do.

Tanelia shook her head, unable to watch the exchange, and stepped through, followed closely by Adasser.

Arianna turned to Ellavorn, and asked, "Would you care to join us on this adventure, Prince of the Elves?"

Ellavorn smiled, "I would be honored."

They joined arms and stepped through. Armen whispered a few words and the portal closed behind them.

To Be Continued…

ACKNOWLEDGMENTS

I would love to thank my daughters: Abby and Cecilia. You three are my whole heart and the reason that I wake up every day. You've encouraged me along this ride and I hope that you can stick with me for at least another two more. I can't tell you enough how much I love you guys.

I want to thank my parents. Mom, Dad, who have always encouraged my interest in writing. You two are the absolute best parents a girl could ever hope for.

To my extended family: My brother, Bill, who is a pretty cool guy. Thank you for the votes of confidence when I needed them. Krista, I love you, girl! Mom-mom, without whom I would not have been able to get this book up and running so quickly. Granny, who gives me a role model to look up to every single day. Aunt Ceil, who I can always count on to give me an honest opinion on things. I know that you won't steer me wrong!

For all of my friends, whether I've known you for years, months, or weeks, you guys are the most amazing group of people ever. I am so lucky to have each and every one of you in my life. I can't imagine my world without any of you in it.

To my editor, Sandra, thank you! You are worth your weight in gold! Check her out on Fiverr (proofreadgirl.)

To my image designer, Vira, you made my vision even better than I imagined. Check him out on Fiverr (Vira_Lanka.)

To my cover designer, Evan Schukis, who not only designed an amazing cover, but also helped me fail Geometry in high school. Love you, Evan!

ABOUT THE AUTHOR

Chrissy White was born and raised in Philadelphia, PA, where she still lives with her two daughters. She has always had a love of reading. As a child, her mother would read "normal" children's stories to her brother and her, while her father would tell them stories from The Lord of the Rings, and other series like them. This inspired a love of fiction and fantasy that still prevails today. She has always loved to write, and has had several poems published by the National Library of Poetry. Throughout high school, she would entertain her friends with short stories. She enjoys baking, spending time at the beach, crafting, trying to paint, and being with her family.

www.ingramcontent.com/pod-product-compliance
Lightning Source LLC
Chambersburg PA
CBHW070204260626
47160CB00002B/443
* 9 7 8 0 9 9 7 8 4 4 9 0 0 *